MURDER
MOST
BRITISH

BOOKS BY HELENA DIXON

MURDER
MOST
BRITISH

HELENA DIXON

bookouture

Published by Bookouture in 2025

An imprint of Storyfire Ltd.
Carmelite House
50 Victoria Embankment
London EC4Y 0DZ

www.bookouture.com

The authorised representative in the EEA is Hachette Ireland
8 Castlecourt Centre
Dublin 15 D15 XTP3
Ireland
(email: info@hbgi.ie)

ISBN: 978-1-83618-139-2
eBook ISBN: 978-1-83618-138-5

For all those who worked to entertain a nation and kept morale boosted.

Keep the Home Fires burning
While your hearts are yearning
Though your lads are far away
They dream of home
There's a silver lining
Through the dark cloud shining
Turn the dark cloud inside out
Till the boys come Home

Lena Guilbert Ford 1914

CHAPTER ONE

LATE OCTOBER 1941

Thankfully, as far as Jane Treen was concerned, no signs of Christmas had yet encroached upon her office. Though already noises had been made, like last year, about decorating to boost morale. The memo to prove it lay before her on her desk. She glared at her previously blank ceiling, at the now faded scrap of red crêpe paper still offendingly drawing-pinned in place from the previous year's shenanigans.

This year she intended to make certain her office remained a celebration-free zone. She could always point to the scrap of paper and claim she had in fact already decorated. Her colleague Stephen sounded insufferably smug when he called a moment later to say she was required immediately by her superior. She strongly suspected he was once again the instigator of the Christmas decorating proposals.

Jane finished her coffee, standing the empty cup next to the overflowing metal ashtray on the corner of her desk and smoothed the creases from her neat dark-grey skirt. She checked her hair was tidy and her lipstick refreshed before making her way along the corridor to Brigadier Remmington-Blythe's office deep inside Whitehall. Stephen, the brigadier's secretary, was seated at his own desk as usual in the outer waiting area as she entered. The room was cooler than her own office and she shivered, wishing she had slipped on her cardigan.

He smirked at her as she walked in, his pencil-thin moustache lifting upwards. 'I say, Jane, whatever have you been up to? The old man sounded quite cross when he asked for you.'

'I'm sure you have work you should be getting on with, Stephen, unless you are too busy sending round memos about Christmas decorations,' Jane said tartly as she walked briskly up to the brigadier's door and knocked.

She had scarcely been back at her desk for more than a couple of days after her last assignment. One which had gone well, and she was pretty certain that she personally had done nothing to earn the brigadier's ire.

'Come,' the brigadier's stentorian bark sounded through the panelled wooden door.

Jane straightened her narrow shoulders and entered.

'Ah, Jane, take a seat.' The brigadier indicated one of the plain wooden chairs in front of his desk.

She closed the door behind her and complied with his instructions. The brigadier, a brisk elderly man in his late sixties, regarded her thoughtfully from beneath his bushy silvery eyebrows.

'Righto, I won't beat about the bush, Jane. We have a tricky situation on our hands.' He looked keenly at her, and she sensed he was judging his words carefully. That alone made her feel slightly uneasy. Usually, the brigadier would just dive in and say whatever was on his mind. In fact, she had often thought a moment's reflection before speaking would have been better.

'One which you may be uniquely placed to help us resolve,' the brigadier continued.

Jane did not like the direction this conversation was taking.

'Your mother is staying with Stephen's mother, I understand?' Although phrased as a question, Jane knew that her employer was fully aware of where her mother was residing. He had obviously been doing some research.

A recent incendiary bomb had damaged the roof of her mother's apartment. Her mother, Elsa, had decided that living with her best friend, Rosemary, who happened to be Stephen's mother, was much more convivial than living with Jane. This was something Jane herself heartily approved of since she and her mother were not the best of friends.

Elsa was American and well known as a singer and actress. She had opted to remain in Britain at the start of the war and could regularly be heard on the radio. Since the start of the conflict she had been regarded as one of the nation's sweethearts. She and Jane's father had divorced several years ago and Jane had been close to her father right up until his death the previous year. She had never been close to her mother.

'Yes, sir, I believe she is.' Jane hadn't actually heard from her mother directly since her rapid departure from Ashbourne in Kent a scant week or so earlier. She had heard constantly, however, from Stephen who seemed to feel it incumbent upon him to keep her updated on her mother's life.

The brigadier raised one eyebrow at her response before rising from his chair to pace about the office. Jane knew this was a habit he had whenever he was either thinking deeply or was about to broach a difficult subject. She had a nasty feeling that if it concerned her mother, it might well be the latter reason.

'You are aware that the site of Broadcasting House was changed? That after the damage caused by the last bombing raid they are now recording and broadcasting from several locations?' The brigadier swung around to face her.

'Yes, sir. I understand Tooting to have been mentioned.' Jane knew the exact locations were being kept secret. Even MPs in the House of Commons were unaware of the exact locations. She was vaguely aware that Maida Vale and Bristol were in use amongst other places. Control of information, however, was vital to the war effort and keeping up morale, so all was rumour and speculation.

Everything the public saw and heard was strictly controlled, from what appeared in the newspapers, to the radio broadcasts and on the newsreels in the cinemas. Her mother regularly worked on the programmes which were broadcast for radio, both live and recorded. Elsa had also been filmed several times for the newsreels entertaining the troops and leading singalongs in the shelters. Some of the films were being used to raise funds in America for the war effort.

'Tooting, eh?' Brigadier Remmington-Blythe smiled into his moustache. 'You understand that it is vital that we keep broadcasting. Any disruption to the Home Service creates unease, even panic amongst the civilians. The Overseas Service too is essential.'

'Yes, sir.' Jane wondered where this was leading.

'Just lately there have been a few security breaches at the Home Service HQ. Two foiled attempts to take the service off the air and, even more worrying, tampering with the programmes. Attempts have been discovered to insert hidden messages useful to enemy agents. One of our own agents working undercover has already alerted me but she has since gone silent. This is obviously hugely worrying and we are making discreet attempts to trace her whereabouts.' The brigadier continued to regard her steadily.

'I see. Do we have any clues as to who may be behind this?' Jane's mind started racing with possibilities.

'Not as yet. The agent I mentioned left a message to say she had evidence to present. We need to get someone else in there, in the studios. A fresh face who would be above suspicion and could dig around. Now, I heard that you have accompanied your mother as her pianist before?'

Jane's eyes widened with surprise. 'I have, sir, yes.' This was not what she was expecting.

'Good, good. I would like you to accompany your mother as her pianist for her next round of recordings and events. Her regular accompanist is about to be unwell. I have already contacted Arthur and his man Benson and sent them what information I had to date. They will assist you with whatever else you uncover. The content the saboteur managed to insert into the programming was a hidden code. Arthur's expertise in this field may be invaluable to try and trace the route of the codes and their intended recipients. 'I'm sure I need not remind you of the importance of this task, Jane. Or its confidentiality.' The brigadier's gaze sharpened.

'No, sir, but how will you persuade my mother and manage to keep her quiet about this?' Jane asked. She tried to keep the faint, rising tide of panic at the brigadier's request under control. Elsa was not known for discretion.

'The contracts your mother has already signed for the concerts and the play she is to appear in cover that aspect. She will be told that I have given you time off to assist her as her work is vital to keep up morale. Her usual accompanist will, as I said, be unavailable. Stephen has assured me that she will find that plausible. You must ensure that the broadcasts air as planned, and that no disruption is created. You also need to prevent the insertion, however subliminal, of propaganda from the enemy designed to derail the war effort.' Brigadier Remmington-Blythe sat back down on his chair making it creak under his weight.

'I understand, sir.' Jane wished she had brought her cigarettes with her into this meeting.

'This may be dangerous, Jane. Control of the airwaves is clearly a priority for the enemy right now.' The brigadier leaned back and surveyed her levelly. 'Speak to Stephen about seeing your mother on your way out. He knows a little of this obviously but not the full extent of what you will be doing. You, Arthur and Mr Benson remain a secret cell within this department.'

'Sir.' Jane rose. She was clearly being dismissed.

'Thank you, Jane,' the brigadier's voice softened slightly as she placed her hand on the office door ready to leave.

'Well? Have you been demoted to the typing pool?' Stephen greeted her as she re-entered the outer office and closed the brigadier's door.

Jane longed to remove the supercilious smirk from Stephen's face. She knew he was enjoying every moment of this. 'The brigadier has instructed me to contact my mother as she is apparently in need of my help.' She kept her tone even and cool.

'Pop around tonight for dinner. Mother will be delighted to see you and Elsa will be too, I'm sure. Say sevenish?' he suggested.

'Lovely,' Jane agreed, forcing a tight smile onto her face.

She walked along the corridor past the typing pool back to her own office. Once the door was safely closed she promptly reached for her cigarettes and took a seat at her desk. She had accompanied her mother before on tour many years earlier when she had been scarcely out of her teens. It was not a memory she looked back on with any fondness.

Elsa had introduced her to everyone as her younger sister and turned her into an unpaid servant. Thankfully her father had been alive then and had come to her rescue when Jane had telephoned him from Carlisle in floods of tears.

She blew out a thin stream of smoke and wondered how her mother would take the news that Jane was to be her new temporary accompanist. Normally, her mother had a rather pleasant elderly man called Michael who played for her. It seemed that the brigadier had taken care of this issue for the time being.

No doubt she would discover a little more at this dinner party at Stephen's mother's apartment. As if she didn't see enough of Stephen at work, now it seemed she was to spend her precious leisure time with him too. Not a thought she relished.

The previous Christmas he had made yet another pass at her during the small office party. A dig in his ribs and a heel on his foot had been required to get her message across that she wasn't interested in him. Despite this, her mother still seemed to be keen on promoting a romance between them. Jane sighed and stubbed out her cigarette. It was going to be a very trying evening.

At Half Moon Manor in Devon, Arthur Cilento listened carefully to his instructions from the brigadier. He had already received several documents in the post earlier that day from the brigadier's office.

The curtains were drawn in his study to comply with the blackout and the desk was illuminated by a green glass-shaded brass desk lamp. A small fire crackled in the hearth to warm the space. It was almost six o'clock and Arthur guessed the brigadier was working late once again.

'Yes, sir, I understand. Benson and I will, of course, be on standby to assist Jane. I've begun to go through the papers you sent.' Arthur had been a little disappointed by the simplicity of the code used in the materials supplied by the brigadier.

Since childhood he had been severely asthmatic and had been declared unfit to enlist. His academic skills at solving difficult puzzles and complex mathematical problems had seen him being valued by the brigadier's department. His work had begun before the war and now was even more valuable.

Benson, his faithful manservant, stood close by listening in to the call. He, like Arthur, also worked for the department. Now in his early sixties, Benson was an astute individual who provided Arthur with medical assistance when required. He also carried out various other tasks not normally found within a servant's terms of employment.

'Jolly good. I know that Jane's relationship with her mother is somewhat strained,' the brigadier said.

Benson, who could clearly hear the brigadier due to his habit of shouting into the telephone, lifted his eyebrows slightly at this.

'Yes, sir,' Arthur agreed, having witnessed Elsa and Jane together during their most recent assignment in Kent.

The conversation was briefly halted. Arthur gathered from the muttered conversation and exclamations on the other end of the line that something both shocking and untoward had occurred.

'I'm afraid I have to go. Something has occurred which may make this assignment much more dangerous,' the brigadier sounded unusually perturbed.

'Is everything all right, sir?' Arthur realised that was an absurd question.

'It seems there has been a death, a murder which is almost certainly connected to the job I have just allocated to you and Jane. I'll speak to Jane shortly, and she can brief you when we know more.'

'Very good, sir.' The call ended and Arthur replaced the telephone receiver back on its stand.

'That sounded most perturbing, sir,' Benson observed as Arthur tried to gather his thoughts.

'Yes. It seems that Jane might be taking great risks if the brigadier's fears are correct.' Arthur looked at his manservant.

'Indeed. I shall ready the firearm and prepare bags should we be required to travel to London at short notice,' Benson said.

'Yes, I think that may be wise.' Arthur slumped in his seat as his servant left the room.

From what the brigadier had just said it appeared that the previously simple assignment of cracking codes and finding a saboteur may just have become a hunt for a murderer.

CHAPTER TWO

Stephen's mother, the Right Honourable Rosemary Carter, lived in a large five-bedroomed apartment in a smart area of Kensington. Jane's mother was one of Rosemary's closest friends and it seemed to be suiting them both to have Elsa stay while her own flat was being repaired. Jane was relieved to not have her mother residing at her flat, something which would not have been good for either of them.

Jane battled the end of working day crowds back to her own compact apartment in a less fashionable area to feed Marmaduke, her fluffy one-eyed ginger cat. Once Marmaduke had been mollified with some pilchards, she fastened her windows, put up her blackout and turned on a lamp.

Jane selected a gown from her limited wardrobe, applied her lipstick and set off again in the grey, cold air of a London night. The blackout made getting around doubly difficult since taxis were often in short supply. Many of them had been converted to tow fire appliances and acted as couriers. The buses too often had their routes changed depending on any bomb damage or reconstruction.

By the time she reached Stephen's mother's flat, Jane was

cold, damp and thoroughly out of sorts. A hail shower as she left the bus had turned into sleet. The buses had been full, and her route had involved a large diversion. She could only hope that dinner would not drag on and she could escape before returning home became a complete nightmare.

Rosemary's elderly maid let her into the flat and took her winter coat and the headscarf she had used in an attempt to keep her hair dry. The hall of the flat was warm, and she could hear the sound of music and laughter coming from one of the rooms.

'If you'll follow me, miss,' the maid said, once Jane had smoothed her hair and pinched some colour back into her cheeks with the aid of the gilt-framed mirror near the front door.

Stephen was in evening attire at the small cocktail bar in the corner of the room, silver shaker in hand. His mother, dressed in dark-green satin, was seated beside the fire while Jane's mother, Elsa, was dressed in dark blue shot with silver on the other chair.

'Janey pie, how was your journey? You should have come here straight from work with Stephen.' Her mother set down her martini glass and leapt up to kiss her cheek. 'My, you feel cold, come nearer to the fire and get warm. Stephen will mix you a drink.'

Jane obeyed her mother and stood closer to the cheery blaze in the hearth feeling distinctly underdressed for the occasion. Since it was not practical to wear an evening gown on the bus she had opted for a mid-calf length serviceable fitted dark-chartreuse dress.

'There you go, Jane, dear heart.' Stephen pressed a martini glass into her hand.

'It looks a foul night out there,' Rosemary observed. 'I took a peek earlier before Pearson drew the curtains.'

'Yes, I think it's becoming quite foggy. Hopefully that may deter any raids tonight.' Jane could only pray the drizzle, and smog, would put off any enemy action. She had no desire to end up sheltering in one of the public shelters or underground stations for hours on end.

'Dinner is ready, madam,' Pearson, the maid, announced from the doorway.

'Marvellous. Do come through then, Jane.' Rosemary took her son's arm and led them through into a comfortably furnished dining room. The table was set with fine white linen and crystal glasses. A bowl of clear soup was ready for each diner.

Jane took her place between her mother and Stephen and sniffed the aroma appreciatively. It had been a long time since her meagre lunch of a cheese sandwich and an apple. At least being invited to dinner meant she hadn't had to cook.

Elsa appeared determined to be amusing, regaling the table with a story about a singing dog at the lunchtime concert she had been part of earlier in the day.

'We can discuss our new working arrangements after dinner, Janey, honey. It's so good of Stephen to have come to my rescue.' Elsa flashed one of her brilliant smiles in his direction.

Pearson had just cleared away the soup bowls when the sound of a telephone ringing could be heard elsewhere in the apartment.

'Oh, who on earth could that be during dinner?' Rosemary asked.

Her question was soon answered when the elderly maid reappeared in the dining room. 'There is an urgent call for you, Miss Treen.'

Jane jumped up and placed her linen napkin down on top of the table and apologised briefly to her hostess before following the maid. The only person who knew she would be at Stephen's apartment was the brigadier, so she guessed something serious must have occurred.

'Jane, thank heavens. Are you alone?' the brigadier's voice

boomed into her ear. She glanced around the deserted drawing room. The maid having returned to continue clearing and serving the next course of their meal.

'Yes, sir, go ahead.' The door to the hall was closed and there was no one else in the flat except Stephen and their mothers.

'I received a message shortly after you had gone for the evening. It came in whilst I was talking to Arthur. Tabitha Moore, a young woman from this department, has been found dead under a pile of rubble not far from Tower Bridge.'

Jane tried to recall Tabitha. 'She was the pretty girl we recruited from the typing pool last year. Spoke French and German. She was on a mission in town, wasn't she?' Jane had not been looking after Tabitha, but she had overseen the girl's initial training.

'Yes, that's the girl. She was murdered, strangled, and her body hidden under the rubble. No doubt the killer hoped it would be assumed she had been killed by the blast. Unluckily for them the chappie that found her knew better and called the police.' The brigadier sounded troubled.

'I see, that's awful.' Jane was slightly at a loss about why her employer had called her urgently to tell her this news, sad though it was.

'Tabitha was the agent I spoke to you about earlier. The one I said we were trying to find. She was the one who picked up on the problems we spoke about,' the brigadier explained.

Jane suddenly felt quite sick, and she gripped the telephone receiver a little tighter. 'I understand.' She knew the brigadier was being cautious in his speech in case there was anyone else listening on the line.

'Tabitha was engaged to Leo Cavendish. He also works at the place we spoke about. Now as far as I know she hadn't told him what she had discovered but I can't be certain of that. I believe she must have been on her way to see us when she was killed. I'll dig up what I can and ask Arthur to come into town early tomorrow. Meet me in my office at eleven o'clock sharp before you accompany your mother to rehearsals,' the brigadier said.

'Yes, sir.' Jane replaced the receiver with a shaking hand. Their new mission had suddenly taken on an unexpected and deadly twist.

She took a moment to compose herself before returning to the dining room. Pearson was starting to serve the main course of some kind of chicken dish, padded out with vegetables and more potatoes. The delicious aroma made her stomach rumble appreciatively.

'Is everything all right, Janey pie?' her mother asked as Jane retook her place at the table.

'Yes, perfectly. Just an administration question that couldn't wait.' Jane avoided Stephen's gaze and smiled at her hostess. 'This looks delicious, you must ask your cook to give me the recipe.'

Elsa snorted and picked up her knife and fork while Stephen eyed her curiously. Conversation continued about the difficulties of obtaining food throughout the dessert of apple crumble and custard. Jane risked a furtive glance at her wristwatch when dinner was finally finished, and they retired to the drawing room once more for coffee.

Jane lit up a cigarette, ignoring Stephen's belated offer of a light, and seated herself on the sofa. She still had to discuss arrangements with her mother about acting as her accompanist.

'I must say, Janey pie, I was surprised you were going to assist me with my recording sessions and concerts.' Her mother was perched elegantly on the edge of an armchair, her china coffee cup in one hand and the saucer in the other. 'I can't say I'm not grateful though. It's difficult to get someone who knows the nuances of a piece. Everyone seems to be working for ENSA these days. It's very inconvenient when one doesn't know which Tom, Dick or Harry is going to arrive to play for you.'

Jane gave a tight smile. 'What time do you need me tomorrow for rehearsals?'

'Around two would be fine. There's a lot to get through. I'll just get you the address.' Her mother set down her delicate china cup and saucer before producing a small evening bag. She took out a tiny notebook and scribbled the directions down with a gold propelling pencil. 'There you go, sweetie.'

Jane took the note and glanced at it. She had a vague idea where the building was that her mother had jotted down. She was sure that was where the service had always been based. If so, then they must not have moved out for long.

'Thank you. I'll meet you there. I presume you already have your music?' She hoped Elsa wasn't expecting her to run around London tracking down sheet music. It wouldn't be the first time she'd done such a thing.

'Yes, I have everything we need. You might need some practice though. I know you played in Kent, but this is for broadcasting.' Her mother gave her a doubtful look.

'I'm sure it will be fine,' Jane said. 'That is what the rehearsal room is for after all.'

Her mother shrugged as if not really believing her and Jane bit back the retort which had risen to her lips.

'It was so good of you, Stephen, to use your influence to help me.' Elsa fluttered her eyelashes in his direction.

'We shall enjoy listening to you both, won't we, Mother?' Stephen drawled looking at Rosemary. 'I had no idea until recently that you were so talented, Jane. A concert pianist, eh? What will the department do without you while you're assisting Elsa?'

Jane extinguished her cigarette with some force. 'I expect you'll do what you usually do, Stephen.' She didn't add the words very little, but his eyes narrowed at the saccharine-sweet implication of her words.

'Well, it's a good thing we are not all flitting about the place,' he retorted.

'I must say they have given me quite the workload. Guest appearances and all kinds of things. The penalties of being a star, I suppose,' Elsa grumbled, but Jane could see her mother was secretly pleased.

'Speaking of workloads, I'm afraid I must get off. I have a lot of things to get through tomorrow before I meet you for rehearsals,' Jane said as she placed her coffee cup and saucer down.

It was just after nine and if she hurried and the fates were with her, she could be back in her own flat by ten o'clock. She really didn't wish to be out during the blackout any later than that. Not on her own. She was quite used to being out and about but the smog and the dark with the risk of raids made her edgy.

News of Tabitha's murder was also most unsettling. The crime rate had risen sharply with the lack of street lamps and the low numbers of policemen. Criminals and opportunists had been quick to take advantage of the situation.

'Oh, must you go? You've only just got here, Janey,' her mother protested. 'I had hoped we might have had a game of bridge or something.'

'I'm sorry, Mother. The smog was rolling in from the Thames when I arrived and with no lights it's not a pleasant journey home.' Jane rose from her seat.

'You can always stay here overnight,' Rosemary said. 'There is plenty of room.'

'That's most kind of you but I need to get back for my cat. It was a lovely supper and so thoughtful of you to invite me.' Jane moved purposefully towards the door of the drawing room.

'Stephen will walk you to your stop and wait with you. I assume you came by bus?' Rosemary looked at her son.

'Yes, I don't care for the underground, and it gets dreadfully crowded these days with people trying to use it as a shelter.' Jane wrinkled her nose as she recalled the smell and the amount of people in the stations. The bus might be riskier and not reliable but at least she was above ground.

'I'll get my coat.' Stephen unwound himself languidly from the armchair.

'Thank you.' Jane wasn't certain she really wanted or needed Stephen to escort her. She suspected he might try fishing to discover why the brigadier had telephoned. Or make a fresh renewal of romantic overtures towards her.

She followed Stephen out into the hall where he retrieved her hat, coat and scarf, before putting on his own things. Elsa and Rosemary came out to see them off, her mother offering her carefully powdered cheek for a kiss.

'Do take care, Janey, honey. I so wish you would stay. I'm sure that darn cat of yours would be all right for one night,' Elsa grumbled.

'Bye, Mother, I'll see you tomorrow.' Jane followed Stephen out and quickly closed the door before any light could show and get her hostess in trouble with the wardens.

Once out on the city street the darkness seemed to envelop them like a cloak. The air smelt of coal fires and ash mixed with the soupy scent of stagnant water. The smog made it even harder to see than usual and Jane was forced to concentrate on where she was walking. The sleet from earlier had left the pavements slippery underfoot. She had no desire to trip on a paving stone or twist an ankle going down a kerb.

The traffic going past sounded muffled as the few cars and buses crawled along at a snail's pace unable to see more than a few feet ahead of them. Stephen walked by her side between her and the road.

'I hope your bus will still be running,' he said as they navigated around an unlit metal lamp post.

'Yes, I hope so too. I should be in time for this one.' Jane didn't bother to try and look at her watch. It would have been a waste of time in the darkness.

Eventually they reached the stop. There was no one else there and she hoped she hadn't missed it.

'I'll wait with you. If it doesn't come then we can go back to Mother's and try for a taxi,' Stephen said.

'Thank you.' Jane was grateful for his company. Despite her earlier thoughts on the matter, it was reassuring not to be alone on such a horrid night.

'I won't ask you what the old man wanted as I know you won't tell me anyway.' Stephen paused. 'Just be careful, Jane. This war business is getting worse.'

Jane glanced at him but couldn't make out his features in the smog. 'Thank you. Yes, it is. I suppose all we can do is hope that a breakthrough is coming soon,' she said.

There was the muffled sound of an engine and Jane let out a sigh of relief as the familiar shape of the double-decker bus rumbled into sight. The bus stopped and several people alighted, grey and black shapes in the mist.

Stephen handed her up onto the platform of the bus. 'Goodnight, Jane.'

She made her way to a seat and proffered her coins to the conductor. A shiver ran through her spine as she took her ticket and tucked it inside her glove. She wished she could ignore the cold spear of worry that had assailed her when the brigadier had telephoned. It seemed to have sparked something deep inside her, a dreadful feeling of fear, and Jane was not someone who scared easily.

CHAPTER THREE

Arthur and Benson boarded the early train from Exeter into London's Paddington Station. As usual the carriages were jammed full. Soldiers on their way to various places, businessmen heading for the city and housewives clutching baskets and bags hoping to find more goods in the city than in their small towns and villages.

The brigadier's second telephone call yesterday evening had come as Arthur was enjoying his night-time cocoa, while listening to the wireless beside the fire. They were now expected for a briefing at the brigadier's office at eleven o'clock. It seemed they were also to prepare themselves to remain in London for a time.

Benson had performed his usual miracle of managing to pack at short notice and they had boarded the train with minutes to spare. Benson taking charge of Arthur's medical equipment and a gun which lay concealed under the false bottom of the bag.

Arthur was still uncomfortable about Benson's suggestion of packing the gun. Firearms always made him uneasy, even though there was a war on. They arrived at Paddington and

Benson set about finding a taxi to transport them and their bags to Whitehall.

They would be early to see the brigadier, but Arthur thought it might be prudent to see Jane ahead of the meeting. She might have more information which would be useful to their investigation. Hopefully, she might also have information about where they were to stay and how long the investigation was estimated to take. From what the brigadier had shared the previous evening the case had taken an even more dangerous turn.

Benson had seemed quite chipper since discovering that Miss Treen's mother was also involved in the investigation. It had come to Arthur's notice, after Jane had pointed it out, that his manservant had something of a crush on the singer. Personally, Arthur found Elsa Macintyre self-centred and a little tiresome.

A taxi finally secured, they made their way through the busy streets to Whitehall. Their route took them past sites of more recent bomb damage. The craters where buildings had once stood with teetering walls papered with fragments of floral wallpaper and remnants of tattered curtains always saddened him.

Once at Whitehall they made their way to the main reception desk and enquired if Miss Treen was in. They were commanded to take a seat, and someone would be down to collect them. Arthur took a chair next to Benson under the watchful eye of the receptionist as she dialled an internal number on her black desk telephone.

A minute or two later the lift doors opened in the lobby near the desk and Jane appeared, neat and precise as usual in a smart grey two-piece suit.

'Arthur, Benson. Our meeting is at eleven.' She consulted the small silver watch on her wrist. 'You are a little early.'

'We came on the early train. We thought it might be useful

for the three of us to compare notes before we see the brigadier. There may not be much time afterwards if you are assisting your mother,' Arthur said.

A cloud crossed Jane's face. 'Ah, you've heard about that then? Better come upstairs to my office. Leave your luggage behind the desk.' She led the way to the lift, and they were soon walking briskly along the long corridor that led to Jane's domain.

Arthur felt himself becoming breathless simply trying to keep up with her. Why she always had to walk so swiftly he had no idea. She unlocked her office door and showed them inside. Her desk was neat and orderly as usual with only the empty coffee cup and full ashtray betraying that she must have been at work for quite some time already that morning.

'Please take a seat. I can probably go and scare up some tea if you would like a drink?' she offered as she took her own place behind the desk.

Arthur sat down as Benson a trifle reluctantly took the chair next to him. He refused the offer of tea. 'I know the brigadier will give us a full briefing but what do we know about this young woman who has been murdered?' Arthur asked. 'Obviously the brigadier only gave me the bare bones of what happened when he called.'

'Tabitha Moore was a typist here in the pool. She was spotted as being intelligent and quick, with a talent for languages. We recruited her for internal surveillance. I trained her but was not subsequently her handler. It seems she was assigned to the BBC headquarters. The Cabinet had become concerned that there was insufficient scrutiny of the broadcast content and that it was at risk of subversion. Hidden coded messages could be inserted giving signals to the enemy and there was a risk of sabotage. The fire at Swansea and some of the near misses have been a huge concern.'

Arthur nodded. He knew the broadcaster had lost studios at Swansea to fire. Bristol had also come under attack, as had London. Since those had been from external sources, he had not considered there might be an internal risk.

'Tabitha, as I understand it, had been monitoring and collecting data to ensure internal security. No one was aware of her mission so far as we know. Ostensibly she worked in reception, oversaw contracts and assisted her now fiancé, Leo Cavendish, to manage the site and the staff. The brigadier will no doubt tell us more about what he thinks Tabitha had discovered.' Jane leaned back in her seat.

'She had let the brigadier know that something was wrong?' Arthur mused. 'And this may well be why she was murdered?'

Jane nodded. 'It seems likely. The brigadier believes she was on her way to the department. Her body was discovered under rubble from a raid that took place a couple of days ago. I've been told she had been strangled. No doubt someone hoped it would be thought she had died in the raid.' She passed him a slim file which he shared with Benson. The photograph of a pretty dark-haired young woman was on the first page.

Arthur went cold as he looked at the image of the murdered girl. This was a part of the war work he struggled with. Facts, figures and numbers were one thing but seeing a face of someone who had been killed was something else. 'I see.'

'The brigadier has arranged for me to act as accompanist for my mother while she records some programme content for the corporation. Some will be live, others will be recorded.' Jane toyed with an open pack of cigarettes on her desk.

'How is your mother, Miss Treen? Erm, Miss Jane,' Benson hastily corrected himself at the glare from across the desk. Jane had consistently asked his manservant to address her as Jane, but Miss Jane had been as far as she had been able to persuade him to unbend. And that was done reluctantly.

'My mother is quite well, thank you. I dined with her last night. She is still residing with her friend Rosemary while her building has the repairs made to the roof,' Jane replied.

'How do you feel about working with your mother?' Arthur asked. He knew all too well how tricky the relationship between the two women could be. While they had been staying in Kent on their last assignment he had seen how the land lay between them.

'There is a war on. My personal feelings are neither here nor there on the matter.' Jane avoided his gaze, her tone studiously neutral.

Benson opened his coat and examined the silver fob watch which hung from a chain on his waistcoat. 'It's almost eleven.'

Jane rose from her seat and Arthur and Benson followed her back out along the corridor to the brigadier's office. Stephen was busy typing in the outer office as they entered. His brows rose when he saw that Jane had company.

'The brigadier is expecting us,' she said as she rapped on the door of her superior's office.

'Come!'

At the familiar sound of the brigadier's bellow, Jane opened the door, and they went in, closing it once more behind them. Brigadier Remmington-Blythe was not alone. A man wearing the khaki uniform of an army officer was with him.

Arthur noted the man bore the rank of colonel as they were directed to sit in front of the brigadier's desk. The brigadier had his hands clasped loosely behind his back as he addressed them. 'I should like to introduce you to my colleague, Colonel Hardacre, who has special responsibility for ensuring the security of our broadcasting channels. Colonel, Miss Treen, Mr Cilento and Mr Benson have already had a preliminary briefing on the situation in hand. Perhaps you could expand on what has happened.' He inclined his head towards the younger man.

'Certainly. If you would all please be seated.' Colonel Hardacre surveyed them keenly as they obeyed his instruction and sat on the chairs in front of the desk. A man in perhaps his mid-forties he had sharp eyes and a businesslike air about his person. 'Miss Treen, I believe you knew Tabitha Moore?'

'Yes, sir. I was responsible for arranging her initial training, although I did not supervise her placement and was unaware that she had been posted to Broadcasting House,' Jane said.

'Hmm, and you now have been told why she was posted there?' the colonel asked.

'Yes, sir,' Jane confirmed.

'Mr Cilento, I believe you are something of an expert with codes and mathematical puzzles and patterns? And you have seen a few of the documents from the studios already?' He turned his attention to Arthur.

'Yes, sir. I have worked with the navy, the air force and at a specialist site on just this kind of work.' The initial papers he had received had not appeared complex. Arthur wondered where this line of questioning was going. He could see why Jane would be ideal to place as a mole within the broadcasting organisation but it was harder to see where his own role would be.

'Tabitha Moore alerted the brigadier and myself via her supervisor that she had uncovered something significant at Broadcasting House. We know this was either something connected with the various sabotage incidents that have occurred lately or to do with using the programmes themselves to send coded information which could assist the enemy. She sent us a few documents but indicated more were to follow,' Colonel Hardacre said.

'She had been due to come here two days ago. She never arrived. Her fiancé, Leo Cavendish, who was also her boss, reported her missing to the police. He was unaware of her exact role. As you can imagine there was little the police could do at that point in time. We were also trying to locate her. Her body was recovered yesterday afternoon as they removed some rubble from a bomb site not far from Tower Bridge,' the brigadier said.

'And it was definitely murder, sir?' Jane asked.

Colonel Hardacre nodded. 'I'm afraid so. The girl was strangled with her own scarf. Cavendish is distraught and, since her body was identified, is making all kinds of wild accusations.'

'You are sure he was not aware of her assignment?' Arthur asked.

'We had not believed that he was but from his actions since Tabitha was found we think she must have either told him something of her mission or he has guessed something else was afoot. He obviously knew she was based here previously.' Colonel Hardacre's face was grave.

'If he did know then it's highly likely that others may have found out. Her entire mission would have been compromised,' Jane said.

Arthur sensed her turning the matter over inside her mind. It was clear to him that Jane's position as her mother's accompanist would be regarded with suspicion. It had to place Jane's own safety at great risk.

'What accusations is Cavendish making?' Arthur asked.

'That our department is responsible for her death. He asserted this to the police yesterday evening. Then he claimed that someone higher up is a traitor, and Tabitha was silenced to protect them. He was here first thing this morning causing problems,' Colonel Hardacre said.

'I see.' Arthur rubbed his chin thoughtfully. 'What happens now then, sir? Jane is due to enter Broadcasting House purporting to be her mother's pianist. Surely this will immediately be seen to be false? Her safety could be at risk,' Arthur said.

Jane flashed him a glance and he knew she had been thinking along the same lines.

'I agree,' Brigadier Remmington-Blythe said. 'However, I think the plan should go ahead. If questioned Jane should make it clear that she is there to protect other performers who might inadvertently be at risk. If she is known to be part of this department, although she may find out less, the potential trade-off might be that she is safe. It may also force whoever is behind this into action.'

'Then surely that makes it more dangerous, not less,' Arthur said. 'You are using Jane almost as bait to try and lure this person or persons out.'

The brigadier looked at Colonel Hardacre. 'We have considered this possibility. Therefore, we will need you to step up your own role in this.' He looked at Arthur.

'I don't follow.' Arthur had an uneasy feeling that his job was about to become much more complex and dangerous.

'It might be useful for you to also be on hand at Broadcasting House as a technician if required. Your file indicates that you are skilled at various small electrical tasks and adjustments. It provides a good excuse for your presence should the need arise. Another possible ruse may be that you and Miss Treen perhaps feign a romantic connection. Lunch or tea with an admirer would give you the perfect ruse to be close at hand.' The colonel ignored both Jane and Arthur's dismayed expressions at his suggestion.

'And me, sir?' Benson asked.

'I wonder if you might consider a janitorial position, Mr Benson. I think whoever is behind Tabitha's death and whatever else is going on will be focused on Mr Cilento and Miss Treen. This would allow you to move around the place almost unnoticed and at times which may not be open to the rest of your team,' Colonel Hardacre said.

Benson nodded. 'That seems very sensible, sir. I would be honoured to participate.'

'Good show. Right, I shall get off and let you all get cracking. You will report to the brigadier, and he will let me know how things are progressing. Good luck.' The colonel took his leave.

'Arthur, I have arranged accommodation for you and Benson in a vacant apartment in the same block as Jane's flat. As you know she resides in a townhouse with ten units in the building. You will be on the floor below her. A hotel would cause too much interest if you were being watched. This way you can work together after hours without attracting attention.' The brigadier handed Benson a set of keys with an address tag attached. 'In the flat I have also arranged for you to be able to listen to the last three days of broadcasts before Tabitha was killed. We believe there may be something in those broadcasts which is significant. Transcripts are also ready for you.'

'Thank you, sir.' Arthur could see this job was going to take a lot of painstaking work, both mentally and physically.

'Do any of you have any further questions?' the brigadier asked.

The three of them shook their heads and were swiftly dismissed. They made their way back to Jane's office.

'What number apartment has he given you?' Jane asked.

'Six, Miss Jane,' Benson said.

'Yes, that's the floor below me. Mine is ten, you probably remember from when you were there in January. I have to shoot off in a minute to meet my mother at the rehearsal rooms. I suggest you both go to the apartment and settle in. It will give you the chance to listen to the broadcasts and study the papers.' Jane looked at Arthur. 'I'll call in and see you both when I finish at the rehearsal rooms.'

Arthur thought Jane's plan seemed a sensible one. They left Jane to finish off her paperwork before going to meet her mother and made their own way back out of the building.

Benson succeeded in hailing a taxi and gave the address to the driver. The townhouse where Jane lived was a large Victorian building built of red brick. Once a grand house it had been subdivided into apartments. They had stayed overnight before in Jane's flat back in January when they had worked on their first case together. At least this time one of them wouldn't have to sleep on a lumpy sofa. Even better, as far as Arthur was concerned, he wouldn't have to live with Jane's cat.

CHAPTER FOUR

After Arthur and Benson had departed Jane finished the work she had at hand, leaving her files for Stephen. She hurried out into the street. There was a bus due and if she got a move on she should be able to catch it. According to the timetable and the map she had consulted, it ran quite close to the address her mother had provided.

The smog was still present as she huddled into her serviceable dark wool winter coat, wrapping her knitted scarf over her nose and mouth. The air held an acrid tang, reminiscent of the fires left by the incendiary bombs and the coal fires used to heat the houses. The murkiness even managed to dull the bright advertisements in the shop windows advertising festive gifts.

Jane squeezed onto one of the last vacant seats on the bus and paid the conductress for her ticket. The window was steamed up with condensation which was smeared off by a small child wearing woollen mittens perched on his mother's lap.

Thankfully, mother and child disembarked after a couple of stops before the child could place his grubby mittens on Jane's coat. At least the child's mother had refrained from trying to engage her in conversation so that was one small mercy at least. She was not in the mood to exchange pleasantries with strangers. Her mind was on the task ahead.

The bus stop was just across the road from the address her mother had given her. Bush House was a handsome distinctive white building with no name plaque on the exterior. It had a distinctive dome with statuary above the entrance. Any previous damage appeared to have been repaired.

Jane disembarked and hurried across the road avoiding the traffic. She straightened her coat and skirt before heading up the shallow flight of steps and through the revolving wood and glass door. It seemed that the Broadcasting Service had returned to its previous home despite having some services located elsewhere.

She entered a large lobby with a marble tiled floor. In the distance she heard the faint sounds of someone playing a violin and a man singing. A motorcycle dispatch rider hurried past her on his way out of the building. Jane approached a dark-haired young woman who was seated behind a very large desk.

'Hello, I'm here for rehearsals with Miss Elsa Macintyre. My name is Jane Treen, I'm her pianist. She is expecting me.' She refrained from saying she was Elsa's daughter. She wondered if the girl was a replacement for Tabitha, drafted in at short notice.

The girl consulted a large diary before looking at a blackboard attached to the wall beside her. 'Oh yes, Miss Treen. Please sign in here and then Miss Macintyre is in room nine, up the stairs and turn right.' The girl indicated a flight of stone stairs at the side of her desk.

'Thank you.' Jane signed in the visitors' ledger and headed up the stairs to enter a long, narrow corridor. The large glass windows had all been taped in the familiar crisscross pattern to minimise glass shattering and causing damage should a bomb land nearby. Heavy, black-lined curtains were in place for night-time.

She passed a brown door marked with a number eight and heard the sound of violin music grow louder. Further down the corridor she found another brown door marked with a nine and pushed it open.

Her mother was already there, dressed elegantly in a fitted pale-blue French suit and standing beside a black baby grand piano. A leather case of sheet music was open on the top of the piano stool and her mother was talking to a handsome man in his early forties.

'Janey, honey, do come and meet Reggie. He's the band-leader you often hear playing most Friday evenings with his little dance band.' Elsa greeted her with an air kiss on both cheeks before stepping aside to allow Jane to shake hands with her mother's companion.

She gathered the man was Reginald Bosun, a Friday night favourite who played most of the popular hits of the day. He was also on air quite often either as a guest on other shows or when presenters played his music.

'Delighted, I'm sure. Elsa was just telling me that you had to step in at the last minute. Such a shame about Michael falling ill.' Reggie gave her a lascivious look, holding her hand just a fraction too long to be comfortable.

'Yes, it's most unfortunate for him, still I've played for her before.' Jane extricated her hand and resisted the urge to wipe her palm on her coat.

She moved over to a row of coat hooks and hung up her hat, scarf and coat.

'Reggie was just helping me sort out some songs. It's a tad early for Christmas music but variety is the key really. It wouldn't do for all of us to keep on performing the same old things,' her mother said as she turned back around.

'Luckily, Elsa has such an exquisite voice she can tackle most songs.' Reggie smiled at her mother.

'You're too kind, but I thought maybe since Janey pie might be a trifle rusty accompanying me we should choose some simpler music to begin with,' her mother said.

'Whatever you think is best,' Jane agreed and made sure she stood at a comfortable distance from Reggie. She suspected he fancied himself as something of a ladies' man.

'These are the ones we shall be performing as guests on Reggie's band show slot.' Her mother thrust a bundle of sheet music towards her. Jane cleared a space on the piano bench and sat down so that she could study the music.

'Now if any of these are too difficult, just say, you'll find that we're all friends here,' Reggie said.

'I'm sure I shall be fine, thank you,' Jane replied in a cool voice.

The songs her mother had selected were mostly ones she had played before, although admittedly for her own amusement. Accompanying her mother to her satisfaction would no doubt be more difficult. She set the first piece of music on the piano and flexed her fingers ready to warm herself up with a quick run-through.

She played a few bars and then played through to the chorus. It was one she knew fairly well so she hoped she would manage it without too much trouble. 'Right, do you want to make a start?' She looked at her mother.

'Of course, honey, let's go from the top then.' Her mother stood at the side of the piano and Jane played the introduction.

Much to her annoyance Reggie appeared to be lingering around like a bad smell as she accompanied her mother right through the piece. He broke into a series of hearty handclaps as her mother sounded the last note.

'Oh, I say bravo, Elsa, my dear. Magnificent.' He beamed at her mother.

'One tries.' Her mother bestowed a gracious smile on him. 'That was quite adequate, Janey, honey, although I think you might have fudged that middle part of the chorus a little.'

'Would you like to go again?' Jane disregarded her mother's criticism knowing that no matter how perfect her playing she would still find fault.

'Once more, please, honey,' her mother directed.

Jane gritted her teeth and played through again.

'Much better, darling,' Elsa pronounced. Jane thought it had sounded much the same as the first time but said nothing.

'Let's try the next piece.' Elsa replaced the music on the piano with another sheet.

The practice session continued and much to Jane's annoyance, Reggie showed no inclination to leave. The afternoon dragged on with Jane biting the inside of her cheek so hard she thought she would draw blood in her attempts not to be rude to her mother. Finally, she heard the blessed rattle of the tea trolley entering the room.

An elderly woman in a blue cotton pinafore duly poured them all a rather insipid cup of tea from the chrome urn. She also bestowed one plain biscuit on them as if doing them a huge favour. Jane accepted her cup with a sigh. It was too much she supposed to expect coffee.

At least the break meant she could stretch her fingers and light a much-needed cigarette, while her mother conferred with Reggie. She had barely lit up when the rehearsal room door opened again.

An older lady with dyed auburn hair wearing a cabbage-green twinset and multiple strands of amber beads hurried into the room.

'I say, Elsa, have you heard the news about Tabitha? It's quite dreadful, isn't it? Did you know, Reggie? The poor girl is dead. Murdered!'

The woman came to a halt and peered at Jane as if trying to place who she might be.

'Yes, I heard when I arrived. It's quite awful, isn't it?' Reggie replied.

'She must have been attacked by some ruffian during the blackout.' The woman clutched her strings of beads dramatically to her scrawny bosom. 'One feels so unsafe these days. You never know who may be lurking about.'

'That's very true,' Elsa agreed.

'Poor dear Leo, he must be absolutely distraught. They were so recently engaged as well.' The woman shook her head.

'Quite.' Reggie's tone was sympathetic.

'I wonder if they will catch whoever did it? I heard that the murderer hid her body on a bomb site.' The woman tutted as she spoke.

'It will be difficult for the police I expect, especially if it is some random bloke lurking about in the dark waiting to prey on innocent young women,' Reggie said, causing her to squeak in dismay.

'One never knows. Perhaps someone may come forward, a witness perhaps,' Jane said as she looked about for an ashtray.

Not finding one, she tapped the ash from her cigarette carefully onto the edge of her saucer. The auburn-haired woman stared at her.

'Do you really think so, Miss erm...?' She hesitated.

'Miss Treen,' Jane said. 'Well, why not? It's surprising, isn't it, what people do see sometimes. They might not have realised the significance at the time but if the police make an appeal, well, one never knows.'

'I suppose so.' The woman still sounded doubtful. 'Are you an artiste, Miss Treen?'

'Jane is accompanying me as Michael, my regular accompanist, is ill,' Elsa explained. 'Jane, honey, this is Miss Frances Fellowes.'

Jane noticed her mother was still not willing to admit their relationship.

'Oh, I see. Have you worked with Elsa before?' Frances asked.

'Yes, I have, although not for some time,' Jane said. 'Are you an artiste as well, erm, Frances?'

The older woman gave a nervous titter. 'Oh yes, I regularly play piano for a good many other singers and for Reginald here at times. Elsa, my dear, you know I would have assisted you if you had said.' She gave Jane a slightly doubtful glance as if uncertain of her abilities.

'Aw, Frances, sweetie pie, you're just too good. I know how busy you are, honey, so Janey here offered to help me out. You aren't offended I hope?' Elsa asked.

'Oh no, not at all. Yes, you're right, I do have a large workload. I suppose Miss Treen here has all the correct documentation?' Frances asked.

'Of course, my papers are in my bag if you need to see them, and do please call me Jane,' Jane offered. Fortunately, her prior experience of working with her mother in the past meant the brigadier had pulled strings to push through all necessary accreditation for Jane's eligibility to perform.

'Oh no, no, no. I didn't mean to imply you were not accredited, my dear. It was just I didn't recognise you and I've been on the circuit for a very long time,' Frances replied hastily.

'Frances here is quite the old warhorse.' Reginald chuckled at his own joke while Frances glared stonily at him.

'Janey played for me before the war, on the continent and on a theatre tour of Britain,' Elsa explained. 'Do any of the other regulars know about Tabitha?'

'I saw Jenny Jackson and Vincent Vaughn this morning. They were frightfully cut up as you might expect,' Reggie said.

'Quite. I wonder if Ernie knows?' Frances said. 'He must have been in to do the children's slot.'

Jane guessed that Frances must mean 'Uncle' Ernie Simons, who was a popular children's entertainer.

'I guess so,' Elsa agreed. 'Louisa, the new girl on reception, would have told him.'

'Oh dear, well, I had better let you get back to your rehearsal. Reggie, are you performing later or are you here for a recording?' Frances looked at the bandleader.

'The boys are due to arrive soon. I'd better go up to the studio.' Reggie looked at his watch.

He said his goodbyes to them and headed out, followed by Frances.

Jane placed her empty cup down on a nearby windowsill. 'I suppose we should continue. How much longer do we have the room booked for?'

'Only another forty minutes. Now, we may be recorded live tomorrow lunchtime with that new second number. It's a guest appearance on Ernest Simons's show so it needs to be bouncy and upbeat. We should run that one again to make certain you have it.' Her mother rearranged her music.

'I take it you all know one another quite well?' Jane asked as she took her seat at the piano and flexed her fingers.

'We usually end up doing the same shows over and over, you know. The headline stuff. It fits in around the news and the other things like the plays. I think the public grew tired of listening to Sandy on his organ,' Elsa said disparagingly.

Jane knew she was referring to a popular entertainer who had frequently been called upon to play in the various scheduling gaps. This had been very obvious during the early days of the war.

'The lunchtime thing tomorrow is a concert for the troops. Ernest is the compère. Parts of it are being filmed. I've agreed to do a few tunes, some drive for something or other.' Elsa peered critically at Jane's face. 'Honey, you really could be almost attractive you know with a little effort. It's important if the camera lands on you. Maybe if I used my tweezers on your brows. Stop you looking so tired. The boys will expect a little glamour, you know.'

'No, thank you, Mother,' Jane refused firmly, aware of her mother's fondness for attempting to change her appearance.

Elsa shrugged. 'Suit yourself, Janey. Just make sure you make some effort, wear a nice frock or something instead of those tweed things. I must say I was thrilled the brigadier has given you some time off to help me. It was such a shock when Michael said his doctor had advised him to rest. Stephen said he'd speak to the brigadier, and he said you could be spared. After all, there are plenty of other secretaries and it's a good thing Stephen has some influence in his department.'

Jane bit her tongue once more and hoped this assignment would end swiftly before she murdered her mother.

CHAPTER FIVE

Arthur discovered the brigadier had been most efficient in setting up the small flat in Jane's block. The building was on a pleasant tree-lined residential street and was mainly occupied by professional people. The apartment was identical in layout to Jane's, except her kitchen was at the rear of the flat and this one overlooked the street. Benson set about unpacking and Arthur settled down to begin studying the huge pile of transcripts which had been left for him.

Fortunately, the task was made slightly easier in that some of the suspect sentences had already been marked in pencil. He noticed that all of these seemed to be pasted in or fastened over the top of the original lines. There was a lot to go through, however, as well as hours of material to listen to.

Benson received a telephone call shortly after lunch and informed Arthur that he needed to go out.

'I shall return shortly, sir. It seems I have to make arrangements for the janitorial position.'

Arthur, deep in the transcripts, nodded his agreement. A moment later he heard the front door close, and Benson was gone. The suspect scripts had transmission dates on the top and a date next to the changes in pencil. He made notes as he looked through and noted the date of the changes matched the transmission dates. None of the dates on the changes to the scripts seemed to have been made in advance of transmission. He wondered how the changes were made and when the studios received the scripts. If they were couriered in from Whitehall or done internally via telephone instructions to someone.

There were crossings out and red pen markings in the margins or newly typed paragraphs, pasted on or clipped in place over the originals. Arthur worked methodically through them trying to identify who the authors may have been and who was responsible for alterations. He wasn't certain if all of the changes were suspicious or just certain ones. His next step would be to listen to what had been aired to see if they matched the scripts. A tape machine with headphones had been supplied for this purpose.

After a couple of hours, he grew tired and set the papers down. He removed his wire-framed spectacles and pinched the bridge of his nose trying to ease the pressure building in his forehead. He decided a cup of tea might be helpful and wandered into the small and sparsely equipped kitchen.

There was a pint of milk and a small tin containing loose tea on the kitchen side. He filled the kettle and set it on the electric ring to boil. The kitchen window offered a view over the front of the building down onto the street below.

Outside it already seemed to be quite dark. The murky smog Jane had mentioned from the previous evening had not fully cleared and seemed to be coming in more densely once more. On the pavement opposite there was a large London plane tree. A few tattered orangey-red leaves clung to its spiky branches. The rest lay in drifts on the pavement and in the gutter, rapidly turning brown as the end of the year moved closer.

He wasn't sure what caught his eye to begin with, but he

was suddenly certain that he was being observed. He pretended to be busy at the sink getting his cup and saucer and spoon ready, warming the teapot with a spot of water from the almost boiling kettle. There was a man by the tree, loitering near where the railings had once been. Arthur spooned some tea into the brown china teapot seemingly not looking in the direction of the stranger.

He made the tea discreetly watching his watcher. After a minute he grew tired of the game and locked eyes briefly with his observer. The man immediately adjusted his hat to shade his eyes and hurried off down the busy London street.

Arthur finished making his pot of tea, applied a jaunty red knitted cosy to the pot and carried it back into the sitting room. He set the simple tea tray down with a sigh and wondered if Benson had discovered any biscuits in the cupboards. The initial documents he had been sent while still in Devon had been much simpler than these more recent ones.

He didn't like the business of the man spying on the entrance to the flats. He could be friend or foe. Was he looking for Arthur himself or was it someone waiting for Jane? One never knew these days. It could be someone sent to ensure their safety or someone with rather more malicious intent. Either way it made him uncomfortable, and he would be glad to see his manservant return.

Jane was exhausted both physically and mentally by the time she let herself into her flat. The journey back from the rehearsals on the buses had been arduous with much hanging around at freezing stops and being jammed on the overcrowded transport.

Marmaduke, her one-eyed marmalade cat, strolled out into the hall to meet her as she took off her hat and coat. He twined himself around her legs meowing a greeting. Jane ignored the stray orange hairs on her precious stockings and bent to caress him.

'Darling Marmy, come on and I'll find you something nice for supper.'

She shivered as she entered her kitchen since she always left the window slightly ajar while she was at work. The cold air was a small price to pay since it allowed her cat access to get out via the black iron fire escape to the small area of parkland behind the apartment block. Marmaduke liked to prowl around the scrubby laurel bushes hunting for mice and small birds.

The window was fitted with a lock to prevent it from being forced so it took her a minute to undo the fastening and drop the pane back into place. She turned on the electric ring and put her kettle on to boil while she prepared a bowl of food for her cat and refilled his water dish.

Once Marmaduke was fed and she had a cup of coffee she wandered into her compact sitting room and sat down for a restorative cigarette. She needed a few minutes' peace before she headed out again to call on Arthur and Benson to see if they had made any progress.

She pulled out a notebook and made a list of the names of the people she had met and heard mentioned during the afternoon. Reggie Bosun, Frances Fellowes, Ernest Simons, Vincent Vaughn and Jenny Jackson. She exhaled a stream of cigarette smoke and added Leo Cavendish's name to her list.

It might at least provide a starting point, depending on what Arthur had discovered in the transcripts and the tapes. The scripts might well have those names on them which would help them to see if the same people kept cropping up. She knew Arthur well enough to know he would have already begun to go through the material the brigadier had said he would supply.

There had to be something in there that Tabitha had recognised was wrong. Something she had been about to reveal before she had been murdered. Jane shivered again and extinguished her cigarette in a small, blown-glass ashtray. She finished her coffee and saw her cat was settled before setting off for Arthur's temporary accommodation.

She slipped on her coat and took the back service stairs down to Arthur's floor. She was less likely to encounter any of her neighbours this way. She wasn't in the mood to make polite, casual conversation about smog or food shortages.

Benson answered the door to her knock after he had first checked through the small peephole to see who was there.

'Brr, it's a cold one tonight,' she said as she hurried inside the narrow hall, relishing the comforting wave of warmth emanating towards her from the sitting room.

'Indeed, Miss Jane, please go through.' Benson disappeared towards the compact kitchen as she hung her coat on a hook.

Her stomach rumbled as she caught a whiff of something delicious, reminding her that she had eaten very little at lunchtime and her own supper was probably likely to be pilchards on toast.

Arthur was seated beside the fire. A recording machine was at one side with a set of headphones and a pile of papers covered a low table in front of him.

'Hello, Jane. I thought you'd be along soon. How did it go this afternoon?'

She sank down on the armchair opposite him with a sigh. 'Mother was as tiresome as ever and I met a few very interesting people.' She produced her notebook from the pocket of her cardigan and tore off the list she'd prepared upstairs. 'Here, I don't know if any of these names feature in the scripts or the recordings.'

Jane passed the paper across to him and he scanned the list. 'Hmm, interesting.'

'Reggie Bosun was ensconced with Mother when I arrived.

He's quite smarmy I thought. Rather thinks of himself as a ladies' man.' Jane looked at Arthur.

'He's quite a big name, isn't he? The bandleader fellow? Does a lot of the light music?' Arthur frowned at the list. 'I've run across his name several times. Who else did you meet?'

'Frances Fellowes, dreadful old bat. She was questioning my credentials to play for Mother. She was also morbidly gleeful about Tabitha's murder.' Jane gave a faint shudder as she recalled the look on the woman's face when she had arrived inside the rehearsal room.

'What does she do?' Arthur asked.

'Pianist I believe, mainly, but she also does sound effects and some prompting. A few speaking lines in plays.' Jane stretched out her slender legs, enjoying the heat emanating from Arthur's electric fire.

'Yes, I think I've seen her name in the scripts too. What are your plans for tomorrow?' Arthur asked.

'Mother is singing at some fundraising drive tomorrow lunchtime for the troops. It's being filmed to ask for money for war bonds or something, I think. Then we have an evening performance of a couple of songs with Reggie's band.' Jane raised her hand and pressed it to her mouth to stifle a yawn. 'Gosh, I'm sorry, I'm so tired.'

'There was a man out the front this afternoon watching the building,' Arthur said.

Jane immediately sat up straight, all her senses on full alert. 'Watching this building? Are you quite certain?'

Arthur nodded. 'Yes, he scarpered pretty quickly when he realised I'd seen him.'

'What did he look like?' Jane was confused. How could anyone have discovered where they were so quickly? Unless they had been looking for her and it was mere chance they had gone when they realised they had been observed.

'Tall, about thirty to forty, smartly dressed. His hat was

obscuring his face so I couldn't tell you much more than that,' Arthur said.

'He might be one of our lot. If the brigadier or Colonel Hardacre felt we might be in danger,' Jane said. She wasn't convinced about that though. She knew her employer pretty well and he would have said if he was setting someone up to ensure their safety. No, this felt different.

'I thought that but I'm not sure. It could be someone who saw us at Whitehall and followed us, I suppose?' Arthur suggested.

'Could be, or a leak from somewhere. Maybe someone who helped set this flat up and sorted the paperwork. It only takes one slip.' Jane met his gaze, and she knew he too was thinking of their first case again.

Then, they had uncovered a network of people working against the interests of the country. It could be that this new case had thrown them back up against the same group. Even though the person who had headed that group of traitors had died, Jane knew that someone would have taken their place.

'I've made a start on these transcripts. The first ones that were sent to me in Devon had a fairly simple code inserted in some of the statements. These later ones, however, seem to be much more complex. I can see there is a pattern there but I'm having to listen to the tapes. The emphasis placed on a word or part of a word could potentially make a difference. I need to be certain about what changes are significant.' Arthur frowned as he spoke.

'Surely though if there were different announcers then the emphasis wouldn't be important? It would need to be the same person so they would know what the message was that they needed to convey. If that's the case, then it should be simple to pick up who the traitor is.' Jane looked at him.

Arthur shook his head. 'I wish it were that simple. No, the messages are encoded in the scripts, and for all I know, possibly in the musical pieces. It's too early to say until I listen to the tapes and compare. They are being delivered by people who are unaware of the hidden content. I just need to establish the pattern.'

Jane sighed and pulled out her cigarettes. She ignored Arthur's frown and looked around for an ashtray. He reached down the side of his chair and placed a small chrome metal one in front of her, moving some of the papers to make a space for it.

'Thank you.' She took care to hold her cigarette so the smoke wouldn't annoy him. 'I have had the most trying day and tomorrow will probably be worse. Is Benson all set for tomorrow?'

'He went out this afternoon to get everything arranged.' The furrows on Arthur's forehead deepened. 'What if your mother sees Benson acting as a janitor at the studios? She could well scupper the whole thing.'

Jane blew out a thin stream of smoke and considered his question. 'Mother is not terribly observant, unless it is something that directly concerns her. I think Benson dressed as a janitor in a place she is not expecting to see him won't register with her at all. It would probably be best if he doesn't speak to her though. As a singer that is one thing she is good at, pinning people down by their voice.'

'Obviously, he'll avoid her where possible. Their paths may not cross at all. He'll be around mostly out of regular hours, evenings and early mornings.'

Arthur moved to ease his shoulders, and she guessed he had spent much of the afternoon crouched over working on the scripts.

Benson entered the room. 'Will you be dining with us this evening, Miss Jane? I have adequate supplies for three,' he said.

'Oh, I couldn't put you to any trouble, Mr Benson.' Jane's heart wasn't really in her protest. Whatever Arthur's manservant was cooking definitely smelled better than anything she was likely to come up with back in her own flat.

'I assure you it's no trouble at all. Perhaps a small sherry while dinner is cooking?' Benson suited his actions to his words.

'Arthur was telling me that you're all set for your new role tomorrow.' Jane tapped the ash from her cigarette into the ashtray.

'Yes, Miss Jane. The brigadier has been most thorough. I shall report for duty at six in the morning.' Benson set a sherry glass before her and poured another for Arthur.

'Arthur was concerned that my mother might recognise you,' Jane said.

'I shall endeavour to keep out of sight of Miss Elsa,' Benson said and returned to the kitchen, coming back shortly afterwards bearing cutlery and tablemats to set the small folding table for dinner.

He set the table for three and Jane extinguished her cigarette. It looked as if she could save the pilchards on toast for another day.

CHAPTER SIX

Arthur rose the following morning to find that Benson had already departed. His breakfast had been left prepared in the kitchen and some fish paste sandwiches were wrapped in greaseproof paper for his lunch on the cold slab.

He opened the curtains and looked out onto the street half expecting to discover the man from the day before. The street, although busy, showed no sign of anyone lurking. Somewhat relieved, he dropped the curtain back in place and concentrated on making his morning tea.

He had just finished shaving and dressing when the telephone rang.

'Ha, Arthur, good show, just the chap.' Arthur recognised the familiar boom of the brigadier's voice and moved the receiver away from his ear.

'Good morning, sir.' He wondered why the brigadier might be calling.

'I thought I should check on progress. I have people here very anxious to know that the wheels are in motion on this business.' He knew the brigadier was being careful about what he said. The telephone line was not secure, and anyone might be listening in to the conversation.

'I've made a good start. The initial items I received in Devon were quite simple. However, the later goods are more complicated. It may take a while to establish the pattern.' Arthur hoped the brigadier would understand him.

'I see. You think they were altered in response to something?' the brigadier asked.

'It's very possible that suspicions had been roused so they became more complex,' Arthur agreed.

He had discussed this with Jane over dinner and she and Benson had both had similar thoughts. The coding could well have been made more difficult if those transmitting it thought that someone, probably Tabitha, was onto them.

'Hmm, I see,' the brigadier said.

'By the way, sir, yesterday I noticed someone outside the apartment block. Do you know if he might have been a friend of yours?' Arthur knew the brigadier would understand this question about whoever had been observing him.

'No, no one I know in your area. What was he like?' the brigadier asked and Arthur thought he detected a slight note of alarm in the older man's tone.

He described the man he'd seen lurking by the plane tree.

'Very good. Keep an eye open in case he calls back. I'll check and see if any of my friends were out your way after all,' the brigadier said. He ended the call.

* * *

Jane set off shortly after nine to meet Elsa at one of the mobile NAAFI canteens operating in the city. The money for the mobile canteens had been principally raised in America and there were several in use now all over London. Elsa had informed Jane that they were to be filmed for a short piece to play overseas showing how the canteens were being used.

Jane shivered and huddled into her coat on the bus. At least the smog had lifted leaving a fairly clear, crisp morning. The bus dropped her a couple of streets from the address Elsa had given her. All around her she could see signs of damage from the bombing raids carried out by the enemy. Scorched brick-work and gaps between buildings leaving the survivors standing like a battered row of jagged teeth.

The mobile canteen had been set up on a cleared bomb site in the East End of London. Next door to the canteen was a church hall, which was where the piano had been set up along with chairs all ready for the troop concert.

Jane had the music for the concert in a black leather case that she tucked under her arm as she walked briskly along, dodging the debris on the pavements and the people all going about their business. Her mother had instructed her to meet her inside the church hall.

She spotted the canteen truck with a queue of five or six people outside it waiting for cups of tea and Bovril to be dispensed. She knew that the small truck also produced hot meals for poor and needy people in the local area and she marvelled at how they managed to do it in such a confined space.

Elsa was waiting inside the hall. The lavish fur collar and cuffs on her coat and mink hat a stark contrast to the poverty all around her.

'Janey pie, about time,' Elsa greeted her, with a brief kiss on her cheek. 'Now, do come and meet Jenny, she is doing a reading in between our musical numbers and Ernie will be performing one of his skits and his stand-up comedy routine.'

Elsa introduced her to a woman of a similar age to her mother. Jenny Jackson was a well-known stage actress, popular in the London theatres. Before the war she had been a star of a touring theatre performing Shakespeare nightly. She was smoking a cigarette and talking to a round-faced, plump younger man.

'Jenny, Ernie, this is Jane, she is my accompanist for today.' Once again Elsa failed to mention that she was Jane's mother.

'Delighted, I'm sure.' Jenny eyed her curiously.

'Pleasure to meet you, Jane.' Ernie at least seemed friendly.

Jane recognised both names from the previous day.

'When are the film crew arriving?' Jenny asked.

Elsa consulted the dainty gold wristwatch she was wearing. 'Anytime now, I believe. The soldiers are also getting here soon so we need to get a run-through going pretty quick smart. Janey pie, hop to it.' She indicated the piano stool.

Jane slipped off her coat and gloves and hung them on a nearby hook before taking her seat at the battered upright. She hoped the piano played better than it looked. She had recurring memories of the brief tour she had done years before with her mother. She had spent hours trying to coax tunes out of instruments that had only been fit for firewood.

She did a test run of scales on the piano wincing a little at a couple of keys that were slightly off. On the whole though she had played many worse instruments.

'Now, here is the running order and the script notes. Apparently, Tabitha had prepared these before she was killed. Louisa, the girl that's taken her place, gave them to me yesterday.' Elsa handed out a flimsy sheet of paper to Jane and the other two performers.

Jane glanced at the running order. The introduction was to be made by Ernie, before her mother made a speech about the value of the mobile canteens. This included thanking the American donors. Then there was the first song, followed by Jenny's reading of some sentimental verse. Ernie was then to thank her, and perform a short routine before Elsa would close the hour with a patriotic singalong with a special thank you to our American friends.

It all seemed quite straightforward, and she could see no added notes or changes. Perhaps because this was to be filmed for the cinema rather than a radio transmission there would be no hidden messages.

The film crew arrived with a small canvas-backed lorry and began to set up for filming. Jane tried to keep her concentration on playing for the run-through of her mother's solo and then the music for the final sing-song.

Outside the hall she could hear a hubbub building as word seemed to have gone around locally about what was happening.

'Right then, we're all set, Miss Elsa, ma'am,' said the man who appeared to be the director, and who, like her mother, was American.

'Fabulous, honey.' Her mother beamed at him and earned herself a sour look from Jenny.

The doors of the hall were opened, and the seats were soon filled by soldiers who Jane guessed had been instructed to attend. The room filled with chatter and cigarette smoke. Once everyone was in place, Ernie set the ball rolling.

He made the introduction and Elsa took to the stage, her appearance drawing wolf whistles and a round of applause from the soldiers. She gave her brief speech and blew a kiss directly at the camera with a saucy wink, before Jane played the music for her mother to sing.

The song was met with wild enthusiasm. Ernie was forced to say a few words to quieten the crowd before Jenny performed her dramatic and moving monologue. This was received well but more quietly. Jane remained at the piano while Ernie ran through his skit.

The jokes were so old it was a wonder they had not grown whiskers, but it seemed to go down well before Elsa returned to the stage to lead the sing-along. Jane found herself feeling unexpectedly emotional during a couple of the songs. It seemed so hard knowing that many of the audience would never return.

Elsa gave her thanks to her comrades at home in the USA and the concert finished. The camera stopped filming, and Elsa was swamped by soldiers requesting autographs and a kiss for good luck before they were ordered out of the hall.

'Thank goodness that's all done. I must admit I was worried how it would go without Tabitha to organise it all. Ordinarily Leo would have stepped up, but the poor man must be devastated,' Jenny said as she watched the last of the soldiers march out of the hall.

Elsa was busy talking to the film crew as they packed up their gear.

'Goodness, yes, although I don't suppose you are too upset, Jenny, darling. You and Tabitha were hardly bosom chums.' Ernie looked at the actress with one eyebrow slightly raised.

'I admit that Tabitha and I had our differences, but I wouldn't have wished the girl dead,' Jenny protested.

'Really, darling, that wasn't what you were saying the other day when you were moaning about her reducing your appearances,' Ernie said as he gathered his things together.

'That was a misunderstanding,' Jenny huffed. 'Anyway, you had your own quarrels with her. You were always trying to get your scripts changed to give you a bigger part.'

'Miss Treen, did you know Tabitha at all? She was our receptionist and organised all the contracts with Leo,' Ernie asked.

'I think I only met her a couple of times,' Jane answered the question truthfully. She had been aware the girl had been placed on an assignment, but she had not been responsible for overseeing her.

'And how do you know Elsa?' Ernie asked as he glanced over to where her mother was openly flirting with the film director.

'I've accompanied her before. I've known her all my life so when Michael had to stand down she asked me if I could help out for a while.' Jane had no wish to draw attention to their relationship. It would only complicate matters.

'Do you know Leo too, Tabitha's fiancé?' Jenny asked as Jane placed her music inside her leather case.

'No, not really. It must be awful for him though, poor man. I heard Tabitha was murdered.' Jane decided to see what response this got.

'Really, darling, I heard it was murder too and by strangulation. She was such a pretty girl. I expect it was some depraved sex pest lurking in the blackout.' Jenny shivered, her hands involuntarily going to her own throat.

'You sound like Frances, darling. Such a ghastly thing to happen though. Poor old Leo. Has anyone seen him since it happened?' Ernie asked.

'Frances was asking that too. You know how she's always hanging around him. I haven't seen him, though I don't know about Elsa,' Jenny said as Jane's mother approached them.

'What's that, honey?' Elsa asked looking at Jenny.

'Ernie asked if anyone had seen or heard from Leo since Tabitha's murder,' Jenny said.

Elsa shrugged and donned her fur hat with care, tidying her curls by looking at her reflection in a speckled mirror on the wall of the church hall. 'Sorry, honey, I haven't. I expect he'll be back in once he's gotten over the shock.'

Her words sounded a little harsh, but Jane knew what she meant. Life was so precarious that no matter how deeply someone might be affected by the loss of a loved one you simply had to get on. There was no time or space to grieve properly. She knew that herself all too well.

They said goodbye to the others and Elsa accompanied Jane outside the hall.

'Janey, I'll see you back at the broadcasting studios later. I promised that darling director I'd go with him for a quick cup of tea.' Elsa glanced back over her shoulder to where the film director was standing waiting for her next to a large black motor car. The truck with the camera crew had already departed.

Jane suppressed a sigh and set off for the bus stop wondering how her mother's beau had acquired his petrol. By the time she arrived back at the apartment block she was both tired and hungry. She decided to drop in and see if Arthur had made any progress before returning to her own flat.

She made her way up the stairs and rang the doorbell. After a few minutes Arthur finally answered the door.

* * *

Arthur was annoyed when the doorbell buzzed, breaking his concentration. It took him a moment to realise that Benson was still absent, and he needed to go and see who was there himself.

'Oh, um, Jane, do come in,' he said, standing back to allow her into the hall. She looked tired and cross.

She hung her hat and coat on the hall stand and followed him into the sitting room. The tape machine was stopped, and he had papers and notes covering every surface. He hastily moved a small pile from the end of the sofa so she could sit down.

Jane sank down with a weary sigh and pulled out her cigarettes. Arthur looked around for the ashtray and discovered it buried under a stack of transcripts.

'How did it go at the concert?' he asked as he placed the ashtray next to her.

'It was my mother, so it was pretty much as I expected. I met Jenny Jackson and Ernie Simons though. There was lots of chatter about Tabitha's murder.' Jane applied her lighter to her cigarette and looked around at the papers. 'It looks as if you've been busy this morning?'

'Yes, I think I'm getting somewhere but it's taking me more time than I'd like,' Arthur admitted. 'Can I get you some tea? Or coffee?' he added, suddenly recalling that Jane preferred black coffee to tea.

'That sounds heavenly. I've only got a short window of time before I have to go back out again ready for this evening's performance for the radio transmission. It takes an age to get anywhere on the bus these days.'

Arthur went through to the kitchen to fill the kettle. He glanced out of the window and instinctively moved back so he couldn't be seen. 'Jane, that man is here again, outside the block.'

She was at his side in an instant. 'Where?' she asked. She too stayed back so she couldn't be seen from outside.

'There, where I saw him the last time, lurking next to the plane tree,' Arthur said.

'Keep watching. I'm going down.' She vanished and he heard the front door before he could stop her.

CHAPTER SEVEN

He stayed in place at the window and saw Jane emerge from the block minus her hat and coat. She headed purposefully across the street dodging the passing cars. The watcher saw her coming and went to escape but Jane was too fast for him. Arthur could only watch as she chased the man down to block his path.

He saw her gesticulating and pointing towards the block before the man turned and they both headed back to cross the road. Arthur frowned and put the kettle on to boil before adding an extra cup to the tea tray. It seemed that Jane was bringing an extra guest to the flat and he would have to save his rebukes at her recklessness for another time.

Arthur hurried through to the sitting room and hastily stashed all of his notes and papers into a pile out of sight, before throwing a cloth over the tape machine. He finished just in time for the doorbell to sound and Jane was back on the doorstep.

'Brr.' Jane shivered as she wiped her feet on the mat and stepped inside the hall. 'Arthur, this is Leo Cavendish. Mr Cavendish, this is my colleague, Arthur Cilento.'

The tall man accompanying Jane took off his hat and, at her urging, hung his coat beside hers on the hooks in the hall.

Jane asked a silent question with her eyes before suggesting to their visitor that he go through into the sitting room.

'I'll finish making the coffee,' Arthur said and left Jane with their guest.

It seemed the man watching the flat from the street was the fiancé of Tabitha Moore, the dead girl. The man the brigadier had said had made accusations against the department and caused a scene at the police station. How had he found them here and what was he doing lurking around outside? He took the whistling kettle off the heat and prepared the coffee. It was harder to come by these days and Benson had struggled to get hold of a tin.

Arthur carried the tray through and set it down on the table before taking a seat. He poured a drink for them all, which Leo accepted gratefully. Arthur studied him carefully, whilst apologising for the lack of sugar. The man looked pale and haggard, dark shadows lay under his eyes as if he hadn't slept for days.

'Thank you.' Leo wrapped his hands around the cup as if glad of the heat.

'What were you doing out there watching the flats?' Jane asked as soon as some colour had begun to return to Leo's pale face.

'I was hoping I'd find out what was going on. I tried going the official route to get answers about Tabitha's death. She'd said a few things that I didn't think much of at the time. I knew she was more than just a receptionist, but obviously she couldn't tell me her other reasons for being at Bush House. Then, when she was killed, I began to wonder.' Leo leaned back in his seat.

'What kind of things did she say?' Arthur asked.

Leo glanced at Jane as if he was uncertain he should enlarge on what he had already let slip.

'Arthur is a member of my team. You may say anything in front of him,' Jane said.

'Tabitha said she was worried about some anomalies she

had noticed in the scripts. I thought she just meant people jostling for airtime. You have no idea of the egos of some of the actors,' Leo said.

'Oh, trust me, I do,' Jane responded with feeling.

'I asked her what she meant, and she wouldn't say. She said she was probably mistaken. This was a couple of days before she was killed. I knew she had come from working at Whitehall, but I had assumed originally that she had just been involved in administration. She told me she had been a typist there.' Leo looked at Jane.

'That's true, she was,' Jane assured him.

'When the police told me Tabitha was dead, murdered, well I kept turning everything over and over in my mind. The suspicion that she had been an agent of some sort and someone in the home security department knew something. That maybe someone there had betrayed her or killed her over whatever it was she'd discovered. The police seemed to think she had been attacked at random. That her attacker had spotted her in the smog and hurt her. I mean, I suppose that could have been the case except I knew there had to be more to it than that.' Leo looked at them.

Arthur frowned. 'Why do you think that?' He was curious to hear Leo's reasoning. He didn't believe there was such a thing as gut instinct. Any wayward feeling in someone's abdomen could usually be traced back to something small that had raised the alarm.

Leo sighed and appeared to consider. 'A random attacker wouldn't have taken time to try and hide her body. Her bag was missing, I allow, but her engagement ring and necklace had not been stolen.' He paused and swallowed before adding, 'She had not been molested in any way.'

Arthur nodded. 'Yes, I see.'

'Then I thought what if it's someone she knew? Maybe someone within her former department at Whitehall? Or someone who had been doing something at Bush House and Tabitha was onto them? I went to the police and then to White-hall and demanded to see someone. They threw me out.' Leo stopped to sip his coffee.

'Leo, you were Tabitha's employer, you knew she had come from the department, and she didn't say anything to you at all about something else being amiss? She only mentioned something about anomalies in the scripts? Was that all she said?' Jane leaned forward in her seat; her earlier weariness appeared to have disappeared.

'My role at the BBC is running programming. I organise the news, any updates from government, official notices and balance the programme of cultural events, morale-boosting stuff and the popular items. Since the television service was stopped and radio broadcasting has become more confined, the role has increased in importance. Tabitha was my right-hand woman in all ways. She oversaw contracts, booked the artistes and ensured they could make recordings and live programmes to fulfil the brief. As you may know we have a core of regular artistes who are quite versatile and are popular with listeners. It builds confidence and that feeling of security. Then we book other acts and plays, etc. around that. She never said anything else about something being wrong,' Leo explained.

'So why do you think Tabitha was concerned? What part of the programme was bothering her? Was it just these supposed anomalies? She could have simply left off any act or artiste that she felt was problematic?' Jane said. 'I heard today that Jenny Jackson was one of those acts who was getting less work.'

Leo's lips quirked up at the corners in a sketch of a smile. 'Jenny is rather fond of the bottle. That was why Tabitha was using her less. She was half-cut most of the time. She kept forgetting her lines and the other actors had to cover for her. We could only use her if we pre-recorded items.'

'Why were you outside the apartment block? What made

you come here? Why look for me or for Arthur?' Jane asked. She sincerely hoped that there had not been a leak from inside the department. No one apart from the brigadier, and she suspected possibly Mr Churchill himself, knew of their small investigative cell.

'I saw your name on the list that Louisa, Tabitha's replacement, had in front of her when she first came to cover after Tabitha went missing. Forgive me, Miss Treen, but your surname is distinctive and Tabitha had mentioned you once before a long time ago when she first came to work with me. I raised my concern to Brigadier Remmington-Blythe that Tabitha's death was linked to national security after her death. Then when I saw your name, I thought there had to be a reason why someone as senior as yourself was accompanying Miss Macintyre.' Leo looked at her.

Arthur coughed gently. 'Elsa is Jane's mother.'

Leo stared at him in disbelief. 'Your mother?' He looked back at Jane.

'Yes, my mother, not my sister or my cousin or any other fabrication she may come up with to make herself seem too young to have a daughter my age,' Jane replied in a dry tone.

'How did you know where Jane lived?' Arthur asked.

'I loitered outside the offices at Whitehall, and I heard Miss Treen give her address to the driver. I made my way here and decided to stake the place out. I knew there was something going on. I realised you had noticed me the other day, but I didn't know if you were part of the department or just a neighbour who thought I was behaving suspiciously,' Leo explained.

'I see.' Arthur supposed the man's explanation was plausible.

'I won't rest until I find out who killed Tabitha.' Leo looked at them and Arthur could see the determination in the line of Leo's jaw.

Jane exchanged a look with Arthur. 'Mr Cavendish, you

realise we are not at liberty to discuss any part of our assignment with you?'

Leo bowed his head for a moment before raising his gaze to look Jane in the eyes. 'Yes.'

'I must also ask that you say nothing at all to any other person working at Bush House. It is imperative that no one knows anything other than I am assisting Elsa. I would also suggest that, unless my mother makes my connection to her public, you also don't mention that to anyone either. Do you understand me?' Jane's voice was firm.

'But you are looking into Tabitha's murder?' Leo asked.

'I can't tell you that,' Jane said.

Leo sighed, studying her face for a moment as if trying to read an answer in her expression. 'Very well, I understand. I will be looking for Tabitha's killer though, Miss Treen. Of that you may be quite certain.'

'I cannot stop you, nor would I wish to, but if your investigation compromises our mission in any way, I shall have you removed. Do I make myself quite clear?' Jane said.

Leo set down his cup and saucer. 'As crystal, Miss Treen. Now, if you'll excuse me, I have to make arrangements with Tabitha's parents for her funeral.' He rose from his chair.

'I'll see you out.' Arthur followed him into the hall to retrieve his hat and coat before letting him out of the flat.

When he returned to the sitting room Jane had lit another cigarette.

'Has he gone?' she asked as Arthur retook his seat.

'Yes, I saw him downstairs and out of the main entrance.' Arthur looked at her. 'You believed him?' he asked.

Jane blew out a thin stream of smoke, taking care to deflect it away from Arthur. 'No, he was lying, at least in part.'

'You noticed?' Arthur had guessed Jane would have picked up on the flaw in Leo's spiel.

'He said he got my address from the taxi after seeing my

name on the list at Broadcasting House. That wasn't possible. My name was only added to the list later once the brigadier made the arrangements. You and Benson took a taxi the day we saw the brigadier in his office. I went to meet Mother by bus. I didn't come home first.' Jane looked at Arthur.

'I thought the same thing. We can only assume that Tabitha must have let something slip. Although it's concerning that he found your address. Do you know which police officer is handling the investigation into Tabitha's murder?' Arthur asked.

'The brigadier did say he had spoken to them. I think it's in the file.' She nodded towards the papers Arthur had concealed.

He uncovered them and found the small folder they had been given at the briefing. 'Ha, yes, here it is. Inspector Winters at Scotland Yard.'

'We need to speak to him.' Jane tapped the ash from the end of her cigarette into the ashtray. 'We also need to let the brigadier know what has happened.'

'He won't be happy,' Arthur warned.

'No, and neither am I. This whole operation may have to be abandoned before it properly gets going. We'll have to see what our instructions are.' Jane took a last pull from her cigarette and extinguished it.

'I'll make the calls,' Arthur offered. 'You haven't much time if you are to get back to Broadcasting HQ.'

'I need to go and see to Marmaduke too. I'll call back this evening. I hope Benson is having more luck.' Jane rose from her seat ready to head back to her own flat.

Arthur walked with her to the door where she collected her hat and coat.

He wished she had left Leo Cavendish on the pavement. 'Do be careful, Jane. Your safety as well as this mission may be in more danger than we realise.'

CHAPTER EIGHT

Jane shivered as she opened her front door and entered her hall. It was already beginning to grow dark, and the air was cool after being in Arthur's apartment. Marmaduke was nowhere in sight as she washed his dish and prepared his food.

She went to the slightly open kitchen window and made the chirruping noises that usually called him in to eat. She was certain he wouldn't be far away. Her cat was fond of food and had an innate sense of timing of when it was likely to appear.

Sure enough, a minute later, Marmaduke eased his fluffy bulk through the gap. Jane pulled the window closed behind him, switched on the light and put up the blackout. It would be late when she returned home, and she wanted to make sure her flat was secure.

Marmaduke permitted her to fuss the top of his head before going to his bowl. Jane hurriedly made herself some toast and jam with a cup of coffee. She wasn't sure if she would be able to get anything to eat while she was out, and her stomach was growling with hunger.

Once she'd eaten and made sure her flat was tidy and that

she had everything she needed for the evening performance, she said goodbye to her cat.

'Now do be good.' She kissed him tenderly on his head while he blinked at her with his one good eye. 'I'll be back later.'

She locked the door and hurried out to wait for the bus once again. The street was busier now as people were making their way home from work. The evening was grey and gloomy with low light and the incipient smog had begun creeping in once more from the river.

Jane huddled inside her coat and pulled her scarf up to cover her nose and mouth. The bus was crowded, and she had to stand for much of the way. One hand holding tightly to the leather strap above her head as the bus bumped its way over the potholes. Her free hand gripping the handle of her music case.

It was almost dark by the time the bus halted at her stop, and she had to fight her way through the crowd to get off the bus. The fog had rolled in and was swirling about now, leaving a noxious smell in her nostrils and an almost oily taste in her mouth despite the protection of her scarf.

She joined a crowd at a crossing point ready to go over to the studio building. There was more traffic than usual, and she supposed it was probably people hoping to reach home before the blackout started.

As she began to cross, she felt someone give her music case a sharp tug. She immediately tightened her grip on the leather handle. She looked up to try and see who was attempting to take her bag, but several grey and black clad figures were pressed in close beside her and she couldn't see who was responsible.

Jane pulled her case closer, bumping it against the box that held her gas mask. They were almost at the kerb now on the opposite side of the road and the group began to thin. Just as she was about to step onto the pavement a hard shove in the small of Jane's back sent her sprawling onto the pavement, knocking her leather music case from her hand.

An elderly lady and a gentleman stopped to assist her to her feet, steadying her and brushing her down.

'My dear, are you all right?' The woman peered anxiously at her through her spectacles.

'Yes, I think so. Someone pushed me.' Jane suddenly realised she had let go of her music case. She looked around on the pavement that was now empty of people except for her helpers. 'My music case is gone.'

'A case?' the man who had assisted her asked.

'Yes, black leather, like a satchel. It has my sheet music inside.' Jane couldn't believe she had been robbed. Her knees ached where she had landed, and her gloves were muddy.

'There's no case here,' the woman said with a frown. 'Can we help you in any way? You look quite shaken up.'

'No, thank you, you've both been very kind. I'm just going to that building there. I'm meeting my mother,' Jane explained as she politely refused more offers of assistance. After a minute or two more convincing them that she was all right Jane limped inside the BBC headquarters.

Her mother was at the desk talking to the receptionist when Jane entered the lobby. A motorcycle courier was with them, clearly having dropped off a package. He hurried past her as she hobbled to the desk.

'Janey, honey, I wondered where you were. Have you hurt yourself?' Her mother hurried over to meet her, a frown on her immaculately made-up face.

'Someone pushed me over as I was crossing the road and stole my music case.' Jane tugged off her soiled gloves, annoyed she hadn't been able to get a look at whoever had assaulted her.

'You've lost the music?' Elsa looked at her with an appalled expression.

'I didn't lose it. It was stolen.' Jane glared at her. Any concern her mother may have had for Jane's dishevelled appearance had been immediately superseded by the missing music.

'Well, how are we going to manage now. This is a fine pickle.' Elsa continued to complain while Jane examined the damage to her precious stockings.

'I think we should be all right. I can play the pieces you selected for tonight pretty well from memory and we have the band so I can look at their pieces,' Jane snapped as she straightened up.

'Well, I hope so. This is live tonight so we can't have any mix-ups. Now, we need to head to the studio.' Elsa pursed her ruby lipsticked lips together and Jane guessed she had taken umbrage at her solution to the problem.

She limped up the stairs after her mother and diverted off to the ladies' toilets to clean up her hands and bathe her knee before going to the studio. It was her first time being in a radio studio and Jane looked around with interest. In one corner there was what seemed to be an enclosed glass booth where an announcer was reading from documents into a large rectangular microphone. A red light showed above the door to the booth and an illuminated sign read '*On Air*'.

Jane assumed the announcer was Vincent Vaughn, one of the regular people who normally delivered the news and the links between the programmes. There was a glass wall with a door behind where she could see the band setting up and a technician checking the microphone for her mother and Reggie Bosun, the bandleader.

The light above this door was green so she went inside. The receptionist followed her and passed a script to the technician who glanced at it and set it aside as the girl departed.

'My dear Jane, Elsa was just telling me about your accident. How dreadful! Can you manage to play by ear, do you think? Or do you need a copy of the pieces?' Reggie asked her as soon as she stepped through the door. 'We have' – he paused to glance at the large clock on the studio wall – 'fifteen minutes to finish preparing and to do sound checks before broadcast.'

'I think I should be all right, if I have a copy of the running order.' Jane forced a brief smile and edged slightly away from Reggie who was standing much too close to her for comfort.

'Of course.' Reggie flashed a greasy smile and delved into a pile of papers handing her one of the sheets.

She limped to the piano and took her seat.

'Now then, places people, not much time!' Reggie announced loudly, getting everyone's attention.

Elsa was already at the microphone harassing what seemed to be a technician about the sound. Reggie shooed the man away as Jane played a few notes and hoped she could remember the music.

There was time for a run-through of three short pieces, two with just the band and one with Elsa and Jane without the band. Reggie, despite Jane's mild distaste for him personally, was good at his job. He soon had everyone as he wanted them just before the studio light turned red and they were live on air.

Jane watched and listened as Reggie introduced the music and Elsa. Reggie linked the songs, told a few self-deprecating jokes and shamelessly flattered her mother. Her nerves quickly dissipated as she concentrated on the task at hand. The hour and a half went by rapidly, and the studio light changed to green for off air.

'That's it then, ladies and gentlemen, thank you all,' Reggie said as soon as he'd bidden farewell to their audience and the light had changed.

Jane breathed a silent sigh of relief. Her knee hurt from where she had scraped it, her fingers ached, and she was tired. All she wanted now was to get home, run a bath and tuck herself into bed with a mug of cocoa and some hot buttered toast. She probably had just enough butter if she was careful until she collected her next lot of rations.

Elsa bustled over to her. 'Well, you fudged a couple of bars, honey, but I don't suppose anyone will notice.'

'Thank you.' Jane kept the sarcasm from her voice. She knew her mother's comment was actually high praise.

'Now, we will need to practise again tomorrow as we have some new pieces to record at the end of the week. I suppose I shall have to try and get some more copies of the music. Really, it's terribly inconvenient. I do think you could have been more careful,' Elsa chided.

'My case was stolen. I didn't misplace it.' Jane had a touch of asperity in her voice. She wasn't looking forward to the journey home again through the fog on the bus alone. Not after what had happened on her way to the studio.

'Well, it's still very annoying, Janey.' Elsa tutted. 'Now, I must find my furs. Reggie is taking me home in his car.'

The band had placed their instruments in their cases and were heading out of the studio. Jane was keen to catch them up in the hope that some of them might be taking the same bus that she needed to get.

'I must go, my bus will be here and if I miss it I'm not sure how I'll get back.' Jane kissed her mother quickly on the cheek and made her escape.

Wrapped up once more against the cold with her gas mask in its stiff cardboard case slung over her shoulder, she hurried down the stairs hoping to see one of the other musicians heading for the bus stop. The reception desk was now deserted, and the lobby was in darkness.

The smog outside the building seemed to envelop her the moment she stepped outside, and an icy chill ran along her spine. It was hard to see anything in the darkness despite the white paint on some of the kerbstones. At least for the return journey she didn't need to cross the road. She made her way along the pavement mentally cursing the blackout.

The bus stop, when she reached it, was deserted, and she wondered where the others had gone. Her mother seemed to have arranged a lift back to Stephen's mother's flat with Reggie, who apparently had a car.

Neither Elsa nor Reggie had suggested they might offer her a lift. On balance Jane decided she would rather risk the smog than a ride home with Reggie. She wasn't keen to let him know where she lived since he, along with the other people she had met, were on her suspects list.

It was eerie standing alone in the dark not being able to see who might approach her. The smog also seemed to muffle sounds so even though her every sense was on full alert she couldn't hear footsteps. She hoped the bus would run on time as her feet were frozen.

Thankfully she spotted the bus looming towards her out of the darkness and stuck out her hand to try and attract the driver's attention. She had no wish to see it sail past the stop due to the driver not having seen her waiting there.

At least this time the bus was much emptier, and she managed to get a seat. Thankfully, she used her gas mask box as a handbag, so she had money for her fare, and her cigarettes and lighter in there.

Finally, she reached the stop near her apartment block, and she got off the bus with a sigh of relief. The smog was slightly less thick, and she looked around the empty street just in case Leo Cavendish or anyone else might be lurking in the shadows. The street appeared deserted, and she hurried inside, glad to be almost home.

* * *

'Miss Jane has returned, sir.' Benson stepped back from the kitchen window where he had been keeping watch, and tweaked the blackout curtain into place.

'Thank you, Benson.' Arthur had been feeling uneasy ever since Leo Cavendish's visit earlier.

He had listened to the radio, to the live broadcast, and once the programme had finished, Benson had been on the alert for Jane's return. Sure enough a moment later there was a soft knock on the apartment door.

'Do come in, Miss Jane. Allow me to take your coat.'

Arthur heard Benson ushering her into the tiny hallway.

'Phew, I am so glad to be back,' Jane announced a moment later as she entered the sitting room.

She looked exhausted and she had a scrape on her knee revealed by a large hole in her stockings.

'You look as if you've had a long day. Can we get you a drink? I believe we have either a small amount of sherry left or there is some Scotch.' Arthur looked at Benson.

Jane wrinkled her nose. 'I'm absolutely flagging so I can't stop long. A Scotch with a splash of water would be welcome though.'

'I listened to the broadcast. I thought you played very well, and Elsa sang charmingly,' Arthur said. 'Nothing seemed untoward either in the introductions or the schedule itself.'

Benson produced a plain glass of whisky and added some water before passing it to Jane. 'Indeed, a most delightful performance.'

'You look as if you've been in the wars rather.' Arthur looked at her knee.

'Tell me about it. I was pushed over as I got off the bus outside the studio. I was crossing the road in a large group of people. The smog was bad, and I couldn't see anyone's features, then someone tugged at my music case. When I reached the kerb I was pushed hard in the small of my back and my case was taken.' Jane took a large swallow of whisky and coughed when the spirit hit the back of her throat.

'You didn't see who it was?' Arthur asked.

Jane shook her head. 'I've no idea, I'm afraid. The bus was busy, I had to stand all the way there and a lot of people all got off at the same time as me. It was rush hour. The visibility was dreadful, and everyone had their faces covered.'

'Did they get away with your music case?' Arthur said.

'Yes, although I'm afraid they will be sadly disappointed with the contents. There was nothing inside except the music Mother had given me.' Jane took another sip of her drink.

'Even so, it's a worrying development. You'll need to let the brigadier know what's happened,' Arthur said.

'Did you speak to him earlier, after I'd gone?' Jane asked.

'I told him about Leo Cavendish and our worries that this assignment was already compromised. Now this latest incident seems to confirm that.' Arthur leaned back in his seat.

Jane twisted around at the end of the sofa to look at Benson who had stationed himself on a small straight-backed chair near the drinks trolley. 'How did you get on today, Benson? Did everything go all right?' she asked.

'Yes, thank you, Miss Jane. I assumed my janitorial duties without seeming to draw any kind of attention. I checked all discarded paper, looked at documents on desks where possible and generally listened in to conversations whilst working,' the manservant said.

'And did you discover anything useful?' Jane drained the last of her whisky after posing her question.

'I learned that Mr Cavendish had quite an argument with the lady who was killed shortly before she left the building that day. It was overheard by several members of staff. Tabitha Moore also argued with a Jenny Jackson the same morning. Miss Jackson apparently was most upset with Miss Moore, accusing her of wanting her gone. Oh, and Mr Vaughn, the announcer, had also quarrelled with Miss Moore,' Benson said.

'Do you know why Tabitha argued with Leo Cavendish?' Jane asked.

'It would appear that he accused her of being secretive and

he suspected her of seeing another man.' Benson gave a small, sheep-like cough.

'That's interesting. Leo didn't think to mention any of this when we caught him snooping around here this afternoon.' Jane looked thoughtful.

Arthur could tell that she was not happy with what they had discovered so far.

'I couldn't discover what the disagreement with Mr Vaughn had been about,' Benson said apologetically.

'Thank you, Benson, we'll find out soon, I daresay,' Jane said. 'I saw him this evening as he was in the booth making the announcements for the news.'

'Could Cavendish have been the one to attack you, Jane?' Arthur asked.

'It's possible, but equally it could have been anyone connected with the radio broadcasts that we've encountered so far. While I was being helped up by a couple of bystanders and looking for any sign of my case, whoever attacked me managed to get away. They could have gone inside the building or even just walked off with the crowd.' Jane took her cigarettes from her gas mask box and lit up.

'The brigadier asked that we remain vigilant and continue for now. I don't know if he will pull us from the assignment when he learns about this latest incident.' Arthur could see that both Jane and possibly Benson were at risk.

His own position was more complicated. He supposed he could continue trying to work out the codes and who had inserted them into the schedules. That work could continue regardless. Jane, however, appeared to be in some danger. Someone knew where she lived and seemed to be trying to discover why she was at Bush House.

CHAPTER NINE

Jane woke later than her usual time the next morning. The whisky she had drunk at Arthur's had combined with her much-needed cocoa to provide her with a good night's sleep. She might have slept for even longer if Marmaduke had not meowed his displeasure at her tardiness with his breakfast.

She fed her cat and opened the kitchen window so he could have free access to the fire escape. Her kitchen cupboards looked decidedly bare, and she knew she would have to make time to go to the grocers to collect her rations. Obtaining food seemed to take up much more of her time these days since there were so many shortages.

She also needed to speak to the brigadier about what had happened the previous day. After making her coffee she sat down and picked up the telephone receiver and dialled the brigadier's number.

'Jane, I was about to telephone you.'

She moved the receiver away from her ear. 'I wanted to update you, sir. I know you spoke to Arthur yesterday but there has been a further incident.' She phrased what she said carefully in case anyone might be listening in to the call. She knew Arthur would have done exactly the same the previous day.

'Go ahead, what's happened?' the brigadier asked.

She told him about the stolen music case.

'Hmm, you weren't hurt, I hope?' he asked.

Jane assured him that she had just been shaken up.

'I see. I'm in two minds about all this, Jane. You must be very careful. It seems that someone has decided they think they know why you are there. The others at the moment appear to be all right. Only Cavendish appears to know about Arthur. Benson's involvement will hopefully have completely passed them by. It's your neck that is on the line. What do you feel?' he asked.

Jane had been thinking about what her response might be to that question ever since she'd woken up.

'I think so long as I remain watchful, I'd like to continue. Mother does need an accompanist, and I may as well stay in my role for a while longer. If anything else happens, then I'll obviously need to rethink,' she said.

'Very well. Be careful though, my dear.' He finished the call on that note.

Jane replaced the receiver and stayed in her chair for a moment longer. She could only hope that she had made the right decision.

* * *

Half an hour later she went to call on Arthur. Benson, she guessed, had already left for his day of janitorial spying. Arthur appeared to have been expecting her as he was quick to come to the door at her knock.

She followed him into the sitting room. 'I've just spoken to the brigadier.' She told him what had been said.

Arthur's expression was grave as he took his place in the armchair beside the fire. 'I can see why the brigadier is concerned. I don't like what's happened so far.'

'I know, neither do I. Still, I have to think of the bigger issues here. Tabitha's murder and even more seriously the potential for sabotage and covert sending of messages via the radio. Those things are bigger than me, Arthur. I have to do my duty,' Jane said.

Arthur didn't look wholly convinced by her argument. 'I telephoned Scotland Yard yesterday too,' he said.

'Did you manage to speak to the inspector in charge of investigating Tabitha Moore's murder?' Jane was instantly on the alert.

'Inspector Winters? Yes, eventually. He's a busy man and hard to track down,' Arthur said.

'Did you learn anything new from him?' Jane asked.

'Not much. I think at first the police had been inclined to chalk Tabitha's murder up to a random attack in the smog by an unknown assailant. It wasn't until Leo Cavendish started to cause a fuss and the brigadier became involved that they had a bit of a rethink,' Arthur said.

'So, Leo went to the police? He wasn't the one who identified her?' Jane was interested to hear what the inspector had said about Tabitha's fiancé.

'No, her father was contacted first as her next of kin since she fit the missing person description. Then, as soon as Tabitha was identified as the victim, Leo went to Scotland Yard and demanded to see Inspector Winters. He created a huge fuss apparently and was making all sorts of allegations, as we know.' Arthur looked at Jane.

'It seems Mr Cavendish is something of a loose cannon. Who was he making allegations against? Did it match what the brigadier told us? Did the inspector say?' Jane asked.

'Inspector Winters took some persuading but eventually he

let slip that our friend, Cavendish, was saying that the brigadier's department could have acted to silence Tabitha. He also made allegations against Vincent Vaughn, the radio announcer.' Arthur leaned back in his chair.

'I saw Vincent Vaughn last night as I said. He was the announcer before our segment, a good-looking man. I didn't get the chance to speak to him.' Jane wondered why Leo Cavendish had thought Vincent Vaughn could have killed Tabitha. Was he the man Leo had thought Tabitha might have been seeing? Benson had said he'd had a disagreement with Tabitha before she had been killed.

'So far it all matches what we knew already. I asked about alibis. Obviously the police had checked out Vaughn and he was probably on air at the time they think Tabitha was killed, but since they can't be absolutely certain of her time of death he still could have been responsible.' Arthur frowned, and she guessed he was thinking about the other possible suspects.

'And Leo Cavendish?' Jane asked.

'He said he was at the radio studios until late that evening and then he got caught up in the raids and sheltered in a public shelter until the all-clear. Of course, it's difficult because of the delay in discovering Tabitha's body and the cold weather. Time of death is a best guess.' Arthur's frown deepened. Jane knew he hated uncertainties.

'So, the field is really wide open then it seems. I presume Inspector Winters did not believe the brigadier was responsible?' Jane raised an eyebrow as she posed the question.

The corners of Arthur's mouth twitched upwards. 'I don't believe Inspector Winters would dare to probe that allegation in too much depth, but he assured me that the brigadier's own movements were accounted for and were entirely satisfactory.' Arthur sobered again and added, 'There is still very much the possibility of someone in the department, however, being responsible for Tabitha's death either directly or indirectly. Leo Cavendish found your address and name from someone.'

'Our suspect list then is quite wide. We know now, thanks to Benson's sterling work, that Leo and Vincent argued with Tabitha the day she was killed. Jenny Jackson was also not on good terms with Tabitha since she feared she was losing contracts. Jenny also said that Ernie Simons had been pestering Tabitha about the scripts,' Jane said.

'It's tricky to know why Tabitha was killed. It could be a personal reason. It would seem it might also be to do with sabotage or coded messages being surreptitiously added to the scripts due to the timing of her death. Which, of course, is why we are involved,' Arthur said.

'Her murder coming right after she hinted to Leo that something was amiss, that surely must be significant.' Jane could see what Arthur meant. 'That could put any of the others in the frame, including Reggie Bosun the bandleader, and even Frances Fellowes. If you could discover the source of the alterations and the code for what was being sent then we might at least discover the traitor.' Jane knew Arthur's task was extremely difficult.

'Then we might learn if the traitor and Tabitha's murderer are one and the same person,' Arthur finished her thought for her.

'We need to know what those arguments Tabitha had with people were really about. I'll do some poking around and see what I can discover.' Jane rose from her chair.

'Good luck today. What time will you be back?' Arthur stood ready to see her out.

'I'm meeting Mother in an hour for more rehearsals ready to make some recordings for future shows. I have no idea what else she may have planned in her diary.' Jane grimaced at the thought.

She went into the hall to collect her hat and coat from the stand.

'Any problems, telephone me.' Arthur assisted her into her coat. 'I can always pretend to be a technician, remember?'

She was pleased he appeared to share her distaste for feigning a romantic connection.

'I'll let you know if I am to be late returning. Here.' She fumbled in her coat pocket before extracting a key and pressing it into his hand. 'It's the spare key to my flat. If I get delayed this evening please could you or Benson go and feed Marmaduke? The window to the kitchen is open for him but he will expect his food.'

Arthur regarded the key as if she had handed him a grenade with the pin removed.

Jane put on her hat and checked her appearance quickly in the mirror. 'Thank you, I must go, or I'll miss the bus.' She left Arthur contemplating the key and ignored his faint protestation as she ran lightly down the stairs.

The smog from last night had dispersed leaving behind weak, watery sunshine. She was still smiling to herself as she boarded the bus. Poor Arthur was not fond of Marmaduke, saying the cat could trigger his asthma. She had no doubt that should she be delayed Benson would be dispatched to attend to her pet.

The journey to the studios was less fraught than the previous evening. It wasn't until she arrived at her destination that she saw there was a problem. A small crowd was assembled on the pavement outside the building, and a fire engine and a police car were at the kerb. Jane got off the bus with a sinking feeling in her stomach.

'Janey!' Her mother spotted her as she crossed the road and waved an imperious hand in the air to call her over.

'What's happened?' Jane hurried to her mother's side.

'Leo discovered a fire in the back office. He tackled it with an extinguisher, but at the same time there was another fire that was more ablaze on the second floor,' Elsa explained as she huddled into her fur coat, wrapping it over to keep out the cold.

'Good heavens, has anyone been hurt?' Jane asked. She looked around for any sign of Benson and hoped he was safe.

'Not so far as we know. No ambulance has been sent for,' Frances Fellowes said as she appeared next to them, her face avid with curiosity. 'Leo was terribly brave to tackle the fire. We're still broadcasting, of course.'

Jane's finely pencilled eyebrows rose slightly at this welcome news. It would be dreadful if there was a disruption to the programme. Preventing disruption to the broadcasts was part of her remit. Public confidence and morale would be severely shaken, which was no doubt the intention of whoever had set the fires.

'Vincent is on air at the moment reading the news, I believe. He started just after Leo found the first fire.'

Ernie Simons came to join their group. 'Has anyone seen Reggie by the by? He was due to meet Louisa about agreeing the schedule for the next few weeks' performances.'

'I've no idea where he's gone. He gave me a lift here this morning. You know I abhor public transport. Jenny might know, I thought I saw her milling about a moment ago.' Elsa peered around at the knots of people on the pavement.

'There she is. Jenny, cooee!' Frances waved to Jenny, and the actress came to join their group.

'Well, what a thing to happen.' Jenny looked at Frances. 'Three fires the fireman said, all in various parts of the building.'

'Three?' Jane asked.

'Oh yes, Leo found the first one in his office and tackled it himself, then one of the janitors found one on the first floor in a cupboard. He put it out and called the fire brigade. Then they found someone had tried to start a third one on the top floor near the fire escape.' Jenny looked pleased to have all the gossip about the incident.

'That's dreadful. They really must get some better security in place here,' Frances said in an appalled tone.

Jane wondered if Benson had been the janitor who had found the second fire. He may even have glimpsed the culprit who had set it.

'I quite agree, whatever is the world coming to,' Elsa huffed. 'Why, any of us could have been injured or killed if those fires had taken hold.'

'Have you seen Reggie at all?' Ernie asked, looking at Jenny.

'No, I saw him earlier before all the alarms went off. He was due to see Leo and that new girl Louisa. I haven't seen him outside.' Jenny looked around as if expecting to see the band-leader amongst the crowd.

'He might be with Leo, I suppose,' Frances suggested. 'I haven't seen him out here either.'

'Well, the fire drama seems to be over at any rate.' Ernie nodded towards the fire engine.

Jane saw the firemen were all boarding the engine ready to depart.

'They may let us back inside the building then. I'm perished waiting out here,' Frances grumbled as she cast an envious glance at Elsa's luxurious furs.

'Where is Leo? He must know what's happening by now and if we can go back inside,' Ernie asked.

Jane spotted Leo standing with his back to them while he spoke to a uniformed policeman. Reggie and the young woman from the reception desk were with him. The fire engine drove away leaving just the black police car parked outside the entrance.

Leo finished talking to the constable then went to the doors of the building under the dome.

'If I could have your attention please, ladies and gentlemen.' Leo raised his voice to address the crowd on the pavement.

The murmurs of conversation died away and everyone looked at Leo to hear what he had to say.

'The fires have all been safely extinguished thanks to the vigilance and bravery of our staff. The police will continue to investigate the causes and to identify whoever is responsible. They will be talking to any of you who may have been in the building at the time of these incidents. The firemen have assured me that we are safe to return inside. I shall, of course, be looking to see how we can improve our security. Please go back in and go about your business. If any of you has any important information which might assist the police then the constable and Inspector Winters here would like to speak to you.' Leo indicated the uniformed officer and a tall, older man in a dark-grey overcoat and trilby hat.

Jane gave the inspector an interested glance. This was the man who was dealing with the investigation into Tabitha's murder. No doubt that was why he had arrived when Leo had called for assistance with the fires in the building.

The crowd started to disperse. Bystanders drifted back about their business and the staff began to make their way up the steps inside the lobby of the building. Jane hung back a little, still looking out for any sign of Benson.

She didn't see him in the groups ahead of her. Reggie had followed Leo inside.

'Janey pie, do stop dawdling. We don't have much time left on our room booking,' Elsa chided in an exasperated tone.

'Miss Treen!' The receptionist was back at her post and called to her as soon as she entered the lobby.

Jane ignored Elsa's tutting and went to see what the girl wanted.

'Miss Treen, a member of the public found your music case this morning stuffed in a hedge in the next street. They brought it here and gave it in. I think they assumed someone here must have lost it.' Louisa handed Jane the black leather case which had been stolen the previous evening.

Jane glanced inside and saw that all her sheet music was still intact. The case itself, although damp from being outside, also appeared unscathed.

'Thank you so much, Louisa. I was worried I might not see it again.' Jane took the case and was about to go and rejoin her mother.

'Miss Treen, might I have a quick word.' Inspector Winters appeared at the side of the desk and beckoned to her.

Elsa folded her arms and pursed her lips in annoyance as Jane turned back to greet the policeman.

'I understand that you were assaulted yesterday evening and your music case taken?' Inspector Winters had a low, well-modulated voice. He drew Jane away from the desk so they couldn't be overheard.

'That's correct, sir, yes,' Jane said.

'I believe we have an acquaintance in common, Brigadier Remmington-Blythe?' The inspector's keen grey eyes scanned her face.

Jane nodded. 'That's correct.'

'I spoke with a Mr Cilento on the telephone yesterday after-noon regarding the death of Miss Tabitha Moore, who also worked here,' the inspector continued.

'Arthur is my colleague,' Jane confirmed. 'He told me of your conversation.'

The inspector gave a satisfied nod. 'Please tell me how your case was stolen.'

Jane gave him a concise report of what had happened. The inspector made some notes in a small notebook. He tucked it back in his coat pocket when she had finished. 'Thank you, Miss Treen. Were you in the building this morning when these fires occurred?'

Jane shook her head. 'No, I arrived when everyone was outside the building.'

The inspector sighed. 'Thank you, Miss Treen. I had better let you go, Miss Macintyre looks eager to be at work.' He inclined his hat towards Jane's mother.

Jane glanced towards where Elsa was waiting. 'If I discover anything useful, I'll let you know.'

She shook hands with the policeman and went to join her mother.

CHAPTER TEN

'Do get a hustle on, Janey. Honestly, making so much fuss over that wretched music case. I assume that's what that was all about?' Elsa glanced at Jane's case as they hurried up the stairs together towards the rehearsal room.

'Yes, and he wanted to know if I had been in the building this morning when the fires started. Were you here then, Mother? You said Reggie gave you a lift,' Jane asked as they reached the landing.

Her mother paused at the rehearsal studio door. 'I think Leo discovered the fire after I'd been here for about fifteen minutes. I came in here and started the warm-up exercises for my vocal cords. Reggie had a meeting booked with Leo, so I assume he must have gone to his office. Then just as you were due to arrive someone, Leo I assume, sounded the alarm and we were all evacuated out onto the pavement.' Elsa frowned at her. 'Honestly, Janey, we really do need better security here. I could have been burnt to death.'

Jane decided it was better not to reply and followed her mother into the studio. She hung her hat and coat on a hook in the wall and her mother removed her furs, draping them over the back of one of the wooden chairs inside the room.

The list that Reggie and her mother had given her of the music required for the upcoming recordings was inside her gas mask box. Jane extracted it and began to sort out the music inside her case.

Elsa resumed her vocal warm-ups, trilling up and down the scales while Jane prepared to play. She had scarcely had a chance to seat herself on the piano bench when Frances entered the studio.

'I say, have either of you spoken to that Inspector Winters yet? He's rather a dish, isn't he? I was just talking to the constable, and I saw Leo having words with Ernie. I don't know what it was all about, but the inspector has taken them into Leo's office.' Frances looked at Elsa and Jane expectantly.

'I'm not certain I follow you,' Jane said.

Elsa, who had paused in her warm-up glared at Frances. 'So, what if he has. Poor Leo is still very distressed about Tabitha, he's short-tempered with everyone, even me.' Elsa sounded slightly incredulous at this latter part of her statement.

Frances looked put out that Jane and Elsa appeared unimpressed by her news. 'Hmm, well I think there is something strange going on.'

'Yes, well someone has tried to burn us alive, Frances, honey. We do need to get on though, as we've lost lots of time already. Is there anything else?' Elsa asked.

'Say what you like but mark my words there is something fishy about this business of these fires coming so soon after poor Tabitha's death. Cursed, that's what this place is. Cursed.' Frances swept out of the room, banging the studio door shut behind her.

'Honestly, are you ready, Jane? We do need to get going now Lady Macbeth has taken herself off.' Elsa scowled at the now closed door.

'Yes, I'm all set.' Jane confirmed which music her mother wished to sing and started the introduction of the first piece.

They had only reached the chorus of the song when the door opened once again, and Reggie Bosun strolled in. He nodded to Elsa and Jane before seating himself on a nearby chair to listen to the rest of the song. His lean, handsome features showed no signs of concern over the recent events.

'Bravo, superb as always, Elsa, my dear.' He clapped enthusiastically when Elsa finished.

'Gee thanks, Reggie, sweetie, you're too kind.' Her mother smiled graciously at the bandleader.

'I say, it's all rather queer this business about the fires, don't you think? I just ran into Frances, and she said Ernie and Leo were closeted in the back office with a police inspector,' Reggie said.

'Perhaps Ernie saw something important,' Jane suggested as she pressed a couple of the keys on the piano.

'Oh my, yes, he could have seen someone near where the fires started.' Elsa's eyes widened.

'Or he may be the suspect,' Reggie remarked with a chuckle. 'A bit of a dark horse, our Ernie. Rather fond of a flutter or two at the bookies. Perhaps someone caught up with him.'

'Oh, Reggie, honey, do be serious!' Elsa tutted.

'Perhaps I am being serious, darling. One never knows these days who one can trust. Any one of us could be a German spy.' Reggie laughed as he spoke.

Jane smiled politely but wondered if there was some truth behind the bandleader's words. She stored away the information about Ernie's gambling to share with Arthur later.

* * *

When the telephone rang in Arthur's flat, he answered with some trepidation. Very few people had the number so whoever was calling obviously had something of importance to impart.

'Good morning, sir.' Benson's calm familiar voice greeted him as he picked up the receiver.

'Good morning, has something happened?' Arthur knew his manservant would not be calling to make idle chit-chat.

'I'm in the telephone box at the end of the road near the studios. There has been an incident here this morning,' Benson said.

Arthur's pulse kicked up a notch. 'What kind of incident? Is Jane all right?'

'Miss Treen and her mother are quite safe, sir. Inspector Winters is in the building now and the problems have been dealt with. The fire brigade has attended to extinguish some small blazes within the building.' Benson was circumspect in his report and Arthur knew he would be wary of giving too many details in case anyone might be listening in.

'Good grief, was anyone harmed in these fires?' Arthur asked, relieved that Jane and Elsa were seemingly unhurt. His first thought had been to worry that whoever had stolen Jane's music case may have tried to harm her in some way.

'Not so far as I know, sir. I will continue with my observations and report back this evening.'

'Thank you, Benson.' Arthur replaced the receiver before the pips had time to sound on Benson's end.

This report was troubling. His manservant had said blazes, so more than one fire had happened. Whatever had taken place had been serious enough for Scotland Yard and the fire brigade to become involved. If Inspector Winters had been dispatched to the studios then he must consider there was the possibility of a connection to Tabitha's murder. Otherwise, a constable or a sergeant would have attended.

He had been listening to the radio while making notes on the piles of transcripts. There had been no disruption from the fires that he had been able to detect in the day's broadcast. Vincent Vaughn had read the news and provided the links between the scheduled programmes exactly as usual. That at least meant the potential saboteur had failed today.

Arthur couldn't shake off the unsettled feeling that now lay across him since talking to Benson. He decided that perhaps a cup of tea might help him to refocus on his task. Once in the kitchen he looked out of the window while filling the kettle.

There was no sign of anyone loitering on the pavement near the plane tree. Even so, he still felt uneasy. He placed the kettle on the ring and set out his cup on the saucer before getting a biscuit from the box.

While he waited for the kettle to boil he moved back to the window, taking care to stand to the side so he could see out without being visible to any onlooker. At first he saw no indication that anyone was watching the block. Still no one loitering, but he was certain that he had seen what appeared to be a nursery maid with a large pram there before.

The kettle whistled and he turned to retrieve it to make the tea. When he came back to his spot the woman with the pram had moved and was gone. Perhaps he had been mistaken, and was simply on edge with everything that had happened so far. Then, as he stood there a little longer, cup and saucer in his hand, the woman returned.

He watched from behind the curtain as the nursery maid slowed her pace when she was opposite the block. She paused and pretended to stop and check on an infant hidden from Arthur's view under the raised hood of the perambulator. He doubted a child was actually inside. It was most likely a well-concealed doll or simply a bundle of blankets. He was now absolutely certain the girl was not a genuine nurse.

Arthur ate his biscuit and continued to watch the woman slowly wheel the pram away. He wondered whose side she was on. Had she been sent by the brigadier or had she been directed to go there by some other agency, less friendly perhaps?

There could be no doubt that they were under surveillance and not just by Leo Cavendish.

* * *

Jane was somewhat annoyed to discover that Reggie intended to stay while she ran through the rehearsal with her mother. She was forced to grit her teeth and bite her tongue while the band-leader gave her helpful hints on her playing.

She was relieved when the session came to an end and the next people to have booked the room arrived, forcing them to leave.

'I say, lunchtime already. Elsa, darling, do you fancy some lunch, my shout? Oh, Jane, my dear, you are most welcome to come along too, of course,' Reggie offered as he held the door open for them to exit.

Jane had no desire to crash her mother's lunch date. 'No, thank you. You two go and enjoy yourselves.'

Elsa snuggled into her furs and beamed at her. 'I'll see you in a couple of hours, honey, ready to record.' She gave Jane a quick kiss on the cheek of farewell and slipped her arm through Reggie's before setting off down the stairs.

Jane breathed a sigh of relief and focused on buttoning up her own coat ready to face the cold. She had seen a small café around the corner from the studios and she intended to take her lunch there. She still had to call at the grocer's later on her way home to collect her rations. Otherwise, both she and Marmaduke would soon be facing an empty pantry.

The crowded steamy heat of the café interior came as a welcome relief after her brisk, chilly walk down the street. The plate-glass frontage was steamed up on the inside and a small child was occupied with drawing pictures in the steam while his mother was distracted.

The tables were fairly full, and Jane was relieved to spot a free space in the far corner near the door to the kitchen. Once she was seated she unbuttoned her coat, drew off her gloves and looked around. There was a lively buzz of chatter in the room and the faint smell of sausages in the air. At least she hoped it was sausages.

Jane picked up the menu card and studied it while she waited for the waitress to come over to her. The elderly waitress approached her and took a pencil from behind her ear ready to write on her pad.

'What can I get for you, duck?'

'Vegetable soup and a roll please, with a cup of coffee.' Jane set her menu back in its stand next to the cruet set as the waitress scribbled down her order.

'Thank you. I'll bring your coffee over in a minute or two.' The woman bustled through the swing door to the kitchen and Jane heard her order being relayed to the cook.

While she waited for the woman to return she was able to take a closer look at her surroundings. The clientele mainly seemed to be working-class women with baskets of shopping, men in cloth caps and older people.

As she glanced around Jane noticed two familiar figures seated together at a table on the far side of the café. Frances Fellowes seemed to be deep in conversation with Vincent Vaughn the announcer.

Jane watched the two of them curiously. From where she was seated it didn't appear to be a friendly conversation. They had clearly finished eating as their plates were empty and pushed aside. Frances was stabbing the top of the table with her forefinger as if trying to drive a point home. Jane wished she could see her expression, but her view was partly obscured by a large gentleman in navy overalls and a bulky pea coat.

The waitress came back to Jane's table and placed a thick white china cup and saucer with a small stainless-steel coffee pot and jug of steamed milk in front of her. 'Soup'll be out in a mo, duck,' she said before returning to the kitchen.

Jane looked back across to Vincent and Frances. Vincent had appeared quite languid before while Frances had been animated. Now though, she saw his cheeks redden and he pursed his lips, clearly unhappy with whatever Frances had said.

He appeared to listen to her for a moment longer before pulling some money from his wallet. He dropped the cash onto the table and stood up quite abruptly, the legs of the chair scraping on the wooden floor.

Vincent left. The sound of the bell on its coiled spring above the door announcing his departure and bringing the waitress back out. She went across to Frances to clear their plates, obviously noticing the empty chair.

Jane watched as Frances paid for the meals before collecting up her bag and hurrying out of the café herself.

The waitress brought out her order and placed the bowl of soup and a side plate with her roll in front of her. Jane sniffed appreciatively. The soup smelled good and looked nice and thick. There was even a sprinkle of chopped parsley on top. Frances had disappeared from view, the bright crimson colour of her knitted scarf no longer visible through the steamed-up window.

Frances hadn't struck Jane as being a particularly tactful woman but even so, whatever she had said to Vincent had clearly upset him. She wondered if they had planned to have lunch together or if they had been forced to share a table because the café was full. She dabbed some of her roll into the soup.

Her mother was no doubt dining in a much more luxurious establishment. It seemed clear to Jane that Reggie was yet another of her mother's admirers. Having men take her mother to lunch or dinner, present her with flowers, chocolates or gifts was nothing new. Elsa certainly always took it for granted.

Elsa was also very skilled at milking her admirers for all they could give. Reggie certainly appeared happy enough to provide her mother with lifts and to take her to lunch. Jane sighed and finished the last of her soup feeling much better now she had eaten. While she liked her independence, she couldn't help wishing that just every once in a while she could be whisked off somewhere nicer than a small café.

She smiled to herself as she poured her coffee. Stephen had often offered to take her out and her response had always been a constant no. Perhaps on balance she would stay the way she was and put up with travelling by bus and eating soup.

CHAPTER ELEVEN

Once she had finished her lunch she walked slowly back to the studios. Hopefully they could get the recordings wrapped up quite quickly. She really needed to get back and fetch some groceries before the shops closed or there was nothing left on the shelves.

Elsa was waiting for her at the desk in the lobby. A uniformed man with a peaked cap stood next to her wearing a badge labelled security.

'Janey pie, honestly, where have you been? I've been standing here for ages.' Elsa scarcely gave her time to come through the doors. A glance at the large, wooden-framed clock on the wall behind the desk told Jane she was actually early. She guessed Reggie must have delivered her mother back at the studio earlier than expected.

'I'm not late, Mother. I doubt we could even get into the studio until they are ready for us,' Jane remarked.

Elsa disregarded her comment. 'Anyhoo, honey, we now have to have these passes or this nice gentleman here won't let us in the building.' Elsa batted her eyelashes at the young security guard calling a fiery blush into his cheeks.

'Passes?' Jane asked.

'I have one here for you, Miss Treen,' Louisa the receptionist interjected. She held up a small card. 'You just need to
sign it and sign your name here to say you've received it.' Louisa
offered her a sheet of paper and a pen.

Jane duly located her name on the list and signed for the
pass. 'This is new.'

'Leo's doing, darling, after what happened this morning.
Orders from on high apparently,' Elsa said.

'Yes, we all have to be more vigilant,' Louisa said as she took
the pen and the signing sheet back from Jane.

'Well, that does seem jolly sensible,' Jane remarked.

Elsa sniffed dismissively. 'I don't know, honey. Still, any
improvement is welcome, I guess. Anyway, what studio are we
in again?' she said, turning back to the receptionist.

'Number six, Miss Macintyre. The technicians should be
set up for you by now if you'd like to go on up.'

Elsa gathered her furs around her and bestowed a last
smile on the young guard before making her way to the stairs.
Jane followed behind her. The studio they had been directed
to wasn't one Jane had been in before. It was smaller than the
others and divided in two. On one side was a soundproofed
booth complete with piano and microphone. On the other side
there were two technicians with a set of unfamiliar
equipment.

Jane assumed they would direct them when to stop and
start as they recorded the pieces for use in future programmes.
It was all a little daunting.

'Good afternoon, are we all ready to record? Miss Macintyre, um, Miss, er, Treen?' The older of the technicians looked
at his list to find Jane's name.

It was clear he recognised Elsa.

'Perfectly, honey. I'm sure you'll make me sound just
wonderful.' Elsa beamed at him and hung her furs on the hooks

inside the galley. Jane hung her own coat and hat beside them before following her mother into the studio area.

Once Jane was seated at the piano and her music set up, the technicians requested she play the introduction to the first song so they could check the recording levels. Once they were happy, they then asked Elsa to sing the first few bars so they could make sure everything was set up correctly to record.

The technicians then went through the running order and explained how the recording session would work. It was made clear that they were intending to capture the recordings in one take for each song. There was no time or materials to waste on re-recording items unless there was a major error.

Jane flexed her fingers and waited for the signal to start. She hoped she could get through the session without any mistakes. She knew that Elsa would be sure to let her know at the end about any errors she might make, even if the technicians were happy with the recordings.

There was a pause after the first song while the technicians listened back to the recording to make certain they were happy.

'How was your lunch with Reggie?' Jane asked to make conversation with her mother while they waited.

'Oh, it was fine, honey. A darling little place that Reggie knew. It's so nice to be treated like a lady these days,' Elsa said. 'We had to come back here a little earlier than we planned though. Reggie needed to meet up with Leo. They should have done it this morning but what with the fires and all they didn't get a chance to discuss everything apparently.' She gave a shrug of her elegant shoulders.

She didn't ask Jane about her own lunch arrangements and the technicians signalled they were ready to resume before Jane could ask Elsa anything else. They continued to work their way through the songs they had rehearsed earlier in the day. By the time everything was done Jane was exhausted from concentrating on the music.

'I had better go and see if the girl on the desk can get me a cab,' Elsa said as she collected her furs. 'It's all so difficult these days. I'm surprised you don't bring the car up from Kent to run around in.'

Jane knew there was no point in suggesting to her mother that she could take a bus like everyone else. Or in pointing out that she had nowhere to park a Rolls Royce or any petrol to put in it.

'Is Reggie not free to take you home?' Jane asked as she buttoned up her coat.

Elsa pulled a face. 'I don't know what his plans were after his meeting with Leo. Still, he's been very good today at offering me lifts.'

Jane walked with her mother back down the stairs into the lobby.

'I'll see you tomorrow then, Janey pie. We have that lunchtime concert, remember?' Elsa kissed her cheek before turning to the receptionist to request a taxi.

Jane went to make her way out of the building before realising she must have dropped one of her gloves. Mentally cursing herself for her own clumsiness, she hurried back upstairs to look for it. She knew both gloves had been in her coat pockets when she had come back from lunch.

She retraced her footsteps along the darkened corridor. The technicians had finished and gone and the studio where they had been recording was in darkness. Jane knew the blackout time would be earlier now the days were so much shorter, and she was conscious that the various shutters and drapes would all be put into place very soon.

She scoured the marble-tiled floors for any sign of her missing glove. After not seeing any sign of it, Jane turned around to go back along the corridor. As she walked she continued to look for her glove in case she had missed it on the way to the studio.

The route took her past one of the other rehearsal rooms. This one had a window made of reinforced glass that opened onto the corridor. To her relief she spotted her glove lying on the ledge. Someone had obviously seen it, picked it up and placed it there.

Jane pounced on it gleefully and prepared to hurry downstairs ready to catch her bus. As she claimed her glove she glanced inside the darkened studio. What she thought she saw made her stop and change her mind. She stuffed her glove in her coat pocket and went to try the studio door.

The door was unlocked and opened easily, spilling a small amount of light into the room. At first she wasn't sure if her eyes were playing tricks on her as she stared at the figure slumped in a chair at the far end of the room. Jane gasped and hastily snapped on the light switch beside the door. As the bright white overhead light flickered into action she saw her initial suspicion was correct. Jenny Jackson was half sitting, half lying sprawled out of a chair, her head lolling to one side.

Jane approached her slowly, unsure at first if the woman was really dead. Or if she had passed out: a small empty gin bottle lay on the floor at the woman's feet. As she grew closer, the thin wire tight around the woman's throat, her bulging eyes and blue lips were obvious. This wasn't due to drink; the actress had been strangled.

She quickly looked around for any indication of who may have been in the studio with Jenny. Apart from the bottle lying on its side, a tiny pool of gin beside it, there was no sign of anything else being out of place.

Jane stretched out a tentative hand and touched the dead woman's cheek; she was still warm. She must have been killed very recently. Jane didn't bother to try for a pulse: it was all too obvious that she was too late to assist the unfortunate woman.

There was a noise at the entrance of the studio and Jane

shot round prepared to defend herself if the killer had returned to the scene of the crime. Instead, Benson stood in the doorway in his brown janitorial overalls, his sharp eyes surveying the scene.

'Oh dear. I take it she's dead? Best go down and alert the police, Miss Jane. I will remain here until you return,' he suggested.

Jane nodded. 'Thank you, Benson. Don't let anyone in until I or the police get back here.'

She tore her gaze away from Jenny's body and rushed past the manservant to get down the stairs to the lobby. The shocked and horrified young receptionist telephoned Scotland Yard, and the security guard went up to Benson.

Inspector Winters arrived speedily. Benson had switched off the light in the studio and closed the door, guarding it with the new security man until the police came. Leo Cavendish, alerted by Jane, accompanied her and the inspector up to the studio.

'Good Lord.' Leo turned away as the light was switched on once more and he glimpsed Jenny's body.

'Please wait out here, sir, with Miss Treen and these gentle-men. A constable should be along in just a moment.' Inspector Winters's expression was grim as he entered the studio to examine the scene.

Jane exchanged a glance with Benson as Leo turned his back on the room, crossing the corridor to look out through the other window to the dark street below. His face was grey, and he looked as if he might be sick. She sent the guard back downstairs.

The uniformed constable arrived to join the inspector and Jane could hear a faint buzz of conversation coming from the stairs. She could only assume that word that something was wrong had reached the few remaining workers who were still inside the building. They had probably gathered in the lobby by the reception desk.

Jane drew Benson discreetly to one side. 'We need to let Arthur and the brigadier know what's happened,' she said.

'I'll pop out to the telephone box, Miss Jane.' Benson glanced at Leo Cavendish as Jane quietly agreed.

Benson slipped away as a short man in a crumpled suit and bowler hat carrying a brown leather medical bag arrived on the landing. He went to join the constable and the inspector in the studio.

Leo Cavendish appeared to be trying to pull himself together. 'That's so shocking. Poor Jenny.'

'I know. I thought I was seeing things. The room was dark, and I picked my glove up from the ledge and glanced inside. That was when I saw her.' Jane's gaze drifted to where the police and the doctor were huddled around the body inside the now brightly illuminated room.

Leo swallowed and she saw the Adam's apple bob in his neck just above his collar as Inspector Winters came out and approached them.

'Perhaps we could adjourn to your office for a moment, Mr Cavendish,' Inspector Winters suggested.

'Yes, um, certainly.' Leo seemed glad to be getting away from the scene in the studio.

They left the constable and the doctor to their tasks and went downstairs. The new security guard was engaged in dispersing the small group who had gathered around the reception desk. The young receptionist looked pale and anxious as Leo let them all into his office.

'Louisa, could you organise some tea?' Leo asked her before guiding Jane and the inspector into his office. The room still smelt of smoke from the earlier fire and she noticed there were scorch marks on the side of the desk.

'Of course, Mr Cavendish,' Louisa agreed, and Leo closed the door as Jane took a seat in front of his large, plain wooden desk.

Jane took out her cigarettes and Leo promptly offered her a light before lighting his own cigarette. The inspector refused when offered one. She hoped Benson had managed to get to the telephone box to alert Arthur and the brigadier to the news of Jenny's death.

'Where's the security guard gone? We should ask him about anyone entering or leaving the building recently,' Jane asked as Inspector Winters took a seat.

'Security guard?' the inspector asked. 'Did you have someone here this morning?'

'No, we employed someone after the fires. He has literally only been here since lunch. We used an agency.' Leo rose from his seat and went back out into the lobby.

He returned a minute later. 'Louisa is looking for him.'

Jane frowned. 'He was there a minute ago. I presume Louisa also has the lists of people signing in and out of the building?'

'Miss Treen.' Inspector Winters coughed and glared at her.

'Yes, yes, she does, they are on the desk.' Leo rose once more and fetched the sheets, handing them to Inspector Winters. He glanced apologetically at Jane as he did so.

Inspector Winters looked over the list in front of him. 'Miss Treen, you and Miss Macintyre left your studio ten minutes or so before you discovered Miss Jackson's body, is that correct?'

'Yes, ten to fifteen minutes. We left the studio and came down to the lobby, chatted for a moment, then I realised I had lost one of my gloves. The technicians had followed us down and they left while Louisa was organising a taxi for my mother.' Jane finished her cigarette, extinguishing it in the glass ashtray on Leo's desk.

'Your mother?' Inspector Winters looked confused.

'It's not common knowledge but, yes, Elsa Macintyre is my mother,' Jane said.

The policeman's brow cleared. 'Did anyone else exit through the lobby while you were there?' the inspector asked.

Jane shook her head. 'Not that I recall.'

'Did you pass anyone else or see anyone in any of the rooms on your way back upstairs?' Inspector Winters looked at her.

'There was no one in the corridors or on the landing. I didn't hear anything but, of course, one often can't inside the studio rooms. I only saw Jenny because someone had discovered my glove and placed it on the window ledge for that room. There are only a few rooms that have those windows onto the corridor,' Jane explained.

'Yes, those studios and rehearsal spaces have no outlook outside the building, so they rely on borrowed light from the corridors. Only a few rooms are set up in that way,' Leo confirmed.

'I wouldn't have even glanced in that room had my glove not been on the ledge. I had been scouring the floor to try and find it so hadn't looked at that level up until then,' Jane said. 'Even then, it was dark, and I thought I had imagined seeing someone sitting in there. I don't even really know what made me open the door to check.' She paused and thought about what had happened. 'I think there was something slightly odd about her posture and that there was no light on.'

There was a bump on the office door and Leo stood up to let Louisa in. Her hands were full with a tea tray which she set down on the desk. 'I'm sorry to take so long. I was looking for the guard while the kettle boiled.'

'And?' Inspector Winters asked as the girl straightened up.

'I can't seem to see him, but he went off a minute or two ago to patrol around the building,' Louisa said. 'He can't be far away.'

'You haven't seen him since? He hasn't come back down?' Inspector Winters asked in a sharp tone.

'No, sir.' Louisa looked anxious.

The inspector hurried out of the office muttering an oath under his breath.

'I say, what the devil is happening?' Leo was on his feet once more peering out through the office door to see where the inspector had gone. Louisa looked as if she were about to cry.

'I expect he will be back in a moment. He's not been gone long.' Jane lifted the lid of the polished chrome teapot and stirred the tea leaves inside before closing the lid again. She guessed the inspector had gone to dispatch one of the constables to search the building for the missing guard.

She hoped nothing bad had befallen the man. He had scarcely been in post for a day.

'Should I have stopped him from going to check the other floors? Should he have stayed in the lobby?' Louisa asked.

'No, of course not, my dear. Please don't fret. Now, I suggest we pour our tea and wait for the inspector to return,' Jane said in a firm tone. She had no patience with histrionics and knew she needed to keep the young girl's mind on other matters.

Leo turned away from the door and came back inside the office. 'Yes, we'll no doubt know more in a moment or two.'

Jane poured Louisa some tea. 'Take this back to your post and keep a sharp eye out for anyone leaving or entering as you would normally,' she suggested and ushered the girl out of the room.

The receptionist took her cup and saucer and obeyed without arguing. Jane suspected she was glad to be safely out of the office and back behind her desk. Jane saw that Benson was unobtrusively ensuring the blackout shutters were all in place in the lobby.

He caught her eye and gave a discreet nod. Jane took that to mean that he had alerted the brigadier and Arthur to Jenny's murder.

There was the clatter of feet on the stone stairs and one of the uniformed constables hurried to the reception desk.

'Call an ambulance. The security guard has been attacked.'

CHAPTER TWELVE

Leo set down his cup, spilling his tea into the saucer as he strode out into the lobby. Jane followed, hard on his heels.

'What's happened? Where?' Leo asked as the constable finished talking to the operator and replaced the telephone receiver.

'Upstairs, floor above where the actress woman was killed. We found him stuffed inside a cupboard.' The constable's cheeks were pink from his rush downstairs.

'Is he all right? Is he alive?' Jane asked. This was a most unexpected turn.

'The doctor is with him now, miss.' The constable took off back up the stairs.

Leo went to go after him, but Jane placed a restraining hand on his arm. 'No, let him go. The inspector will be down shortly. We do not wish to impede whatever is happening up there.'

She would have liked to have gone up there herself but knew that they would only be sent away and would not learn anything useful. She had no doubt that Benson would do his best to ascertain what had happened and would report to her later.

Leo hesitated. 'Very well.'

Jane guessed he didn't have the stomach to find out what had happened to his new employee.

The ambulance arrived and two men took a gurney to the porters' lift. Jane drank her tea before it could get completely cold. It had been a long day, and she was cold and weary now. Leo hovered anxiously near the reception desk until the ambulance men came back with the guard strapped to the gurney.

A crisp white crêpe bandage was secured around his head and his eyes were closed. Jane thought she saw dried blood on his ashen cheekbone. Inspector Winters reappeared in the lobby and ushered them both back to the office.

'I'm afraid your tea will be cold,' Jane apologised as the inspector retook a seat behind the desk.

'I am used to it,' he assured her and drank it with a grimace.

'Will the guard be all right?' Jane asked as she sat down and smoothed the fabric of her skirt across her knees.

'The doctor thinks so. It seems someone hit him over the head from behind and stuffed him inside a cupboard. He didn't see who did it. He was just recovering his wits when the constable heard groaning. He opened the storeroom door, and the poor fellow rolled out at his feet.' Inspector Winters had taken his notebook and pencil from his pocket. 'My men have conducted a search and there's no sign of the culprit.'

'What is happening here today?' Leo asked, but no one answered him.

'Now then, where were we? Ah yes, Miss Treen, you saw and heard no one and noticed nothing out of the ordinary before you discovered Miss Jackson?' Inspector Winters asked.

'That is correct,' Jane reaffirmed her previous statement of her movements.

'I take it that you didn't pass the guard going about his duties either?' He peered keenly at her.

'No, he was downstairs when Mother asked Louisa to call

her a taxi. He came up to the studio when I told the girl on reception to telephone you.' Jane was succinct. 'Then I sent him away when you arrived. He dispersed the group in the lobby, and I presume he then went to patrol the building which was when he must have been assaulted.'

She caught a glimpse of the time on the inspector's watch and realised she was too late to acquire any groceries on her way home. The shops would all have long closed. The blackout would have started too if they were much longer. The shutters had already been put in place around the building and the white markings on the kerbs would not give much help if the smog had rolled in again from the Thames.

The policeman glanced down once again at the signing sheets. Jane also took a good look, trying to read them upside down on the desk. She saw several names she knew on the sheets. Ernie Simons had signed in an hour before Elsa had signed out. Vincent Vaughn was also in the building. Frances Fellows had signed out just two minutes after Reginald Bosun. Both of them had left only a few minutes ago. That must have been while everyone was looking for the guard and Jane had been with Louisa in Leo's office.

The inspector asked the same sort of questions of Leo. He said he had been in his office for much of the afternoon but hadn't seen or heard anything out of the ordinary. He had been clearing up after the fire and completing paperwork to file a report on what had happened. Louisa also hadn't seen or heard anything until Jane had raised the alarm.

After a few more questions Jane found herself dismissed. She refastened her coat, tugged on her gloves and prepared to set off into the dark beyond the lobby. She had barely slipped outside when a male figure detached himself from the wall and came to greet her.

'May I escort you home, Miss Jane?'

'Benson, thank you, yes. I expect the bus may be quite full

at this time.' She accepted his proffered arm gratefully and they made their way through the darkness to the stop.

There was no opportunity to discuss what had happened since there was a knot of people waiting for the bus. Once on board, Benson secured her a seat whilst he stood holding on to the metal pole near the exit to the bus.

They made their way slowly across the darkened city until they reached the stop near Jane's apartment where Benson assisted her to dismount.

'I do hope Arthur has seen to Marmaduke,' Jane said as they finally entered the building. 'He likes his food at a regular time.'

Benson's lips twitched at this, but he didn't comment.

'I'll go and check on my cat and then come down to you and Arthur so we can discuss what's happened,' Jane said.

'Very good, Miss Jane,' Benson agreed as they parted on the stairs.

Jane hurried up to her flat and hoped Arthur had followed her instructions. She let herself into the flat and Marmaduke emerged from the kitchen gloom mewing a welcome. She pulled off her gloves and dropped them on the hall table before bending to scoop up her beloved pet.

She cooed endearments into Marmaduke's battered ears before entering her kitchen to see that Arthur had indeed been in and shut the window. She drew the curtains and switched on the light. An empty sardine tin lay on the draining board beside the sink. It had been washed out ready to go into the metal collection.

Relieved, that Arthur had clearly put his own discomfort to one side to attend to her pet, she set her cat back down.

'I have to go right out again, Marmy, but I won't be long, I promise.' Jane ensured her drawing-room curtains were closed and the blackout fabric in place before turning on her lamp. She then picked up her keys once more and set off back down to Arthur and Benson's flat.

* * *

Arthur had been waiting for his manservant and Jane to return. The telephone call Benson had made from the call box had been short and slightly cryptic, forcing him to wait for their return to obtain the details.

He was tired and grumpy after spending hours both listening to and poring over transcripts of the radio broadcasts. He glanced at the clumsily applied bandage on the back of his hand.

Jane's wretched beast of a cat had been very ungrateful when he had reluctantly prepared his food. Marmaduke had displayed his displeasure with a sharply clawed swipe on the back of Arthur's hand. Arthur hoped the drops of his blood had added to the epicurean taste of the stupid cat's sardines.

The sound of Benson's key in the lock was very welcome and he set his work aside ready to greet his manservant.

'Good evening, sir. My apologies for the delay in returning home. If you could excuse me for a moment while I change, Miss Jane will be along shortly. She is attending to her cat.' Benson's gaze rested briefly on the bandage covering the back of Arthur's hand and his eyebrows rose slightly.

'Of course, Benson. It sounded as if you and Jane have had quite a day.' Arthur set about tidying up more of his papers in anticipation of Jane's arrival.

He set the ashtray close to her chair and went to the kitchen to fill the kettle. He suspected Jane would require coffee and Benson tea while they told him what had happened at Bush House.

The kettle had just begun to whistle when Benson appeared in the kitchen clad in his normal formal day wear. 'Shall I make the refreshments, sir?'

The manservant smoothly edged him out of the way as a tap

sounded softly at the front door. 'I believe that will be Miss Jane.'

Arthur left his manservant to it and went to let Jane in. She looked tired, he thought as she stepped into the hall and closed the door behind her. There were lines at the corners of her eyes and she was less brisk than usual.

'Thank you for seeing to Marmaduke,' she said, then looked at his bandaged hand. 'What happened to you?'

'Your blasted cat, that's what happened to me.' Arthur led the way back into the sitting room and took his usual spot near the fireplace. Jane perched herself on the chair opposite him.

Benson carried in a wooden tray laden with crockery, a small teapot and a cafetière for Jane. He went to pour Jane her coffee and she waved him away with a grateful smile. 'I can see to myself, thank you, Benson. You must be exhausted.'

'Thank you, Miss Jane.' Benson promptly poured tea for himself and Arthur before seating himself on a small armchair near Arthur's seat. Jane poured her own coffee.

'Right, I think we should have a full debrief about today,' Jane said in a brisk tone as she stirred her coffee. She ran through the series of events. The morning fires, the appointment of the guard, Jenny Jackson's murder and the assault on the guard. She kept her outline brief and succinct.

Jane also told them what she had witnessed between Frances and Vincent in the café at lunchtime and Reggie's information about Ernie's gambling.

Arthur listened attentively. He passed on his own information about his suspicions that the apartment block was still under surveillance.

'I would suggest then that great caution is required from all of us,' Benson said. 'Miss Jane, do you think that any of these incidents could be connected to the network we started to uncover earlier this year?'

Arthur had almost forgotten the network of saboteurs and

fifth columnists who were actively seeking to betray their own country. They had encountered a well-organised group on their first case together back in January. The discovery had led to the brigadier forming them into a secret department to root out and solve just such crimes.

'I think it has to be a possibility. Either directly linked or a separate cell,' Arthur said.

'I agree. It may be someone acting as a lone cell.' Jane frowned. 'The surveillance may be friendly. It may have been arranged by another department unknown to us, since our own operations are covert within the organisation.'

Arthur nodded slowly. He could see what she meant, the surveillance could indeed be from a rival department within the War Office. The Admiralty or air force or some other department who had flagged their activities as suspicious.

'I think we should treat all of them as hostile until proved otherwise.' He looked at Jane and could see she agreed.

'I wasn't in the building at the time of the fires. Do you know what happened?' Jane looked at Benson.

'I believe the second fire was discovered when someone noticed smoke coming from the first floor from inside a cupboard. While that was being extinguished, I was on the top floor when I found a wastepaper receptacle had been set alight. I dealt with that as the fire brigade and the police arrived to finish extinguishing the seat of the initial fire inside Mr Cavendish's office,' Benson explained as he sipped his tea. 'Mr Cavendish had deployed an extinguisher already but there was quite a quantity of smoke.'

'I looked at the signing sheets when I collected my pass. All the suspects from Tabitha's murder were present in the building at the time of the fires. They were also all present when Jenny Jackson was murdered,' Jane said.

'I don't suppose you noticed anything suspicious when you

discovered the fire on the top floor?' Arthur looked at his manservant.

'Not really, I'm afraid. I had seen Mr Simons a few minutes earlier in conversation with Miss Jackson. They had appeared to be arguing over something. I also saw the bandleader, Mr Bosun, huddled together with Mr Vaughn. Mr Vaughn looked quite angry, but he didn't seem to say anything. They were all not too far from the blaze so could have set the fires. Miss Fellowes was also not far from the blaze in Mr Cavendish's office I believe. The receptionist mentioned it to Inspector Winters when I was in earshot,' Benson said.

Arthur drummed his fingers on the arm of his chair. 'The murder method for both Jenny and Tabitha was the same. Both women were strangled.'

'Both were linked to Bush House and the same group of people,' Jane added. 'How are you doing with the codes? Is there anything there that could shed any light on the motives behind the murders?'

Arthur knew she really wanted to know if he could trace who may have been trying to embed codes favourable to the enemy within the broadcasts. 'I have managed to identify and eliminate our own hidden codes. The ones we are transmitting to the resistance groups overseas. At least, I believe I have worked out most of those. Some of them are quite nonsensical but I suspect with the aid of a code book they would be vital to those groups.'

'What about the other codes? The enemy ones which we think Tabitha had uncovered?' Jane asked. She placed her empty coffee cup back on its saucer and returned it to the tray before lighting one of her infernal cigarettes.

'I think I may have found what Tabitha spotted. It's not a code in the way we have used them. We tend to insert a nonsensical phrase into something at certain times or during certain broadcasts. For example we may insert something in French perhaps which, if translated, says something like Mariette is walking her rabbit. With the aid of a code book, this could mean destroy the bridge at Nouville.' He looked at Jane to see if she was following him.

She nodded as she blew out a thin plume of smoke.

'Most ingenious, sir,' Benson agreed.

'Now, the enemy seems to be sending information in a different way. I've looked at the transcripts and listened to hours of programming. The messages are sent in different shows and in different ways. I suspect that these are most often transmitted innocently by the programmer. The performer involved is participating unwittingly in the transmission,' Arthur warmed to his theme, shuffling forward slightly in his seat.

'Such as?' Jane asked.

'One of the ways is through the alteration of the scripts. Last-minute small changes removing usually a common phrase and replacing it with another.' Arthur delved into the pile of papers he had moved to one side. 'Here.' He passed a script to Jane.

She took it from him and asked, 'What am I looking at?'

'You see there a typewritten slip of paper is loosely attached over the top of an original announcement?' Arthur pointed to where a thin piece of paper, curling up at one end was fixed to the script, half covering the original line.

'Yes?' Jane frowned and looked at him waiting for him to explain.

'That's one I unpeeled to see what the change had been. There are two methods of changes being made to the scripts. The handwritten ones by and large all seem genuine alterations. They are written in different inks by different hands. I haven't discovered anything that leaps out at me amongst those. These typewritten changes, however, are different. I think these are the ones Tabitha was concerned about,' Arthur said.

Jane extinguished her cigarette and frowned at the script.

'The original line is in a story Ernie Simons is reading to the children. *"Hop little bunny, hop-a-long home. The sun is setting and you're all alone."* Then this replacement line is *"Hop little rabbit, to the burrow you go, light up the lamps and set the burrow aglow."* Both rhyming but you believe the new line is some sort of signal?'

'I checked the broadcast date of that script. I think that line was a tip-off for a bombing raid we carried out resulting in a huge fire at a target inside Germany. Burrow is the name of the city in code. There are more just like it.' Arthur turned to the pile ready to show her more examples.

'No, I can see. If the relevant changes are typewritten then I assume we need to know who has access to a typewriter?' Jane asked.

'Leo Cavendish has one in his office which is also used by the receptionist. I believe other people may also use it on occasion,' Benson said.

'Leo is often out of his office, and it doesn't seem to be locked,' Jane agreed. 'Have you seen any other typewriters in the building?' She looked at Benson.

'There are some in an office on the top floor. Again, the room is unlocked. Various secretarial staff utilise the machines if last-minute news comes in or information which the government wishes one of the announcers to transmit,' Benson said.

'That doesn't help us much to narrow things down.' Jane looked at Arthur as if she expected him to have a solution.

'Forgive me, sir, but are all the changes being made using the same machine?' Benson asked.

'I don't follow?' The creases on Jane's brow deepened as she looked at Benson.

'Not every machine is identical, Miss Jane. Some machines may not replicate the letters in the same way. May I?' The manservant held out his hand for the script.

Jane passed it over so he could study it.

'If you look, Miss Jane, the letter A on this alteration is missing a bottom portion of the letter in the same place each time. It gives a small break.' Benson showed Jane and Arthur what he meant. 'If we compare other examples we can see if our culprit has a preference for the same machine and we can try and identify which one is being used,' he explained.

'Yes, I see. If they do use the same machine, then once we have found which one it is, we can see who is using it. It may lead us to the traitor and potentially our murderer,' Arthur said.

CHAPTER THIRTEEN

Benson went to the kitchen after announcing that he would prepare something for their supper. Jane and Arthur applied themselves to the stack of scripts with the typewritten alterations. They looked at the letter As for the small break in the formation of the letter and any other clues that could identify the machine which had created the slips.

Arthur turned on an extra lamp and balanced his spectacles on his nose as he squinted at the papers. Jane applied herself to sorting through the piles and tried to ignore the empty feeling in her stomach currently being made worse by the delicious smell now emanating from the kitchen.

'Well, Benson's theory is right. It seems that the majority of these slips were generated on one machine.' Arthur leaned back in his chair. He lifted up his spectacles to pinch the bridge of his nose as if to relieve the effort of concentrating so hard.

'Yes, it certainly looks that way. Now the original transcripts themselves seem to have been typed by a different machine or machines.' Jane had checked the originals to see if they too had the same tiny telltale fault as the alterations.

'Do we know where the original scripts come from? Are

they all from the same source? Whoever made the changes must have seen them in advance to know how to make the changes,' Arthur said.

'The scripts with the alterations are all either stories – like the one about the rabbit – or government urgent information broadcasts. The government ones come via courier. I think the stories are decided in advance but the scripts are only finalised on the day.' Jane tried to recall what she had managed to observe during her short spell at Bush House.

'Tabitha must have spotted the changes but as receptionist and Leo's secretary, would she have seen the alterations before or after they were broadcast or both?' Arthur looked at her.

'I don't know. I think the changes must have been done at the studios. I don't think they would have arrived by courier with the alterations otherwise the story scripts wouldn't have the alterations.' Jane frowned.

'Would the new receptionist... What did you say she was called? Louisa? Would she be able to tell you? It would be good to confirm our theory,' Arthur asked.

Jane shuffled the papers back into a neat pile and set them aside. 'I can try and find out. Mother has a lunchtime concert tomorrow so I'm not due to go to Bush House. I'd have to go later and find some pretext for being there.'

Benson entered the room with the things to set the table ready for supper.

'Oh, do let me do that. You've had such a long day, and I am so grateful for you cooking tonight. I had intended to try and get some groceries on my way home. My cupboards are very bare at the moment even without the rationing,' Jane said as she took the cutlery from the manservant to set their places.

'It's no trouble, Miss Jane.' Benson smiled at her and returned to the kitchen.

A few minutes later he returned and invited them to take their places at the table before serving up a plate of mashed potato, vegetables and a small serving of what appeared to be some sort of meat.

Jane ate hungrily while Arthur, as usual, picked his way slowly and methodically through his plate, inspecting every morsel on his fork. She refrained from commenting and placed her cutlery down on her empty plate with a satisfied sigh.

'Thank you, Benson. That was just what the doctor ordered.'

'The pleasure was all mine, Miss Jane.' Benson finished his own meal, and they waited for Arthur. 'It has crossed my mind, sir, miss, while I was peeling the potatoes, I wondered what the purpose of the fires might be?'

Jane looked at Arthur. Benson had a point. The fires were not large enough or serious enough to have shut down the broadcasts which must surely be the main object of the enemy. So why were the fires set?

'A distraction, or nuisance perhaps?' Arthur suggested as he examined a piece of carrot.

'A distraction from what?' Jane asked.

'I'm not sure. Perhaps to stop us from poking around asking awkward questions. It also makes me wonder why the guard was attacked. He was on a different floor to where you discovered Jenny's body. He was also attacked after her murder.' Arthur finished his supper and picked up his napkin.

'It seems extremely likely that the attack on him was connected to Jenny's murder in some way. The poor man only started work there that afternoon. If he had seen something suspicious then he might have been on his way back downstairs to raise the alarm or to see the police.' Jane could see what Arthur meant.

'He could have been pursuing someone suspicious? Someone who shouldn't have been there? Perhaps that was why he was assaulted,' Benson suggested as he stood up to collect the empty plates.

'No one mentioned hearing sounds of shouting or running feet. Nothing to indicate that he was trying to raise the alarm or stop someone,' Jane said.

'Then if the guard was attacked by the murderer perhaps the guard may not have realised the killer shouldn't have been on that floor, in that space. Like you said, he was new and didn't know who should be where. He may have been attacked to prevent him from mentioning that fact.' Arthur looked at Jane.

'True, the killer may have attacked him to make sure the coast was clear so he or she could make good their escape. They may have gone up to that floor to avoid detection and then been discovered. I presume having a security guard patrolling the building would be most inconvenient if you had committed a murder.' Jane toyed with the cork edge of her placemat while Benson carried their crockery into the kitchen.

'If the murder was premeditated then, yes, that would be true. The guard was only appointed after the fires this morning. You said Leo had engaged him from an agency.' Arthur looked at her and she could see his clever mind was racing over the possibilities.

'I don't see why else he would have been attacked after Jenny was killed. There are no exits from those levels of the building unless I suppose one were to attempt the fire escape in the dark. He may have seen someone trying to leave that way without knowing why but that seems weak to me.' She couldn't see the scenario she had just described as being likely, although it was possible.

'Do we think the attack on Jenny was planned?' Arthur asked.

Jane shrugged. 'I think it must have been. There was a reason she was killed. She either knew something or had seen something that our murderer did not want to be made known. Something that he couldn't risk her talking about.'

Arthur nodded as Benson returned to the room bearing

some small dishes of what looked like some kind of milk pudding.

'Might Miss Jackson have been blackmailing the murderer?' Benson asked as he set the dishes before them.

'If she had realised they had killed Tabitha?' Jane asked.

'Or if she too had discovered the connection about the altered scripts. Perhaps even seen the killer typing the changes?' Benson suggested as he retook his seat.

'I think the blackmail idea is a good one. Jenny was worried about her hours being cut short and her contracts being reduced because of her drinking. She certainly seemed to need money.' Jane stirred her pudding and decided it was tapioca.

'Perhaps the person she was blackmailing had influence, perhaps over her contracts being renewed if that is what was happening,' Arthur suggested as he too eyed his dessert with suspicion.

'If the guard was attacked to ensure the coast was clear then I presume we can also agree that he probably would have recognised the murderer. If not straight away then definitely later if the culprit works in the building regularly. After all, no one can enter now unless they have a pass as well as signing in at the desk.' Jane spooned up her pudding.

Benson gave a small nod of agreement.

'It seems we still have the same core group of suspects,' Arthur said.

* * *

Jane returned to her own flat after helping Benson with the dishes. She was more than ready to climb into her nightclothes and get to bed. It had helped to talk things through with Arthur and Benson but now she was simply exhausted.

She poured herself a small nightcap of brandy to take with some hot milk. Marmaduke followed at her heels as she moved about the flat. The telephone rang as she filled her hot-water bottle ready to remove the chill from her flannelette sheets before climbing into bed.

'Janey, thank goodness, I've been calling and calling. Where on earth have you been?' Her mother's anxious voice reached her before she could even give her telephone number.

'Mother...' Jane tried to get a word in, but her mother didn't even pause for breath.

'As soon as Frances called me to tell me about Jenny Jackson's murder I started ringing you. I told Stephen that you never go out so when you didn't answer the telephone he offered to come over to your flat. Then when he came back and said there was no reply, I almost rang the police,' Elsa continued.

'Mother!' Jane virtually had to shout to get her mother to stop talking.

'Where were you? I mean, I thought you might have been the next victim with all that snooping about that you insist on doing. Not a bit of consideration for what I might be going through,' Elsa huffed.

'You sent Stephen to my flat because I wasn't answering the telephone?' Jane sat down on the chair next to the hall stand.

'Of course, well not sent exactly. The dear boy volunteered. He is such a sweetheart. He was as worried about you as I was. I mean, honey, first Tabitha, then the fires and now Jenny. To top it all off after Frances called I heard from Reggie and he said the guard had been taken away in an ambulance. He saw it as he was leaving apparently,' Elsa explained.

'And you immediately thought I might have been murdered too?' Jane rubbed her hand across her forehead trying to follow her mother's leaps of logic.

'Well, I had gone off in a taxi and you had disappeared back up the stairs looking for that glove. What was I supposed to think when you didn't pick up the telephone? Honestly, Janey pie, you can be horribly thoughtless,' Elsa protested.

'Well, as you can hear, I am absolutely fine,' Jane said.

'Where were you anyway? You never go out. Were you with that man you took to Kent? The one with the bad chest and the lovely manservant? Oh, Janey, really, you don't have to settle you know. If you would just make a little more of yourself, honey. Stephen is a much better catch.' Elsa prattled on, dropping her voice a little for the last sentence. Jane wondered if Stephen might be in earshot.

'I do go out, Mother. I just don't tell you about it. How did Frances know about Jenny's murder?' Jane asked in an attempt to change the subject away from her mother's interest in her private life.

'She had it from Ernie Simons. He had been in one of the other studios and he and Frances met in the lobby just as the police arrived. Something like that anyway. She said she thought you were involved. That inspector from Scotland Yard and Leo Cavendish. Oh, have they arrested him?'

'Mother, what are you talking about?' Jane's head hurt trying to keep up.

'Leo, have they arrested him? I mean with Tabitha's death and now Jenny. There has to be a connection, don't you think? My, I hardly feel safe. Suppose I'm on the list to be bumped off?' Elsa asked.

'No, Leo has not been arrested. Not to my knowledge. I found Jenny so I was interviewed by Inspector Winters.' Jane realised as soon as she'd spoken that she shouldn't have told her mother about discovering Jenny's body.

'You found Jenny? Oh, honey, what in the world is happening? Oh, is that why your brigadier put you with me as my accompanist? Are you a kind of bodyguard? That's it, isn't it? I *am* in danger. I knew you hadn't been hooked out of that typing pool thing for nothing,' Elsa said.

'Mother, you are jumping to all the wrong conclusions as usual. There is no reason to believe you are in any kind of danger. I work in a department, and I am due some leave. I also have the right credentials to assist you. That's why I'm helping you out while Michael, your regular man, recovers. How did Reggie know what happened to the guard?'

'What? Oh, I don't know. He was there I suppose, or Frances or Ernie told him. I was so upset I wasn't paying attention. It's all so shocking,' Elsa wailed.

'Had Jenny fallen out with anyone, do you know?' Jane asked.

'No, well, no more than usual. She was blaming Frances for snitching about her drinking, and she hated Leo. She thought he should be backing her and giving her more work. She needed the money. She and Vince had a big row over her missing some of her cues, all the usual kind of thing. Why? What's that got to do with anything?' Elsa asked.

'I don't know. That's what the inspector was asking, that's all,' Jane fibbed.

'Oh, well, I'm glad you're not dead, I'd better go and get my beauty sleep. I'll see you at lunchtime for the concert. Nighty night now, and don't let the bed bugs bite.' Her mother rang off.

Jane replaced the receiver and sighed. Her carefully prepared bedtime drink now had a skin on it and her hot-water bottle was still in the kitchen. Marmaduke rubbed himself around her ankles, purring.

'I know, Marmy, darling,' Jane soothed as she went to scoop the milk skin from her drink and to place her hot-water bottle in her bed. She had a busy day again tomorrow and she intended to be first in the queue at the grocers in the morning before her cupboard was completely bare.

CHAPTER FOURTEEN

Arthur too rose early the following morning. He ate breakfast with Benson and made a telephone call to the brigadier's office to secure an appointment for later that morning. He thought Stephen, the brigadier's secretary, sounded unusually cool, even for Stephen, when they spoke.

However, once they had arranged a time and Arthur had hung up the receiver he set about making his preparations. He packed up the transcripts he and Jane had discovered with the alterations the previous evening into a brown paper bag.

He placed the scripts they had discarded as being of no interest into a file and marked it as classified before stowing it in a commonplace cheap brown briefcase. Before telephoning for a taxi, he went to the kitchen to look through the window. He hung back behind the curtain so he wouldn't be observed.

After a few minutes spent watching the street near the plane tree he was certain that there were people watching the apartment block. There was no sign of the nursemaid and her pram. This time the watcher appeared to be an elderly man with a cane loitering around near the tree.

Arthur dressed for the cold weather with his usual care.

The fallen leaves in the gutter had glittered silver with traces of frost, another reminder that Christmas was creeping closer. He stowed the paper bag inside his thick woollen overcoat, wrapped his knitted scarf around his neck and donned his trilby.

He didn't have to wait long in the lobby before his taxi arrived. He noticed the elderly watcher taking note of his appearance. Arthur made certain that the man could hear the address he gave to the driver. He was quite certain that the watcher would swiftly make a telephone call and Arthur could expect something to happen when he reached his destination.

The taxi pulled to a halt outside the offices at Whitehall and Arthur climbed out of the cab to pay the driver. As he did so a young man hurrying past bumped into him, knocking the briefcase from Arthur's hand. The man picked it up and passed it back with a muttered apology before disappearing into the crowd.

Arthur finished paying the driver and continued up the steps into the building to keep his appointment. One thing he was sure of. The briefcase he now carried was not the one that had accompanied him from the apartment. The substitution had been slick but that was no more than he had expected.

The watcher and his henchman had acted swiftly to effect the change. Arthur smiled to himself as he entered the lobby of the building. They would be disappointed and distracted he hoped by the contents of his case.

He gave his name at the desk and made his way to the brigadier's office once the receptionist had confirmed he was expected. Stephen greeted him on arrival in the outer office, his dark eyes sharp with interest.

'Arthur, good morning. The brigadier is still on a telephone call at present. He'll be free shortly.' Stephen offered him a seat.

Arthur thanked him and took one of the chairs near

Stephen's desk. He could hear the dull roar of the brigadier bellowing into the telephone inside his office.

'How is Jane faring?' Stephen asked as he lit up a cigarette.

'Very well, I believe.' Arthur shifted uncomfortably on his seat. He wasn't sure where this conversation was leading.

'Elsa is quite concerned about her. This latest murder at Bush House had her very frightened.' Stephen eyed him through the thin veil of cigarette smoke.

'Yes, I suppose she must be worried,' Arthur responded politely. He was unsure of just how much Stephen knew of their mission. Obviously, he was aware that something was afoot, and that he and Jane were working together on a case. Although he knew that Stephen was probably not fully aware of all the details of their work.

'She sent me over to Jane's flat last night as she wasn't answering the telephone.' Stephen tapped the ash from the end of his cigarette into the small glass ashtray on the corner of his desk.

'Oh, I suppose she must have been out.' Arthur wondered what time Elsa had tried calling. Jane had spent much of the evening having supper in his and Benson's flat while they had worked on the transcripts. He was not about to tell Stephen that, however.

'I see you've injured your hand?' Stephen looked at the dressing Benson had applied to replace the bandage on Arthur's hand.

'Just a cat scratch,' Arthur explained. 'Nothing serious.'

The noise from inside the brigadier's office subsided and a moment later the door banged open.

'Arthur, my boy, come in, come in,' the brigadier summoned him into the office.

Once he was seated in front of the brigadier's desk and the door safely closed, Arthur took the concealed package of transcripts from within his coat.

The brigadier raised his bushy, silvery eyebrows slightly at this but waited for Arthur to explain. Arthur placed the package on the desk and picked up the cheap brown briefcase he had carried into the office.

'I took the precaution of placing the ordinary transcripts in my briefcase in a file labelled classified. On arrival here, someone knocked into me and the cases were switched. I am interested to see what this one contains.' Arthur clicked open the catches to reveal a small bundle of cut up newspaper inside the case.

The brigadier leaned back in his chair making it creak under his weight. 'Smart thinking. I presume you had anticipated an attempt to take the case?'

'The flats are still under observation. I don't know who by. I don't know if this is connected to Leo Cavendish or is another department attempting to determine what we are doing. The other alternative is, of course, the enemy, potentially part of the same organisation we encountered in January.' Arthur looked at the brigadier.

'I can assure you that whoever is watching you is not from this department,' the brigadier said.

'Jane and I assumed that whoever it might be was potentially hostile, so we have acted accordingly,' Arthur assured him.

'A wise decision it seems given the latest incidents. I presume the contents of that paper bag are the reason you wanted this meeting?' The brigadier leaned forward and tapped the corner of the bag with his forefinger.

'Yes, sir.' Arthur took the scripts from the bag and gave the brigadier a concise report of what he and Jane had discovered the previous evening. He pointed out the friendly concealed messages sent to overseas agents and then the alterations to the scripts which he suspected were hostile and for enemy agents.

The brigadier's expression was grave as he listened and studied the papers. 'It seems that Tabitha's concerns were justified and presumably were what cost her her life. I think this discovery must finally eliminate any possibility that she was killed in a random assault. Then, of course, we now have the murder of Miss Jackson.'

'Exactly, sir. I am also concerned over the fires which were set within Bush House. It seemed clear to us that these were either for nuisance value or to serve as a distraction for something else. Possibly to try to detract us from our mission.' Arthur shuffled the transcripts back into a neat pile.

'Do you and Jane have any leads about who may be responsible for any of these events?' the brigadier asked.

Arthur went through the list they had compiled of their main suspects and showed the brigadier the telltale fault in the alterations.

'Hmm, interesting. I presume Mr Benson will be continuing to assist you in determining which machine and which person may be responsible?' the brigadier asked.

Arthur nodded and replaced the scripts in the paper bag. 'Yes, he is going to try the machines, if possible, today.'

The brigadier raised one of his beetle-like brows. 'Hmm, hmm, and what about Jane? Where is she today?'

'She is assisting Elsa at a concert somewhere in the city this lunchtime,' Arthur said.

'I heard from Mr Benson that she discovered Miss Jackson's body.' The brigadier looked at Arthur.

'That's correct, sir. My understanding is that Benson came across her a moment later. You know too that the security guard was also injured?' Arthur asked.

'I was talking to Inspector Winters just before I called you in,' the brigadier explained.

'Indeed?' Arthur wondered what else the inspector might have said to the brigadier about the guard.

'Yes, he said the guard had been attacked while his men were with Miss Jackson and the doctor. Apparently, he is recovering in the hospital. He didn't see who attacked him. He told the inspector he was patrolling the upper floor when someone came out of a room behind him and struck him over the head. The next thing he remembered was someone dragging him out of the cupboard where his assailant had hidden him. He has so far been unable to shed any light on why he may have been assaulted.'

It seemed the guard's version of events tallied with what Arthur and Jane had worked out with Benson the previous evening. 'It's unfortunate that he didn't get a glimpse of who it may have been,' Arthur said.

'Exactly. I am concerned about the safety of you all. Especially Jane. This murderer has killed twice now, both of his victims are female. I understand from Stephen that Jane's mother is also concerned even though she is unaware of your connections to this case.' The brigadier looked at Arthur.

'Jane is very aware of the risks, sir, as indeed are we all.' He knew Jane would not be amused if she thought the brigadier might pull her from the assignment. He did, however, share the brigadier's concerns for her safety.

The brigadier stroked his chin in a thoughtful gesture. 'I presume that your part of the code breaking is complete for now?'

'Yes, sir. We need to identify the machine and if we are unable to determine who the culprit might be that typed up the alterations, then we may need to set up a trap,' Arthur said.

The brigadier nodded slowly. 'Yes, we need to discover how our chappie is finding out information useful to the enemy though. It's not enough just to block the method of transmission. We need to discover the source and get that plugged up tight too. I'll set Stephen to work investigating the backgrounds and connections of the names you've given me. That would be Leo Cavendish, Vince Vaughn, Ernie Simons, Frances Fellowes and Reginald Bosun, is that correct?'

'Yes, sir.' Arthur could see the brigadier had jotted all of the names down on a pad.

'Leave that with me. Now, keep me informed of anything you feel is relevant and while you wait I want you to keep a discreet eye on Miss Treen. That concert she's playing at today is at Euston Station I believe. A morale booster for the masses. Get along there and keep an eye on things. Keep an eye on her.' The brigadier rose and extended his hand for Arthur to shake.

Arthur shook hands and restored the papers to the inside of his coat before abandoning the briefcase. 'Very good, sir.'

He left the brigadier and returned to the outer office.

'Well, how did it go?' Stephen asked, eyeing him curiously.

'Very well, thank you.' Arthur glanced at his watch. 'I must be off. I have a concert to attend.'

Jane ended up visiting five different shops in her endeavours to find enough food to at least make a few meals. She collected her rations and bought various additional bits and pieces before managing to obtain more tins of pilchards for Marmaduke.

There was just enough time to get back to her flat, stow everything away, apply some lipstick and hurry back out again. She had to run to catch the bus as it was about to leave the stop as she approached, and jumped to make it onto the platform.

''Ere love, you was cuttin' it fine,' the cockney conductor rebuked her gently as he steadied her to prevent her from falling.

'Yes, thank you, I'm sorry.' She smiled gratefully at him and gave him her fare as she sank down on a nearby vacant seat.

She only needed to travel a few stops before leaving the bus for the underground to take her towards Euston Station. The city was busy and the air in the tube station smelt of stale humanity. Jane shuddered and was glad she had not yet been forced to seek shelter there at any time since the war had begun. The government had tried to stop people from heading there when the sirens had sounded since there was a chronic lack of facilities.

Jane thought they might as well have stood on the beach like King Canute trying to stop the tide from coming in. The tube train was as packed as the buses on the surface and she was glad to get off again, ready to track down the venue for this morale-boosting concert.

She hurried up the steps towards the surface, the air around her growing colder with every step. The concourse of the station was crowded. People going about their business, men in khaki uniforms. Jane was aware that she was running a few minutes late. Her mother would not be happy.

Whilst Elsa took quite a laissez-faire approach with most appointment times, when it came to her work she was a stickler for punctuality. Her mother had said that a dais had been set up ready for their performance. She spotted where the crowd appeared to be denser and headed in that direction.

'Jane!'

She turned in surprise at the sound of her name being called from somewhere close behind her. To her astonishment she saw Arthur weaving his way through the crowd to meet her.

'Arthur, what are you doing here? Is everything all right? Is Benson all right?' she asked in some alarm, noting his unusually rosy cheeks above the layer of green wool wrapped around his neck.

'Yes, everything is fine. I had a meeting earlier with the brigadier. He insisted that I come and accompany you here.' Arthur waved his hand in the general direction of the crowd around the foot of the makeshift stage.

'Meet me here, why? What did he say?' Anxiety bubbled up in Jane's stomach. Did the brigadier not trust her to handle the assignment? Had something gone on behind the scenes?

'Everything is perfectly all right. Let's go and find your mother, you must be due on stage soon.' Arthur took her arm and gently turned her back towards the crowd around the stage.

'Yes, I'm late, Mother will kill me.' Jane gave herself a mental shake and forced herself to focus on the task in hand.

Elsa was happily occupied with signing autographs for a coterie of admirers as Jane hurried over to meet her. Arthur followed more slowly in her wake. Frances, dressed in a dark-purple evening gown was declaiming dramatically on the stage.

'Janey pie, honey, is that the time?' Elsa gave an exaggerated squeak of alarm as she looked at the station clock.

'The traffic was very bad, and I only just made the bus and the tube,' Jane tried to explain as her mother extricated herself from her fans.

Her mother smiled cheerily at her admirers, most of which appeared to be young soldiers, before hissing in Jane's ear, 'That is no excuse. These poor boys have been forced to attend to Frances delivering Shakespeare for the last twenty minutes.'

A round of applause broke out from the group in front of the stage and Ernie Simons took the microphone cracking a few jokes, while Elsa and Jane prepared to take their places. Jane set her music on the piano and flexed her fingers. The running order was to be the same songs they had performed at the last open concert a few days earlier.

She peeped over the top of her music and saw that Ernie had succeeded in drawing an even larger crowd to the front of the makeshift stage. Jane looked automatically for Arthur in his green wool scarf and dark-brown hat. She spotted him standing somewhat diffidently at the side of the crowd and instantly felt calmer.

As Ernie handed over to Elsa and joined Frances at the edge of the crowd, Jane noticed Arthur station himself close to them. She forced herself to concentrate as her mother finished her short speech and launched into the first song.

There was no time to pay attention to what was going on below the stage for the next thirty minutes as she was kept busy playing for her mother. The crowd's applause was loud and long accompanied by a good many wolf whistles whenever the music paused.

Finally, Jane played the last note and Ernie bounded back onto the stage to take over from Elsa once more. She joined her mother to take a bow before heading back down the couple of steps at the side to look for Arthur.

Elsa was immediately engulfed by autograph hunters once more and Jane was pressed into service accepting bunches of flowers and a few cards. Arthur fought his way through the crowd to appear at her side.

'That was splendidly done, Jane,' he murmured.

'Thank you.' She never expected anyone to notice her skills as a pianist. People were there to see her mother after all, she was merely in the background. Truthfully, that was how Elsa preferred it. Fortunately, it was also how Jane liked it too.

'Janey, honey, take care of all these, would you? I'll see you this evening. Fundraising supper tonight remember,' her mother called over the heads of the group surrounding her.

'Come on, let's go for lunch and we can catch up,' Arthur urged.

Jane saw her mother suddenly notice Arthur's presence and her lips pursed as if to say something cutting.

'Yes, let's go.' Jane slipped her arm through Arthur's and tugged him speedily away before her mother could speak.

CHAPTER FIFTEEN

Once safely out of her mother's radius Jane slowed her pace knowing that Arthur struggled to keep up with her rapid walking.

'Are you all right?' Arthur asked as he helped her to take some of the posies of flowers, while she stowed the love notes away in her handbag.

'Working with my mother always makes me feel on edge,' Jane said, snapping her handbag shut and adjusting the strap of her gas mask case.

'Ah.' Arthur looked as if he wanted to say more but held his peace. 'Come on, I think there is a Lyons tea room not too far away. We can try and get something to eat there.'

Accordingly, they headed out of the station and into the surrounding streets. Jane was not as familiar with this part of London as Arthur. She had thought they were going to the Lyons tea room but instead Arthur suddenly diverted down a narrow side street and she found herself following him inside a small café.

'Sit down and I'll order us some lunch.' Arthur indicated a

small vacant table with two seats at the rear of the café. Most of the other tables were occupied.

Jane raised her eyebrows but took her seat, glad to put down the floral gifts from her mother's admirers. Arthur went over to the counter and was busy ordering from the rotund man in a large white apron who seemed to be in charge of operations.

Her colleague returned a moment later bearing a tray with two thick earthenware mugs. 'Coffee,' Arthur announced as he set one of the mugs in front of her. He placed the other mug in front of the vacant seat.

'What have you got?' Jane eyed the thin brown liquid inside Arthur's mug with some suspicion.

'Oxo.' Arthur took his place opposite her as she wrinkled her nose in distaste. 'I thought this place would be quieter than the Lyons tea rooms. Less chance of us being overheard.'

Jane glanced around the warm, steamed up café which smelt of cabbage and fried food. 'Yes, you're probably right,' she agreed. There was a gentle rumble of conversation in the café, interspersed with the clink of china and the hiss of steam from the water heater.

Most of the clientele appeared to be workmen, in their late forties and fifties dressed for manual labour with thick navy peacoats and check woven caps. Their faces were tired and grimy and spoke of stress and life spent outdoors. Jane wondered how Arthur had come to discover the place.

'My uncle used to bring me here when I was younger.' Arthur seemed to have plucked the question from her thoughts.

'Oh.' Jane picked up her coffee and took a sip. It was surprisingly good. She tried to recall what little she knew about Arthur from his files back in Whitehall. She had been to his home, Half Moon Manor in Devon, but Arthur never said a great deal about his past. She knew he had been orphaned, and his house had been his uncle's, left to him when his uncle had passed away.

'We would often come to London when I was well. We would visit Greenwich to see the observatory and to attend lectures,' Arthur reminisced. 'He would take me to his club. That was where I first met the brigadier.'

Jane almost choked on her coffee. 'Your uncle knew the brigadier?' she asked.

'Yes, they were in the army together I believe, at least for a time. My uncle was invalided out. He injured his leg, lost part of his foot.' Arthur blinked owlishly at her over the brim of his mug.

'Why did I not know any of this?' Jane asked.

Arthur shrugged. 'I don't know. I suppose I thought you must know. That it would be on file somewhere.' He unwrapped his scarf from around his neck and unbuttoned his coat in preparation for his food to arrive.

The man from the counter placed two large plates in front of them. 'There you go, put hairs on yer chest that will.' He chortled at his own humour as he winked at Jane. 'Sauce is on the table,' he added before walking back to his post ready to serve the next customer.

Arthur helped himself to brown sauce as Jane surveyed the generous portion of spam fritters and chips. 'I ordered for you. The menu is a little limited.'

She had to admit it smelled good and she was very hungry after her busy morning. 'That's all right. This looks good.'

She added tomato ketchup to her own plate and picked up her cutlery. 'You said you had a meeting this morning with the brigadier?' she said as she speared a chip and dipped it in the sauce.

'Yes, I wanted to go over what I'd found in the transcripts. I don't like to go into detail on the telephone obviously.' He told her of the watchers outside their flats and the incident when he had disembarked from the taxi.

'That's very troubling. Quick thinking on your part though.

They will be very disappointed when they go through that file,' Jane remarked, glancing around to ensure they could not be overheard.

'Hmm, perhaps. If they are the enemy they will know we are on to them when they examine that file.' Arthur sliced into his spam.

'Because of the material in the case?' Jane asked.

Arthur nodded as he chewed and swallowed. 'Precisely. If they are from another department, blind to what we are about, then it may distract them for a while examining the contents.'

'What did the brigadier have to say about it all?' Jane looked at Arthur. She hoped he wasn't going to tell her that the brigadier wanted to remove her from the case.

'He is concerned for your safety, obviously.' Arthur met her gaze.

'And?' Jane waited for his response.

Arthur's lips twitched. 'Hence my appearance at your performance. I am instructed to hang around with you. I believe he thinks it may be safer if there are two of us.'

Jane saw the glint of amusement in his eyes. 'Yes, well, you are a most unconventional bodyguard. He isn't still thinking we pretend some kind of romantic connection, is he?' she asked. 'What about Benson? Is he in danger?' She was concerned that he too might well be at risk.

'I don't think that Benson has come into their notice.' Arthur looked thoughtful. 'Hopefully, he may have discovered which machine is being used to type those messages. That could be useful if we need to set up a trap. In terms of safety, the majority of our suspects seemed to be at the station earlier for your performance.'

'That's true,' Jane agreed. 'Only Vince Vaughn and Reggie Bosun appeared to be absent earlier. Although I think everyone will be at this bash tonight.'

'You left out Leo Cavendish,' Arthur reminded her. 'Will all of them be there this evening?'

'So far as I'm aware. It's being held at The Ritz hotel. It's an informal canapés and drinks with the begging bowl being held out for the Red Cross, I think. Reggie seems to fancy himself as being in line for some kind of recognition from the king when all of this is over. Mother says he is one of the prime movers. He will be conducting the band.' Jane finished her meal and set down her cutlery. 'Will you come?'

'I suspect the brigadier would wish me to attend. I do think it might be wise.' Arthur held her gaze.

'It would help if you knew more about the people involved. You could get to know them a little better. I saw you standing near Frances and Ernie while I was playing earlier.' Jane picked up her coffee.

Arthur shifted slightly in his seat as he cut up the last of his spam. 'Yes, I recognised them from their pictures in the newspapers. At least, I recognised Mr Simons. I saw Frances on stage obviously as she took her applause before you went up.'

'Did you discover anything useful?' Jane asked.

'If you mean was I eavesdropping then yes, I did try to listen in case there was anything helpful. They were discussing Jenny Jackson's murder yesterday.' Arthur nibbled on the last of his lunch.

'Well?' Jane was tempted to hit Arthur over the head with the ketchup bottle in an attempt to extract the information from him more swiftly.

Arthur swallowed the last bite of his spam and set his knife and fork down neatly on his plate. 'Ernie seemed to be trying to get information from Frances. He was asking lots of questions. Frances seemed to have a lot of information.'

From what Jane knew of Frances's personality she wouldn't have thought he would have had to have tried very hard.

Frances seemed eager to impart information everywhere she went from what Jane had seen so far.

'Did she have anything much to tell him then? Anything we don't already know? She seems to be a frightful gossip,' Jane asked. 'We know from Benson that Frances seemed to be having words with Jenny just after the fires and that she seemed to be quarrelling with Vincent when I saw them together at lunch. Did she seek out Ernie? Or did he approach her?'

Arthur's brow furrowed in thought. 'I rather got the impression she had sought him out but then he had somehow turned the tables on her.'

'Oh, in what way?' Jane was intrigued by this interpretation of events.

'Frances came off the stage and more or less seemed to loiter and wait around. Once she'd signed a few autographs she kept looking at Ernie. You and Elsa were getting ready then.' The creases on Arthur's brow deepened as he thought. 'Ernie finished his skits and came off. He signed a few autographs and talked to a couple of people who were obviously keen to see him. He seemed to notice Frances hanging around but was edging away from her when she sort of pounced before he could escape.'

Jane nodded slowly. She could envisage the scene.

'I heard her tell him that they needed to talk, and he asked if it was about Jenny's murder.' Arthur started to fiddle with the metal cruets on the table. He lined them up neatly, crushing grains of salt into the tabletop.

'What did Frances say?' Jane resisted the urge to smack his fingers to make him stop.

'She said she was frightened. Ernie gave her an odd look and asked why she would be scared.' Arthur's fingers stilled.

'What kind of look?' Jane was puzzled and she knew Arthur was not always adept at picking up nuances.

Arthur looked at her. 'I don't know. It was just a queer sort of look. Like as if he thought she was making an odd joke.'

'Did you hear them say anything else?' Jane wished she could have overheard the conversation instead of being on stage. This look that Arthur had described struck her as being very interesting.

Arthur leaned back in his chair. 'It was jolly difficult with the music and everyone around me,' he said. 'I thought I heard Frances ask Ernie what he meant, and he said something like, you always seem to know everyone's business. Why wouldn't you know about Jenny's murder. After all, you were there.'

'Hmm, well we know that they were both in the building when Jenny was killed,' Jane said. 'Do you think he was hinting she knew far more about Jenny's death than perhaps she should have?'

'I don't know. He could have meant it that way or he could simply have been telling her off for being so nosy,' Arthur suggested.

'It sounds as if we should try and talk to both of them.' Jane drummed her own fingers thoughtfully on the tabletop. 'We'll try and get talking to them all tonight. It's time we rattled a few cages.'

Arthur looked perturbed. 'That could be dangerous.'

'I know, but we need to start to try and get some answers. If we work together there should be safety in numbers.' Jane looked at her colleague.

Arthur still looked unhappy. She wasn't sure what was concerning him most. The idea of having to attend a party and socialise, or trying to track down a murderous traitor.

'I suppose so. We should go back, Benson will be home shortly, and we may learn more about the typewriter.' Arthur prepared to fasten up his coat.

'Yes, that would be helpful if we knew which machine was

being used.' Jane collected her own things together and handed Arthur his gas mask box.

Arthur wrapped his scarf around his neck and placed the strap of the box over his shoulder. 'I did wonder if we ought to set a trap, once we know which machine is being used.' He collected up the flowers to carry them out.

Jane paused in the act of pushing her chair back under the table. 'I suppose we could. We really could do with finding out who the person is and where they are getting their information from,' she said thoughtfully.

Arthur stood aside and waited for her to walk out of the café ahead of him. 'It would be ideal but at the end of the day we need to catch a murderer as well as stopping any more potential harm coming to our troops.'

Jane led the way out of the café and waited on the pavement for Arthur to close the café door. He joined her and offered her his arm.

'Shall we try for a taxi?' he asked as they walked back towards the station concourse.

'We could take the underground and the bus,' Jane suggested.

From his expression Jane took that as a firm rejection of her idea. 'We do have all these flowers.'

'Very well, we may be lucky,' she agreed.

As they approached the rank it seemed that their luck was in and before long they were speeding through the busy streets on their way back to the apartment block.

CHAPTER SIXTEEN

Jane was silent on the journey across London and Arthur would have liked to have known what she was thinking. There was no sign of any watchers outside the block as the taxi pulled to a halt. He wondered if their observers had been satisfied with the briefcase switch.

He paid the cabbie as they climbed out of the car while Jane carried her mother's flowers. The air was considerably colder now than it had been when they had set off and he thought they might well have a touch of frost later. He wasn't looking forward to the evening ahead.

Jane arranged to meet him later so they could travel to Reggie's party at The Ritz together. He agreed to telephone her when Benson arrived back if he had any news. He let himself into the flat and immediately went to turn on the electric fire. The sitting room had grown cold while he had been gone.

Arthur switched on the table lamp to dispel the gloom and decided to draw the heavy curtains early. It was already growing dark outside, and it wouldn't be long until the blackout anyway. He had collected a newspaper whilst at the station and settled himself down to read whilst waiting for Benson to arrive.

He had just opened the newspaper when he heard the familiar sound of a key in the lock. He set his paper aside and went to greet his manservant.

'Benson, how was your day?' he asked as Benson removed his overcoat and cap, hanging them neatly on the hooks in the hallway.

'Very strange, sir. Most of the programmes being transmitted were pre-recordings with just Mr Vaughn making the linking announcements. The young lady on the reception desk was very jumpy. I think she was relieved when Mr Cavendish supplied another guard from the agency to patrol the lobby,' Benson explained as he changed his shoes.

'Did you get the chance to try out the typewriters?' Arthur asked as Benson moved into the kitchen to fill the kettle ready to place it on the ring.

'Indeed, sir. It took a little subterfuge, especially to try out the one in Mr Cavendish's office. However, I managed to take samples from each machine, and I have labelled them all for your perusal.' Benson produced several thin slips of paper from the bib pocket on his brown janitorial coveralls. 'I believe the machine in the office on the upper floor is the one with the match.' He focused his attention on setting up the tea tray and warming the pot.

Arthur carried the papers back into the sitting room so he could study them more closely under the lamp. He saw that Benson had labelled each sample with the machine's location and had typed out a strip of the offending letter so they could look for the break.

'You're right, Benson. It is the typewriter in the top office. Do you know who usually has access to that room?'

The manservant entered the room carrying the tea tray, which he set down on the low table in front of the sofa. 'The door is usually unlocked, and I understand it is for use by the news team and the scriptwriters for last-minute changes.'

'That doesn't whittle things down much.' Arthur frowned as he set the papers to one side.

'That particular room is not used as often as the machines on the other floor. It is rather cold in there and according to Mrs Harrington, the lady who does the tea trolley, it's haunted.' Benson took a seat on the sofa and placed the metal tea strainer over the top of one of the cups.

'Haunted?' Arthur blinked.

'I assume it is because the room is always cold and there have been reports of strange sounds. None of the staff like to go there, especially when it is getting dark.' Benson placidly lifted the lid of the teapot and stirred the contents.

'That was near where the guard was found. No doubt that particular rumour would be of use to whoever is making up these coded messages,' Arthur said.

'Undoubtedly, sir.' Benson poured them both a cup of tea and added milk.

'I went to see the brigadier this morning.' Arthur told him about the briefcase, explained what had been said in his meeting and what he had done afterwards.

'I agree with the assumption that Miss Jane could be placing herself at some risk by continuing the investigation.' Benson stirred his tea.

'I seem to have been seconded to accompany her for safety's sake. This includes attending a fundraising gala at The Ritz hotel this evening,' Arthur explained.

'Very good, sir. Will you wish to dine before leaving?' Benson asked.

Arthur shook his head. 'Jane and I enjoyed the delights of spam fritters at a late lunch. She assures me there will be canapés this evening.'

'Then perhaps a sandwich at suppertime on your return,' Benson suggested.

'Thank you, I hope you will take the evening off?' Arthur

suggested. It was always difficult to persuade Benson to take time for himself. He knew though that the janitorial duties he had been undertaking at Bush House must be tiring.

'Thank you, sir. I do have a new gardening journal which I would like to peruse,' Benson agreed, sipping his tea and looking quite chipper at the idea of an evening of leisure.

* * *

Jane plodded up the stairs to her flat carrying the flowers from earlier. Her usual brisk pace slowed by the weariness she could feel stealing into all of her limbs. Still, a nice strong coffee, a sit down and time spent with Marmaduke would soon revive her.

She stopped at her front door. She switched the flowers to her other arm and opened her handbag to retrieve her keys. As she did so she thought she heard a faint sound from inside her flat. She paused to listen more closely. Surely, it couldn't be Marmaduke. He was normally out at this time of day, timing his return with her usual time home from the office.

The sounds were unclear at first. She pressed her ear to the door wondering if she had been mistaken. Then she heard a distinctive creak which she knew was the door of her wardrobe. She had intended oiling the hinges since they had dried out over the winter and the squeak annoyed her. Someone was inside her flat.

There was no real time to think. Arthur would be of little use and by the time she had fetched him the burglar might be gone. She knew no one was likely to be home in the neighbouring flats. They all worked long hours in the city or had moved when the blitz had been at its height.

She placed the flowers down. Her hands now free and her mind made up she inserted the key in the lock and quietly unlocked the door. She knew that she had a large sturdy black umbrella in the stand just inside the hall. Jane pushed the door open and reached in to grab the umbrella. At least now she had a weapon.

She entered the hall and crept along the short distance to her bedroom door which was standing slightly ajar. The interior of the room was gloomy as the light outside was fading fast and her room rarely got any afternoon sunlight anyway. She watched as the shadowy figure of a man clad in black moved around her room.

The intruder opened the drawer of her bedside cabinet, and she tightened her grasp around the heavy wooden handle of the brolly. The man sifted rapidly through her drawer and closed it. It seemed he was uninterested in her Bible, or the cough sweets she kept in a small metal tin. He also ignored the small black square velvet jewellery box she had stowed in there.

She flattened herself back against the wall to remain out of sight as he turned to start searching the drawers of her dressing table. Her heart thumped in her chest and her palms were sweating. She was curious about what the man might be looking for. Was he just a run-of-the-mill burglar? It didn't seem that way. Or was he looking for something in connection with their case?

Before Jane could decide what to do Marmaduke came sauntering along the hall from the direction of the kitchen. He rubbed himself lovingly against her legs leaving his usual trail of orange hairs adhering to her stockings. There was a sound from inside the bedroom as the burglar slid open another drawer.

Marmaduke's back arched as he looked through the open door. His fur stood on end, and he hissed loudly at the intruder. Jane froze in horror as the intruder whirled around. Marmaduke sprang up at the man, claws first, still hissing.

'Argh, get it off me!' The man flailed about trying to extract the angry orange ball of fur from his face.

Jane had no intention of getting between Marmaduke's claws and the intruder. So long as the man didn't harm her beloved pet she felt the burglar was getting his just deserts. The burglar flailed about while Jane looked for an opportunity to whack him with her umbrella.

The man staggered past her out into the tiny hall, making for the front door. Marmaduke leapt clear just as the man managed to open the door. Jane seized her moment and hit the fleeing burglar hard over the top of his head with the wood and steel brolly.

The man half turned before dropping like a sack of potatoes at her feet. He landed among the flowers, scattering petals everywhere. Jane bent and checked the man's pulse to ensure she hadn't killed him. Her own pulse was racing. She then picked up the telephone receiver from the hall table and dialled Arthur's number.

'Benson, please could you and Arthur come up straight away. I have an urgent problem.' She replaced the receiver without giving the manservant the opportunity to respond.

Marmaduke purred throatily about her legs looking very pleased with himself, while Jane kept an eye on the unconscious man.

'Good heavens, Miss Jane.' Benson arrived on the landing first, his face paling at the sight of the man sprawled on the floor half in and half out of her flat.

'What on earth?' Arthur appeared behind his manservant, breathing noisily from his rush up the stairs to her landing.

The burglar groaned and stirred so Jane gave him a small kick in his shoulders with the toe of her shoe. 'Give me a hand to get him inside. We'd better find out who he is before we call the police.'

Arthur and Benson half dragged and half carried the now semiconscious would-be burglar into the sitting room of Jane's flat and deposited him on her sofa.

'What happened?' Arthur panted, sitting down heavily on

one of the armchairs. She could hear the telltale squeak of a wheeze coming from his chest as he did so.

'I caught him trying to rob my flat.' Jane scowled at the man who lay groaning with his head against one of her silk-covered cushions. Stray pink and purple flower petals clung to the stranger's dark coat.

'What happened to his face?' Benson asked, looking at the plethora of bloody scratches covering the man's head, hands and neck. He quickly frisked the man's pockets to see if he had stolen anything. Nothing was discovered.

'Marmaduke didn't like the look of him.' Jane bent to caress her cat who was now sat calmly washing his paws at her feet.

The burglar groaned loudly, and his eyelids fluttered open. He was a middle-aged man of nondescript appearance and a slightly receding hairline. The kind of man one would pass by in the street without even noticing, Jane thought. No doubt something which was useful in his line of employment.

Benson had gone to check in Jane's bedroom to see if anything had been disarranged or placed ready to steal.

'He appears not to have disturbed anything, Miss Jane, that I can see. A very considerate housebreaker,' Benson reported before heading to the kitchen.

He returned bearing a glass of water. 'I have closed your kitchen window. It was wide open, the lock you had appears to have been forced.'

Arthur shivered. 'I thought it was chilly in here.'

Jane turned on her electric fire. She was relieved that his breathing seemed to be settling down once more.

The erstwhile burglar stirred on the sofa and attempted to sit up. Benson thrust the glass of water in his direction.

'My head is splitting. What happened? Where is that infernal cat?' The man took the glass with a shaking hand as he blinked and looked around as if trying to clear his head.

'I rather think we are the ones who should be asking you the questions. Like what were you doing in my flat?' Jane asked.

The adrenaline from earlier was rapidly leaving her system now the immediate fright was over. Her knees were shaking, and she longed to sit down and have a cigarette. She knew though, that she needed to appear cool and unruffled.

'I weren't doing anything.' The man's expression became shifty, and his eyes darted nervously from side to side as if searching for an escape.

Benson, however, had stationed himself firmly in front of the closed door of the sitting room. 'I think you should answer Miss Jane's question.'

The man took a sip of water and wiped the back of his hand across his mouth. He winced as he caught one of the scratches Marmaduke had inflicted on him. 'I'm saying nothing. You can't keep me here.' His gaze glanced across Arthur and settled on Jane. 'No harm done. I didn't take nothing.'

'Who sent you? What were you searching for?' Jane asked.

'I don't know what you're on about, lady. I happened across a wide-open window on the fire escape. Ain't nobody sent me for nothing.' The man took another gulp of water as he spoke.

'Really?' Jane asked. 'How very peculiar considering my flat has been under surveillance for the last few days. A coincidence?' She glared at the intruder. 'What's your name?'

The man gave a nervous laugh. 'Name, rank and serial number, is that what you want?'

'So, you admit you are in the employ of a service. Which one?' Jane's tone was now icy.

'Albert Finch, and I ain't in no service. I'm more what you might call freelance.'

Jane thought she detected a slight note of pride in the man's reply. 'Then who is employing you, Mr Finch? I strongly suggest you tell me the truth before I pick up that telephone and you end up in a whole world of trouble.'

'I don't know what you're talking about, lady.' Mr Finch placed his glass down on the table as if he was about to get up from his seat.

Benson's hand, firmly on his shoulder kept him in his place. 'I strongly suggest you answer Miss Jane's questions.'

The man began to look acutely uncomfortable as he glanced first up at Benson, then across to Jane, before settling on Arthur. 'Look, it's like I said. Times is hard and I got a family. I spotted an opportunity and took a chance.' He spotted Marmaduke sitting beside Jane and scowled. 'I weren't counting on no devil cat and whatever hit me on me head.' He raised his hand to tenderly touch a spot on the back of his skull, wincing as he did so.

'Rubbish. You were here looking for something in particular. You ignored my pearls and the antique gold chain and locket my father gave me. I watched you. Now, who sent you here and what were you looking for? This is your last chance to come clean.' Jane narrowed her eyes.

'You're out of your tree, lady. I ain't saying nothing.' Albert pressed his lips firmly together.

'Very well. I think I had better call the brigadier before I telephone Inspector Winters at Scotland Yard.' Jane went to walk towards the door and Benson moved slightly aside to allow her through.

'Here, now don't be hasty. No need for the police.' Albert Finch shifted in his seat.

'Well?' Jane rested her hand on the door handle.

'I might have been asked to look for any papers like,' Albert said.

'Papers?' Arthur asked.

'Yeah, by this bloke down the pub. He said somefink about scripts from shows. He give me this address and told me to bring anything I found to him at the Dog and Duck tonight.' Albert looked at Arthur.

'And you must think we fell out of last year's Christmas tree,' Jane scoffed. 'I'll go and make those calls.'

'No, all right.' Albert seemed to be working himself into a sweat. Small beads of perspiration were on his temples. 'Look, lady. There's no harm been done. Just let me go and I'll forget all about you and that cat assaulting me.'

'I don't think that you are in any position to bargain, Mr Finch,' Jane said and went out into the hall.

CHAPTER SEVENTEEN

Once Jane had gone from the room, Albert Finch appeared to deflate. He eyed Marmaduke warily. Not that Arthur blamed him looking at the damage inflicted on Albert's face by Jane's cat. Marmaduke lazily stretched himself out in front of the fire. The silence in the room was broken only by the pop of the metal bars expanding in the heat of the fire.

Arthur rose and closed the blackout. He switched on the silk-shaded table lamp while they waited for Jane to return. She was back in the room in a matter of minutes.

'I have notified the department and Inspector Winters is on his way over here. Apparently, Mr Finch, it seems that you and he are old acquaintances,' Jane said, looking at the erstwhile burglar.

'Well, I hope as he brings some aspirin with him. My head is killing me. I could sue, you know, for assault,' he muttered as he gingerly touched the swelling on his scalp.

'I should like to hear you in court explaining how you came to be in my home to be assaulted,' Jane remarked.

It didn't take long for the inspector to arrive. 'Finch, up to your old tricks again, I see,' the inspector greeted the burglar, eyeing him grimly as the constable who had accompanied him got the man to his feet. 'What happened to you?' He looked at the wounds now dried and scabbing covering Finch's hands and face.

'That dratted cat. Demonic it is, went for me like something possessed.' Albert Finch glared at Marmaduke and then at Jane.

Inspector Winters raised one eyebrow. 'Sounds fair. Now, let's get you to the Yard and you can explain what you were really doing here.'

The constable led the handcuffed man from the room.

'I take it you know Mr Finch well?' Arthur said.

'Indeed. He's a professional burglar. You said he gave you some cockamamie story about someone paying him to look for documents in your flat?' The inspector looked at Jane.

'That's correct. I don't know if there is any truth in it or if his presence here may be loosely connected to the murders at Bush House,' Jane said.

'We'll see what we can shake loose from him back at the Yard,' the inspector said. He raised his hat and wished them all a good evening before heading out after the constable.

'Are you all right, Jane?' Arthur asked.

He saw her hand was shaking slightly as she attempted to light her cigarette.

'I am a little shaken up,' she confessed with a small smile. 'At the time I was more worried about poor Marmaduke. If he had hurt him, I don't know what I would have done.'

'In that case it's a good thing that there was only an umbrella to hand, Miss Jane,' Benson remarked with a wry smile.

'Yes, thank you both for coming so quickly.' Jane's gaze fell on her beloved pet who was now busily engaged in cleaning his front paws once more.

'If you don't feel up to going to this fundraising thing at The Ritz tonight...' Arthur started to suggest.

'Oh no, we must go. It's the perfect opportunity to try and work out who could have wanted both Tabitha and Jenny dead and why.' Jane looked appalled at his suggestion that they not attend the party. 'Besides which my mother will be expecting me. She sent Stephen here last night because I didn't answer the telephone. Can you imagine the fuss if I don't turn up at The Ritz.'

'Stephen did mention your mother was concerned for your safety,' Arthur agreed. He would have greatly preferred a night at home. Socialising, having to make small talk in a great smoke-filled saloon, was his idea of hell. The only thing that could possibly make it worse would be if he was expected to dance.

Jane rolled her eyes at this statement. 'Right, I suppose we had better get ready. Time is getting on and I don't suppose getting there this evening will be easy.'

'I can try to organise a taxi, Miss Jane,' Benson offered.

'That would be excellent, thank you,' Arthur hastily agreed. He knew that otherwise Jane was likely to suggest they took public transport.

The only thing worse than being compelled to attend this blasted gala would be having to travel in the blackout at this time of year in full evening wear on a bus.

* * *

Once Arthur and Benson had returned to their flat, Jane spent a little time with her cat. She treated Marmaduke to a small tin of salmon she had put by for a special occasion.

'You were so brave,' she cooed as she placed the dish on the kitchen floor.

She had only rarely seen her pet behave the way he had done today a couple of times before. Both times it had been men that he had attacked and on each occasion it had been when he had perceived a threat.

Jane often wondered if, when she had found him alone and injured as a kitten on the bomb site, he had been maltreated. Although who could not love a cat as wonderful as Marmaduke she had no idea. Even Arthur appeared to be warming to him.

She retrieved the battered remains of her mother's flowers and stuffed them in a large glass vase. It seemed a shame to just throw them away even if they were now worse for wear. After checking that all her belongings were intact and secure she ran herself a bath, adding some of her favourite and precious rose-scented bath salts to the water. She had just stepped in and started to relax when the telephone rang in the hall.

Muttering under her breath she hauled herself out of the water and hastily wrapped herself in a towel to go and answer the call. If it had not been for the earlier incident with Albert Finch she would have ignored it, reasoning that if it were important the caller would have telephoned again.

'Jane, not disturbing you, I hope?' The brigadier's voice bellowed in her ear, and she held the receiver a little further away.

'No, sir, just getting ready for this fundraising gala at The Ritz tonight,' she lied as she looked at the small puddle of water forming around her feet on the cold tiled floor of her hallway.

'Splendid, yes. Arthur is going with you I hope?' the brigadier asked.

'Yes, sir.' Jane wished he would hurry up and get to the point of the call. Her carefully measured bathwater was growing cold, and her toes were frozen.

'I just heard from Winters at Scotland Yard. He has your burglar chappie. It seems this Finch was employed by one of our departments. The Admiralty, unbeknown to us, had some concerns and made their own arrangements. They were onto the code business. It seems you and Arthur were suspicious.' The brigadier was clearly attempting to be circumspect with the information he was giving her.

'Are they responsible too for the briefcase?' Jane asked.

The brigadier chortled. 'So it would seem. Arthur certainly foxed them there. Anyway, my dear, take care and let me know if you discover anything else interesting this evening. Toodle-pip.' He rang off still clearly amused at having pulled the wool over the Admiralty's eyes.

Jane plodded back to the bathroom and released her bath-water. There seemed little point in getting back in now. She towelled herself dry unsure if she should be amused or cross that the Admiralty had clearly considered her and Arthur a risk to national security.

It was hard enough battling the enemy without having to tackle one's own side. Since she had grown cold while taking the brigadier's call, she slipped on her dressing gown and went back into the sitting room for a few minutes to warm up in front of the electric fire.

She stared into the glowing orange bars of the fire for a few minutes until she started to feel better. She had never been the kind of person to feel sorry for herself. Now though, after the last few days and facing an evening with her mother and a reluctant Arthur, she couldn't help but feel just a twinge of self-pity.

Arthur was ready and waiting for her at his flat when she went downstairs. He scrubbed up quite nicely in evening attire. His usual rumpled clothing for once not in evidence and his hair tamed into some sort of order. Jane wished she had a nicer frock to wear. All her dresses were starting to show their age now and she lacked the skill with a needle to be able to perk them up.

'The car should be here for us in a moment. We had better go downstairs and wait in the lobby. Benson had the devil of a game to arrange a lift for us.' Arthur wrapped himself up in his dark woollen overcoat and his usual layers of scarves before escorting her downstairs.

'He has also arranged for this car to collect us from the hotel just before midnight. He thought it best to secure him for the return,' Arthur said as he opened the rear door of the taxi to allow her to climb inside.

'That was very thoughtful of him. It's a good thing we can claim it back on expenses. It will cost a fortune, most of the cabs are in service as extra fire tenders at night. Let's hope that we don't have any raids tonight,' Jane said as Arthur went around the car and joined her on the back seat. The fog had closed in from the river again and she could see the tiny shards of ice already forming on the bottom of the car windows.

Fortunately, The Ritz hotel was not too far away although it was situated in a much more expensive part of London than Jane's flat. The taxi pulled up outside. Arthur came around to assist Jane from the taxi.

'This place always looks so smart in peacetime.' Jane looked up at the creamy stone walls of the hotel frontage. The sash windows all now dark and blank while the faint sounds of music drifted out to them on the pavement. A uniformed doorman stood at the entrance waiting to greet them.

'Let's get inside, it's freezing out here,' Arthur suggested, and they walked in under the canopy.

The elderly doorman took them through into the foyer. Once the outer door was safely closed, they passed through a second door into a well-lit foyer. He directed them down the hall to the rear of the hotel where they left their coats in the cloakroom.

The music was louder now they were inside, and Jane could hear a saxophone. The hall was very grand with marble floor tiles and antique busts in the alcoves. They walked down and were almost at the door to the rooms where the party was being held. It suddenly burst open and a pretty young woman in a gold evening gown stumbled giggling into the corridor.

'Oopsy.' She laughed apologetically as she passed them,

clearly on her way to the cloakroom. The music had grown louder with the opening of the door and Jane could smell the faint scent of tobacco.

The scene inside reminded Jane of happier days before the war. Reggie was engaged in conducting a small group of musicians near the floor-length dark-green velvet curtains which she guessed must cover the windows. A female singer in a glittering, gold gown was singing.

Overhead, crystal chandeliers sparkled, couples were dancing, and the room rang with music, chatter and laughter. People were drinking, smoking and mingling. It was hard to believe that across the Channel a hard and desperate war was being waged.

'I can see your mother.' Arthur inclined his head in the direction of the band. Jane suppressed a groan. As usual Elsa, glamorously dressed in a chartreuse gown, was surrounded by a coterie of admirers as she held court near the dance floor.

'Ha, Miss Treen, I see you made it here safely.' Ernie Simons appeared at her elbow. He looked slightly glassily at Arthur.

'My, um, friend, Arthur Cilento. Arthur, this is Ernie Simons.' She was a little foxed at how to introduce Arthur. She could hardly say he was her colleague when she was pretending to be her mother's accompanist. The idea of pretending he was her boyfriend didn't appeal either. It might raise more questions than it answered since she didn't think acting was one of Arthur's skills.

'Delighted.' Ernie shook Arthur's hand vigorously. 'Are you a musician like Jane?' he asked.

'No, I'm an electrical technician,' Arthur said.

Ernie didn't appear impressed by Arthur's reply. Jane was pleased that he had remembered the brigadier and Colonel Hardacre's other suggestion. At least should Arthur need to enter Bush House he had a pretext for doing so.

Ernie turned back to Jane. 'Elsa is over there by the band. You should get a drink and join her. There is a rumour that Princess Elizabeth may drop in this evening.' He tapped his forefinger against the side of his nose in a knowing gesture.

'Really, how terribly exciting,' Jane said.

Ernie leaned his head closer to hers in a conspiratorial fashion. 'Elsa told me that you were the one who found poor Jenny. That put Frances's nose out of joint by the way. You know she loves to be first with the gossip. By crikey though, that must have been pretty ghastly for you.'

Jane could smell the sour scent of alcohol on his breath. 'Yes, it was rather. Such a dreadful thing to happen. I don't suppose anyone feels safe right now.'

'Frances has been telling just about anyone who'll listen that she thinks Leo Cavendish is behind it all,' Ernie said. 'She has this theory, and you know she was creepily obsessed with Leo.'

'Leo? Why Leo?' Jane asked.

'Well, Tabitha died first, didn't she? And now Jenny. He is the one person closest to both of them. Jenny could have discovered he murdered Tabitha and, well, then she had to go too.' Ernie looked surprised that Jane hadn't worked this out herself. 'Then again it might be that he gave Frances the brush off and she's trying to stir things up.'

'Surely Leo wouldn't have murdered Jenny at Bush House if he were guilty of harming Tabitha? That would be rather foolish,' Jane pointed out.

Ernie scratched his chin and looked thoughtful. 'No, you have a point there. Unless, of course, he had no choice. She could have been about to blow the whistle on him and there was no time to be lost.'

Jane looked at Ernie who now had a pleased expression on his round amiable face. 'I should have thought there might be other people who could have killed both Tabitha and Jenny,' she said.

'Really?' Ernie's eyes widened. 'Who?'

'Well, Frances for one. There wasn't much love lost between her and either Tabitha or Jenny from what I've heard,' Jane said.

Arthur was busy pretending he wasn't paying any attention to their muttered conversation, but she knew he was in fact listening intently.

'Frances?' Ernie looked surprised. 'It's true she does have a tendency to rile people up the wrong way and she did argue with Tabitha a lot over the schedules. Frances is always after more work. The same as poor Jenny. I think Jenny thought it was Frances who had bad-mouthed her to Tabitha. You know about the...' Ernie mimed putting a bottle to his lips.

'Then I suppose some people might think you could have killed them.' Jane opened her eyes wide.

Ernie drew back, looking mortified at the suggestion. 'Me? Why would I have killed them? Who is spreading such vile lies?' he demanded.

'I don't know who started the rumour,' Jane said. 'I suppose it's easy to disprove if you have an alibi for when they were both killed.'

She watched the colour come and go on Ernie's face. 'Well, no, I don't suppose I do. I mean we don't know exactly when Tabitha died and as for Jenny, I was in the building, yes, but so were lots of other people. Reggie and Vincent, they were both there too.'

Jane gave a slight shrug of her shoulders. 'People are saying you argued with Jenny just before she died.'

'No, that's nonsense, well I mean, Jenny and I often had little spats. She argued with almost everyone. She was rather unprofessional, you know, and she could be very cutting. That's hardly a motive to kill someone,' Ernie said.

'That's very true,' Jane agreed.

'Dear me, I had no idea people were talking and saying such dreadful things.' Ernie looked quite distressed.

'I wouldn't worry about it if I were you. The police are sure to get to the bottom of it all soon,' Jane reassured him.

'I hope you're right,' Ernie said. 'If you'll just excuse me, I rather think I need a drink.'

CHAPTER EIGHTEEN

'You are quite merciless when you get going,' Arthur remarked, looking at her with a mix of wonderment and fear.

Jane shrugged. 'We need to stir things up a little if we are to get some answers.'

Arthur considered that there was a difference between stirring things up and applying gunpowder to a hornet's nest.

'Oh lord, Mother has seen us,' Jane said, fixing a smile to her face. Elsa was gesturing to them.

'We had better go over,' Jane said, dragging Arthur with her as she made her way across the crowded dance floor to where her mother was standing.

'Janey, honey, I know it's fashionable to be late but really.' Her mother gave a tinkling laugh as she reproved her, but Arthur noticed Elsa had an icy glint in her eyes.

'Well, travelling in the blackout is not very easy,' Jane said. 'We were lucky to be able to get a car.'

'Oh, and, erm, Arthur is with you, how lovely.' Elsa gave him an insincere smile. 'Dear Mr Benson is not attending?' She glanced around as if expecting the manservant to appear bearing a cocktail for her.

'No, Mother,' Jane said firmly.

In the distance on the far side of the room Arthur noticed Leo Cavendish sitting alone near the bar nursing a whisky glass.

'Jane, shall I get you a drink?' Arthur asked, giving the tiniest of nods towards where Leo was seated. Jane, as he had expected, quickly picked up on his hint. 'Yes please, a cocktail would be wonderful if there is one.'

Arthur made good his escape before Elsa could burden him with any requests while he was at the bar. He had no doubt she would be tutting to Jane about his rudeness in not offering to get her anything. It seemed to him though that this might be the perfect time to talk to Leo Cavendish.

He ordered Jane a cocktail and got himself a whisky and soda from the bar before pretending to notice Leo.

'Mr Cavendish, I didn't expect to see you this evening,' Arthur said, slipping into the vacant seat opposite Leo's.

Leo lifted his head from where he had been studying the bottom of his cut glass whisky tumbler. 'To be honest I would rather not be here. However, I thought perhaps I might find out something about who may have killed Tabitha and Jenny. I keep thinking that it must be someone connected with Bush House, and everyone is here this evening.'

'I see. Perhaps you have a point.' Arthur looked around the room. 'It's very busy tonight. You wouldn't know there was a war on. Did you and Tabitha used to come here often?'

He could see there were several men in uniform on the dance floor as well as civilians. It struck him that it was a good spot to obtain and exchange information.

Leo nodded. 'Once or twice. We would come to dance. It takes your mind off things. In here, like you say, you can pretend there is nothing bad happening elsewhere. It makes everything feel normal again for a while.'

'Have you had any more ideas about anyone in particular who may have been responsible for the murders?' Arthur asked.

Leo sighed. 'I keep thinking all the time. It haunts me. Especially now with Jenny being strangled in Bush House. What is going on there? And why am I not seeing it?' He raked his hand despairingly through his hair.

'I don't know.' Arthur took a sip from his drink.

Leo gazed at him. 'You and Jane, I know you are on some kind of assignment. Have you found anything out? I mean Jane found Jenny's body. She must have missed her murderer by minutes.'

Arthur shrugged. 'She didn't see or hear anyone as far as I know. Who do you think may have killed Jenny?'

Leo blinked. 'I wish I knew. Jenny would annoy people. She drank, that's why Tabitha wasn't keen on offering her more contracts. She'd become unreliable and belligerent. When she was drunk she would be late or slurring her words so then we wouldn't be able to risk her in a live broadcast. It annoyed Reggie, Vince and Ernie no end. She was very bitter about it. I don't know if she accused anyone of, well, telling Tabitha what a problem she had become,' Leo said.

'And had anyone been telling tales to you?' Arthur asked curiously.

Leo sighed once more. 'All of them grumbled to me at some point. Vince because he hates unprofessionalism. Ernie because Jenny was nasty to him over something or other. Frances because Frances just loves to tittle-tattle and she was always trying to take work from the others. Elsa because Jenny annoyed her. Even Reggie because he would end up having to reorder things to accommodate Jenny.'

Arthur picked up the drinks once more. 'I had better go and get this to Jane.' He glanced towards the band. Elsa was busy talking while Jane stood a little apart from her, looking uncomfortable.

'It's hard to believe Elsa is Jane's mother,' Leo said following Arthur's gaze.

'I know. Jane struggles with that idea too.' Arthur smiled and left Leo to finish his whisky.

Jane pounced eagerly on her glass when he reached her and quickly swallowed half of it in a few gulps.

'Steady on, those are quite strong and there's a terrible queue at the bar,' Arthur remarked mildly.

Jane merely frowned at him and edged further away from her mother's circle. 'Trust me, this drink might be all that stops me from making my mother the next victim. What took you so long to get back here?'

'I was talking to Leo Cavendish,' Arthur said.

'And?' Jane looked at him. 'What did he say?'

'Not much. He couldn't really add a specific person or motive to our list. It sounded as if he, like us, thought all of them were a possibility.' Arthur took a sip of his drink and glanced around hoping to spy an open table where he and Jane could sit.

'What about Leo himself as a suspect?' Jane demanded.

'He said he was here hoping to find a lead into who may have murdered Tabitha. I think he thought that might then tell him who had killed Jenny. Unless he was trying to throw me off the scent, he seems pretty genuine.'

'Except we think we know why Tabitha was killed and Leo doesn't know that. That gives us an insight into possibly why Jenny was then murdered. He could still be our killer since he's not going to let on about the transcripts.' Jane glanced round to make sure no one was in earshot even though she and Arthur were speaking in such low voices she had to keep her head close to hear him.

Arthur nodded. Jane was right. They couldn't discount Leo Cavendish.

* * *

Jane took another, slightly smaller sip from her drink. A wave of applause went up from the audience and she realised that Reggie was coming off stage and the hotel's resident bandleader was taking his place.

Her mother swiftly claimed Reggie, linking her arm through his and bringing him into her circle of admirers. He was soon swamped by people asking for autographs and offering him drinks. Arthur nudged her arm, and she looked across to see Vince Vaughn walking towards the group.

'Mr Vaughn, I didn't expect to see you here tonight.' Jane smoothly stepped out and intercepted him.

'They do occasionally let me out of my commentary box,' Vincent said. 'Miss Treen, isn't it? You are working with Elsa?'

'Yes, for a while until her regular accompanist is well and can come back to work. I'm just helping out,' Jane said. 'May I introduce my friend, Mr Arthur Cilento. He is a great admirer of your work.'

Arthur offered his hand to shake. 'You are always so calm and reassuring in your broadcasts. In such troubled times it's a skill to be praised.'

Jane was pleased Arthur had picked up her hint. Vince looked flattered by Arthur's comment. 'That's terribly kind of you. I always think of myself as the grease between the cogs that keeps the programming running smoothly.'

'It must be very difficult especially when you get given last-minute changes or news bulletins to announce,' Arthur said.

'It can be very short notice indeed. You never know what a script might say when it arrives fresh from Whitehall or the Cabinet Office,' Vince agreed.

'It was terrible news about Jenny,' Jane said. 'Were you in the studios when it happened?' She knew full well that he had been. He was usually in his commentary box for much of his shift, but he did go out to use the lavatory and to get drinks or air.

'Yes, I was in all day that day. Horrifying. I heard you were the one who found her.' He looked at Jane.

'It was awful, so shocking. If I hadn't dropped my glove and gone back for it, she may have been there for hours before she was discovered,' Jane said with a little shiver.

'Ghastly. It was lucky for you, I suppose, that you didn't run into whoever did it.' Vincent reached inside the pocket of his dinner suit and offered them both a cigarette. Jane happily accepted, while Arthur waved his hand to decline.

'I know. I didn't think anything of it at the time but when the inspector asked me if I had seen anyone I realised then I must have had a close call.' Jane placed her cigarette between her lips and Vince gave her a light before lighting his own cigarette. Arthur promptly took a step backwards away from the smoke.

'Elsa and Reggie are by the band I see,' Vince said as he waved his cigarette vaguely in her mother's direction.

'Yes. Reggie stepped down from conducting a minute ago. Have you just arrived?' Jane asked.

'Yes, I'm later than I intended, it's so difficult to get places with this confounded blackout.' Vince's gaze seemed to linger on the bandleader.

'It is rather awful. That was how I came to drop my glove. I was rushing to catch the bus before it became too dark and busy. Did you see any of the others that day at the studio?' Jane asked.

Vince glanced over at Elsa. 'Yes, I think everyone we know at some point. Elsa, Reggie, Ernie, Frances, Leo and, of course, Jenny.'

'When did you see Jenny?' Jane asked.

Vince shrugged. 'It was after lunch. I heard her before I saw her. She was arguing with someone in the corridor. I didn't see who it was. I was glad to get back in my booth and close the door. She came in just afterwards to the gallery. She wasn't supposed to be in there so one of the technicians shooed her out. I rather think she had been drinking.'

'You didn't hear what she was arguing about?' Jane said as she sipped the remainder of her drink.

'Not really.' Vince snapped his fingers. 'Wait, yes, I heard her say, you'll regret this. Just you wait.'

Jane gave an exaggerated shudder. 'Perhaps that was why she was killed.'

Vince looked uncomfortable. 'Do you think so? I know it sounds bad, but it was the sort of thing Jenny very often said to people when she was drunk.'

'It's a pity we don't know who she was talking to,' Jane said. 'There are so many rumours flying around about who may have killed her. Some people have hinted it might be Ernie or Reggie. Even your name has come into the frame a few times.'

Vince looked horrified at this suggestion. 'Really, I had no idea. Why on earth would anyone think I might harm Jenny?'

Jane shrugged. 'I don't know. You know what it's like, people love to gossip. I suppose you have an alibi anyway if you were in your booth all afternoon. The technicians would vouch for you.'

Vince shuffled his feet and dropped his gaze momentarily. 'Well, yes, I was in the booth for most of the afternoon, but I did pop out a couple of times. Call of nature and all that.'

'Oh well, I expect the police will catch whoever did it soon. Inspector Winters seems very astute,' Jane said.

'Yes, he does. He would do better talking to Ernie and Reggie though than suspecting me. Reggie is always floating around the building poking his nose into everything. Ernie is as bad. I know they both had words with Jenny recently. I don't know what about. Frances seems to know the most about everything. That wretched woman has a finger in every pie. She's always snooping in Leo Cavendish's office. Since Tabitha was killed she's been even worse than usual. She has the most unseemly crush on him and she's old enough almost to be his mother.'

'She is very nosy,' Jane agreed as she watched Frances wheedling her way through the crowd to join Elsa and Reggie.

'Let's hope you're right about the inspector making an arrest soon. It's becoming a dangerous occupation working at Bush House at the moment,' Vincent said and excused himself to go and greet someone he knew.

'Well, that was interesting.' Jane finished her cocktail and looked at Arthur who was starting to look quite pale.

'You certainly seem to be doing a good job sowing the seeds of discord. Just be careful, Jane, one or more of these people is a murderer and a traitor,' Arthur warned.

Jane knew she was treading a dangerous path, but they had to try and work out who was behind those hidden coded messages betraying military secrets to the enemy. She wasn't sure if that was exactly why Jenny had been killed but she couldn't see how it wasn't connected. It would be too coincidental for both Tabitha and Jenny to be murdered just days apart from one another.

'We need to talk to Frances next.' Jane nudged Arthur with her elbow.

'She's with Reggie and your mother.' Arthur glanced across to where the group were busy chatting together.

Frances, dressed in a rather drab purple dress that drew out the sallow tones of her skin, was right next to the bandleader.

'Well, we do need to tackle Reggie as well,' Jane pointed out.

Arthur looked unhappy as Jane began to weave her way back closer to the group.

'Janey pie, did you get a drink?' her mother called over the heads of her admirers.

A couple of the men turned their heads to glance at her

then turned back again, clearly enthralled by whatever tale her mother was spinning.

Jane held up her virtually empty glass so her mother could see and then edged around the group, so she was closer to Frances and Reggie. Arthur followed somewhat grumpily, she thought, in her wake.

'Miss Treen, Jane, I didn't know you were here.' Frances turned her beady-eyed gaze on her. Jane smiled politely and introduced Arthur as her friend to Frances and Reggie.

'Delighted, I'm sure.' Frances gave Arthur a quick assessing glance.

'Splendid evening, isn't it? Lots of money going into the buckets at the bar for the Red Cross.' Reggie was smoking a cigar, and he waved it expansively in the air as he spoke.

'Most admirable,' Arthur choked as he spoke and turned away to cough.

'We were just talking to Vince Vaughn,' Jane said. 'It's awful isn't it about Jenny's murder. There are so many rumours going around about who may have killed her. I hope the inspector gets to the bottom of things soon.'

'Really, what kind of rumours?' Frances asked. 'I must admit I had heard that Jenny was really a spy, a double agent no less.' She nodded her beak-like head as if to emphasise her theory.

'Oh please, Jenny was always half-cut. If she knew a secret then so would half of London if they poured a gin into her.' Reggie snorted in disbelief.

'Then who do you think could have killed her?' Jane looked at the bandleader.

'I honestly don't know. It could have been a petty thief. The crime rate is dreadful at the moment. Perhaps she disturbed someone going through her bag or something,' Reggie suggested.

'You don't think it's too much of a coincidence after poor Tabitha was killed?' Jane said.

'You think Tabitha and Jenny were killed by the same person?' Frances squeaked. 'I mean I had wondered but it doesn't seem possible.'

'It would be too coincidental if they weren't.' Jane shrugged her shoulders. 'I heard the police are looking into everyone who argued with Jenny before her death. There are several names being bandied about. Including both of you.' She opened her eyes wide and blinked innocently while she waited to see if the bait would be taken.

'Poppycock! Why would I kill Jenny? The woman was a nuisance as she was so unreliable, but murder is a bit rich,' Reggie said scornfully.

'I certainly couldn't have killed her. I know she could be annoying but us thespians need to stick together,' Frances said indignantly.

'Like I said, it was a rumour. Something about Jenny knowing various people's secrets.' Jane gave another shrug and moved away swiftly as if her mother had called her, leaving Frances and Reggie with looks of consternation on their faces.

CHAPTER NINETEEN

Arthur remained where he was when Jane moved away. Both Reggie and Frances appeared to have forgotten his presence.

'What did she mean do you think?' Frances muttered to Reggie as she stared after Jane.

'I don't know. Do you have any secrets, Frances?' Reggie looked amused.

'Certainly not! More to the point do you have any?' Frances snapped. She suddenly seemed to notice that Arthur was still within earshot, although he was busily trying to look as if his attention was focused elsewhere.

Frances frowned and moved away, walking off towards the bar. Reggie's attention was soon claimed by some attractive young ladies. Arthur sighed and hoped Jane would agree that they could return home soon. She had gravitated back towards her mother's circle. His feet were aching inside his highly polished evening shoes and the cigarette and cigar smoke was irritating his chest and throat.

He knew why Jane was going around stirring things up, but he didn't really approve of her strategy. He thought it might well be placing her in danger. It could also be alerting whoever had typed those coded messages that someone was onto them. The last thing they wanted was for that particular traitor to get away.

Elsa was holding court and appeared to have swept Jane back into the midst of things. Jane waved her empty glass at him with an air of desperation. Arthur swallowed the rest of his whisky and plodded off towards the bar to get Jane another cocktail and a refill for himself.

He noticed that Leo Cavendish was no longer at his table and wondered if he had given up and gone home.

'Lucky chap,' Arthur muttered grumpily to himself as he waited for the barman to serve him.

He had just ordered the drinks when a familiar voice sounded in his ear. 'I say, old bean, rather a surprise finding you here. I wouldn't have thought the swinging nightlife of London was at all your scene.'

Arthur turned his head to see Stephen standing beside him looking particularly suave in his evening attire.

'I'm here with Jane. She was keen to support the fundraiser.' Arthur handed over his money to pay the barman.

'Well, I hope you're feeling fit. Jane is a terrific dancer,' Stephen said with a doubtful expression on his face.

'It's very busy here, this evening.' Arthur ignored the implied slight. He hoped Stephen was wrong and that Jane would not be expecting him to ask her to dance. He had never been good at dancing. Not even after the lessons at Miss Mornington's Dance School for young ladies and gentlemen when he had been about twelve or thirteen.

He suppressed a shudder at the memory of having to learn to waltz under Miss Mornington's eagle eye. He had been partnered with a ghastly, round-faced girl called Petunia Waddington who had smelt of stale cabbage and who giggled at nothing. She was also heavy-footed and would often leave him with bruised toes.

'Yes, it's almost always like this but I think one or both of the royal princesses are expected so there are more people here than usual. Reggie Bosun has organised collections for the Red Cross.' Stephen indicated the labelled buckets behind the bar.

Arthur had begun to think the rumour about the royal princesses attending had probably been started by Reggie himself. Probably in a bid to boost attendance at his gala.

'Where is Jane by the way?' Stephen collected his own drink from the barman and turned to scan the crowded ballroom.

'With Elsa near the band. She was with Reggie a moment ago.' Arthur hoped Jane hadn't wandered off. He didn't fancy trekking around the room through the smoky crowd looking for her.

Elsa danced past on the edge of the dance floor as he spoke. She appeared to be being partnered by a handsome young serviceman who was beaming like a Cheshire cat. Arthur sighed and wondered where Jane had gone.

'Well, there's Elsa now.' Stephen smirked and waggled his fingers in greeting as she danced past them.

Arthur took a shot of his whisky.

'And here's Jane,' Stephen remarked as Jane emerged from the dance floor and made her way towards them.

'Stephen, this is a surprise.' Jane accepted the cocktail Arthur handed to her as she approached. 'I didn't know you would be here this evening.'

'Mother wanted to come so I thought I ought to come with her. I can make sure both she and Elsa get home safely.' Stephen took a sip from his drink.

'That's probably wise with the way things are with the blackout and everything,' Arthur agreed.

The crime rate had risen at an alarming rate since the start of the war. The police were stretched to breaking point and the blackout provided opportunities for all kinds of villainy. Even before Tabitha's murder there had been a sharp rise in violent crime.

'Care to come for a spin on the floor, Jane?' Stephen asked as he stepped smoothly in front of Arthur.

Jane took a drink of her cocktail and passed the glass to Arthur. 'Very well. It's been ages since I danced anywhere.'

Stephen's smirk grew wider as he placed his drink on the small table next to where they were standing. 'Mind keeping an eye on these, old bean? Catch you again in a mo.' He swept Jane up in his arms and whisked her off onto the floor.

Arthur took a seat on an empty chair and placed Jane's glass beside Stephen's. At least if Stephen was dancing with Jane he could sit and rest his feet. Although he was rather puzzled at Jane's alacrity in accepting Stephen's offer to dance. Jane disliked Stephen and normally seemed to avoid being in any kind of close proximity with him.

The dance floor was crowded and there was a buzz of excitement near the door which he assumed must mean that Stephen's prediction that one or both of the royal princesses would be present had come true. Both Princess Margaret and Elizabeth were doing their part for the war effort and if the amount of people attending tonight were an indication of success, then Reggie must be raising a fair amount of money for the Red Cross.

He sipped his whisky and wondered if Benson was having a nice peaceful evening beside the electric fire back at the flat. He savoured the taste of the Scotch and thought wistfully of his old tartan slippers warming near the grate. He had a good book he had borrowed from the library too which he was longing to read.

It seemed very unfair that he was having to sit here amidst the crowds and the smoke waiting for Jane to finish gallivanting around the room.

Arthur glanced around at his surroundings and annoyingly could see no sign of either Jane or Stephen. The previous dance must have ended because he could see Elsa now dancing with a different young man. Reggie appeared to be deep in conversation with a group of servicemen. A pretty girl was on each arm. They were laughing and Reggie appeared to be making jokes and entertaining them all.

Ernie was sitting with Vince Vaughn and they appeared to be deep in conversation. Arthur wished he was close enough to hear what was being said as they both appeared to look quite serious. Vince seemed to end the conversation and went to greet a rather foppishly dressed younger man. Something in the familiarity of their smiles and gestures started a chain of thought in Arthur's mind.

There was no sign of Frances or Leo. Arthur sighed and took another drink from his glass. At this rate he would have drunk the contents far too quickly if Jane didn't return soon. He hated rushing food or drink. It was very bad for the digestion, and he knew it would make for a poor night's sleep.

'Arthur, why ever aren't you out the floor dancing with some bright young thing?' Elsa plopped down without warning onto the vacant seat beside him. Her cheeks were flushed and rosy and she was slightly out of breath.

He looked at her in alarm. 'Oh, I don't dance.' He hoped fervently that she wasn't expecting him to take her out on the dance floor.

'Oh pish, everybody dances. Where is Janey? I would have thought you would have been with my daughter?'

'Um, she is dancing with Stephen,' Arthur said.

Immediately a pleased expression settled on Elsa's face. 'Oh, honey, I do hope you don't mind that? Only Janey and Stephen are very well matched.'

'Are they?' Arthur asked. Jane had told him that her mother had kept pressing Stephen on her, much to her annoyance.

Elsa raised her carefully pencilled brows. 'Of course, sweetie. I mean he is from a very good family and Janey would never have to work again if they married. She could give up all this typing and secretarial-type stuff that brigadier makes her do. She's gotten far too involved in it if you ask me since she had that setback right at the start of the war.' Elsa's gaze drifted out to the dance floor, and she waved to one of her friends as she danced past them.

Arthur wondered quite what Jane's mother meant by a setback. He knew Jane had lost someone at the start of the conflict. She had mentioned it once fleetingly in passing but he had never asked her about it. Too many people had lost loved ones, and the loss was often too raw and too personal for discussion.

'I rather think Jane enjoys her work.' Arthur couldn't imagine Jane settling down to a life of domestic bliss. He tried to picture Jane darning socks and ironing shirts and failed dismally.

Elsa gave him a sour look. 'I just would like to see my baby girl settled. It's what every mother wants.'

'I see,' he responded politely and wondered how many cocktails Elsa had consumed. He didn't really see at all why Elsa thought Jane would be any happier married to Stephen than she was now, seemingly quite happily single and living with her cat.

'Has dear Mr Benson accompanied you for your stay in town?' Elsa asked.

'Um, yes. Benson is at home this evening.' Arthur was aware of his manservant's fondness for Jane's mother and Elsa's ability to persuade Benson to wait upon her.

'He is such a lovely man. Do give him my regards,' Elsa said as she rose from her seat. Before he could stop her she helped herself to Jane's cocktail and was soon swept away into the crowd by a group of admirers.

Arthur finished his own drink and resigned himself somewhat glumly to another expensive trip to the bar. He had just placed his empty glass on the table when he saw Jane making her way towards him. At least she was alone with no sign of Stephen. He wondered what she had done with him.

'Phew, I'm parched,' Jane frowned as she looked at the table and saw her drink had gone and only Stephen's drink remained.

'Your mother took your drink. I did try to stop her,' Arthur warned.

'Honestly! What did she want?' Jane remarked crossly.

'I don't really know. I think she just wanted to know where you were,' Arthur said. 'I say, do you think we are going to get much more from this evening?'

Jane gave him a side-eyed look. 'Why?'

'Well, we did tell the taxi to come back at midnight and if we aren't ready then it will just pick up another fare. I don't want to be stranded here and have to walk all the way home. The buses will have finished by now.' He glanced at his watch. It was only eleven thirty, but he guessed it might take them a while to get out of the hotel since they would no doubt have to say goodnight to Elsa before leaving.

'You are just hoping to eat your supper, drink your cocoa and put your slippers on.' Jane shook her head in mock despair.

'There is nothing wrong with that.' Arthur felt decidedly nettled by her tone.

'Very well, let's go and get our things from the cloakroom,' Jane agreed.

'What about Stephen's drink?' Arthur stood and indicated the glass on the table.

Jane shrugged and picked it up. She swallowed the contents in a couple of gulps. 'He owes me,' she said. 'Come on, let's go.'

* * *

Jane looked for her mother as they made their way towards the exit. The room was so busy now though and the air blue with cigarette smoke, she couldn't see Elsa anywhere. Once they were in the wide corridor it was a little quieter and Jane found their cloakroom tickets from her bag ready for the attendant. Arthur looked extremely grumpy she decided as they collected their things.

'We're a little early for the cab. Let's go and sit in the lobby for five minutes. We can ask the doorman to fetch us when he arrives,' Jane suggested.

Arthur agreed and after alerting the door attendant they took a seat on one of the plush, velvet-covered chairs not far from the entrance.

'Do you think it was worth us coming here tonight?' Arthur asked, frowning when she took her cigarettes from her bag.

'I think so. We certainly should have set the cat amongst the pigeons. I just hope we will have rattled some of them enough for us to find out who killed Jenny and Tabitha and who is trying to send those messages.' Jane saw Arthur had started to wheeze so she reluctantly slipped her cigarettes away again. She would have to wait until she was home before she could relax with a smoke.

'I just hope you haven't placed yourself in the firing line.' Arthur looked at her, his expression grave.

'Nonsense, you can't make an omelette without breaking eggs. At some point we have to try and flush our traitor out,' Jane replied briskly. She knew there was an element of risk. Two women had already died but many more people could die if they didn't discover what was going on behind the scenes at the radio station.

'Sir, madam, your taxi is here,' the doorman called to them and they followed him outside the hotel into the unrelenting darkness of the street.

Jane shivered as she scrambled onto the rear seat of the car and Arthur got in beside her and gave the address. The air had turned even colder while they had been inside and there was a shimmering layer of frost coating what little she could see of the pavements and bus shelters as they drove away from the hotel.

There had been several vehicles collecting passengers as they had left, and the streets were surprisingly busy. Jane could only assume it was the time of year when people tried to cling on to the kinds of outings and festivities they would normally have enjoyed in the run up to Christmas.

''Ere, I don't know what this 'ere lunatic behind us thinks he's doin'. If he gets much closer to our back bumper I shall 'ave ter marry 'im. Madman, driving that close in the blackout. You never know when you'm going to 'ave to stop or swerve out sudden like.' The taxi driver squinted at his rear-view mirror.

Jane turned her head to look behind her through the back window. In the darkness she could just make out the silhouette of a car right up close to them.

'He is frightfully close.' She looked at Arthur. It was frightening having the other car so close in the pitch-black city streets.

'I say, would you mind taking a bit of a diversion?' Arthur leaned forward to speak to the driver.

'Where'd you want to go, guv'nor?' the driver asked.

'Nearest police station please.' Arthur settled back in his seat.

The driver looked surprised but took the next turn down a narrow street. 'Righto.'

Unsurprisingly the car behind them continued to follow but dropped back a little as they took a few more twists and turns. Jane's heart bumped against her ribs and she kept hoping their pursuer would give up the chase.

''Ere you am.' The driver pulled the taxi to a stop outside a red-brick building. The car that had been following them shot past and quickly disappeared out of sight. Jane exchanged a glance with her companion.

'Thank you. Can you take us home now, please,' she instructed the bewildered taxi driver.

The driver shrugged his shoulders, and they set off once more, arriving at the dark street outside the apartment block without any further incidents. Arthur paid the driver and he and Jane scurried into the building without speaking. They headed for Arthur's flat and only broke their silence once they were safely inside the front door.

'That was most unnerving,' Jane said as Arthur took off his hat, coat and scarves.

Benson, having heard their return, came into the hall to greet them. 'Shall I make cocoa for three?' he enquired.

'Please, Benson.' Arthur still sounded wheezy, and Jane saw his manservant frown as he turned away to go to the kitchen.

'Let's go and take a seat.' Arthur led the way into the sitting room. 'I don't know if whoever was after us was from the Admiralty or if you have already been a touch too successful in setting off the pigeons.'

CHAPTER TWENTY

Benson carried in a tray containing three thick white china mugs of cocoa. He set them down and then silently commenced setting up Arthur's medical apparatus. The instruments were delicate, and the manservant had to measure the amount of medication required carefully.

'A successful evening, Miss Jane?' Benson asked once Arthur was settled with his tubes and mask.

'We certainly managed to stir things up a little tonight.' Jane told Benson what they had heard and observed during the evening. By the time she had finished telling him about their journey home and the mysterious car that had followed them, the manservant looked quite grave.

Arthur finished his medication and removed his mask as she finished speaking. She was relieved to see he had more colour back in his cheeks and his chest didn't sound so squeaky.

'I told her I considered her actions reckless and I rather think this car that followed us proves my point,' Arthur said, picking up his mug of rapidly cooling cocoa.

'It is certainly a risky strategy, however I do see Miss Jane's point,' Benson said.

'I couldn't see the plate on the car that followed us tonight. It was either a black car or a dark navy. Did you see anything of the driver, Jane?' Arthur looked at her.

'Not really. Whoever it was seemed to be seated low down in the car. They were wearing a hat, and had their coat collar turned up in a way that concealed their face. With no street lamps and little moonlight, I couldn't even tell if it was a man or a woman.' Jane had tried to see if she could get a good look at the driver when they had stopped at the police station and the other car had been forced to drive past them.

'I thought the same thing. I didn't get a good look at them either.' Arthur still sounded grumpy, and Jane thought the cocoa had done little to sweeten his mood.

'Do you think it may have been the other department?' Benson asked.

'The Admiralty?' Jane wasn't sure about Benson's suggestion. It was possible she supposed, if the brigadier had been unable to stop their surveillance in time.

Arthur set his now empty mug down on the cork coaster that Benson had put on the table. 'Maybe, I don't know. To me it felt as if whoever was driving wanted to scare us.'

Jane sipped the last of her drink and wondered if he was right.

'I had the opportunity this evening, while Jane was dancing the night away, to observe what else was going on in the room,' Arthur said.

She looked at him.

'I had one dance with Stephen and trust me it was not a pleasurable experience. I only accepted so people wouldn't find it suspicious.' Jane grimaced at the memory.

Stephen was always far too handsy for her liking when they danced. She had only accepted his offer because she hoped to get close enough to some of the people they were observing to overhear some of the conversations. Dancing had seemed an unobtrusive way of achieving that aim.

'As I was saying I was able to observe the room.' Arthur shot her a glance and continued, 'There were quite a lot of serving officers there this evening. I know it was a charity event, and royalty was expected, but it struck me that if an enemy agent wished to try to gain useful information then the dance floor and bar at The Ritz would be a good place to go.'

'You mean we have been focused on the end point? The point where the information is translated into code and sent?' Jane could see where he was going with his theory.

'Precisely. In order to do that they first have to receive the information from someone, somewhere. When I analysed the messages they referred to all branches of the services. They seemed to warn of planned campaigns or possible resistance actions. That would signify that they are not getting information from a single source,' Arthur said.

'That's true. We have seen already that the Admiralty had no idea of our involvement in anything,' Jane agreed.

'Is there a pattern in the transmissions, sir?' Benson asked, looking at Arthur.

'They seem to run in batches, yes. A few days with several transmissions followed by a gap. So my theory is that after an event such as this evening if enough information has been gleaned, then there will be an increase in coded messages being sent over the next few days,' Arthur said.

'Then we need to work out how to watch the typewriter our traitor likes to use most and see if we can catch them over the next few days. If you are correct, then whoever it is must have gathered something useful tonight.' Jane suppressed a yawn as she spoke. The late hour catching up with her now she had sat down in the warmth of Arthur's flat. 'Shall we meet up in the morning to work out our next steps?' she suggested.

'Do you wish me to go into the studios as usual tomorrow,

Miss Jane?' Benson asked as he collected the mugs to take them to the kitchen.

'I think so, Benson. Obviously, attention is on myself and Arthur, but you are at the moment not in their sights. I can always find you once we have decided what we are about,' Jane said.

Benson bowed his head in acknowledgement and vanished with the crockery.

'I'll telephone the brigadier in the morning about the car tonight.' Jane looked at Arthur who was sleepily rubbing his eyes.

'It would be good to know who was driving,' he agreed.

Jane picked up her things ready to leave just as Benson returned.

'I feel it may be wise to allow me to escort you to your flat, Miss Jane. After the events earlier today, I would feel better knowing you were secure,' Benson said.

'Thank you. I shan't refuse.' Jane smiled gratefully at him. She did feel a little nervous about going home alone even though she was only a couple of flights of stairs away.

She said goodnight to Arthur and walked up the stairs to her flat with Benson accompanying her. He insisted on taking her key and unlocking the door to enter ahead of her.

'Do be mindful of Marmaduke,' Jane warned as she took off her coat in the hall. 'You saw what he did to Mr Finch.'

Benson checked all of the rooms in her flat and returned with Marmaduke at his heels. Jane swooped down to pick up her cat.

'How's my darling, clever kitty?'

'Everything appears to be secure, Miss Jane. Lock the door once I have gone,' Benson instructed her with a gentle smile as she petted her beloved cat.

'Thank you, Benson.' She saw the man out and dutifully locked and bolted her door.

She had anticipated having a hard time falling asleep after everything that had happened but once under the covers with a hot-water bottle, she was soon deep in slumber.

Marmaduke woke her the next morning by leaping up on top of her and noisily announcing his desire for food. After sleepily dragging herself out of bed and feeding her demanding pet, she telephoned the brigadier.

'Followed from The Ritz, you say? And you couldn't see the driver?' Jane moved the telephone away from her ear. The volume of the brigadier's call this early was somewhat over-whelming.

'I'm afraid not, sir. We couldn't get the plate either in the dark,' Jane confessed.

'I'm not surprised. It's as black as pitch out there at night. I'll make some enquiries, see if it was one of our lot. Keep me informed.' The brigadier rang off.

Jane ate a slice of toast for breakfast, treating herself by using some of her precious butter ration instead of the rather horrid substitute the government was keen to get people to use instead.

After fortifying herself with coffee and a cigarette she made sure Marmaduke was comfortable and headed down to Arthur's flat. He answered the door as soon as she knocked, making her wonder if he had been waiting for her arrival.

As they had arranged the previous night, Benson had already departed in his janitor's overalls for the studio.

'Come through, Jane.' Arthur led the way into the sitting room.

She could see at a glance that he had been busy. His note-books were all open and she could see that red ink had been added to his untidy and cryptic pencil notes.

'I take it you were up early?' she asked as she seated herself on the sofa after moving one of his books out of her way. She pulled one of the knitted rugs over her knees to keep herself warm.

'I got up with Benson and had breakfast.' Arthur seated himself in his favourite spot and she saw he had smeared some of the red ink on his jawline.

'Were you looking for something in particular in your notes?' she asked as he settled a cushion behind his back.

Arthur fumbled inside the breast pocket of his jacket and pulled out his wire-framed spectacles. He unfolded them and popped them on his nose.

'Here, look at this.' He found one of the open notebooks and passed it to her.

Jane took it from him and squinted at the page. 'Your handwriting gets worse. It's like deciphering a spider's scrawl. What am I looking at?'

Arthur peered at her disbelievingly over the top of his glasses before taking the notebook back with an exasperated sigh.

'It was what we were talking about last night.'

'Oh, you mean about where the information may be coming from and it being from more than one source?' Jane studied the page with fresh interest.

'Exactly. These are the decoded messages, and I started to group them into the services. N for navy, A for air, and L for land army.'

'I remember you said you had considered the different types of message and you said you thought they were all relating to the different services. Is there a common link?' Jane asked.

Arthur's eyes gleamed behind his glasses and Jane hoped he was not about to give her a lecture on some obscure item he had discovered. If so then she would definitely need to go back to her own flat to get her cigarettes.

'You see the numbers?' Arthur asked.

Jane realised that next to each set of letters he had added a number. 'Dates?' she said, hazarding a guess.

Arthur beamed at her as if she were his prize pupil. 'Bingo. After Benson had gone to work I went through and marked the messages in red. I already had the transmission dates. Here look.' He stabbed his forefinger down on the open page to illustrate pencil headings for each entry.

'Then what are these?' She looked at the new dates and saw they preceded the ones in the headings.

'I tried to think of how we could work out when the information would have been passed over. I wondered if our theory about gathering intelligence at large social gatherings might be correct,' Arthur explained.

'But how would you know what had gone on socially and where?' Jane asked. She had the feeling that she had missed a step somewhere in Arthur's logic.

His smile grew even wider. 'We have the redoubtable Benson to thank for that. He has been dutifully saving every scrap of newspaper since we arrived for the paper collection. He had mentioned that all the papers in the building were taken to a central point in the basement and then collected from there. I went down there this morning and found that there were roughly four weeks' worth of newspapers bundled up ready to be taken away.'

Jane stared at him. 'You went and ferreted through the old newspapers?'

'Just looking at the social columns. It proved most useful. Each of those new dates marks a charitable event or a report of a fundraising event for our forces. They would have been well attended by men home on leave since they were in a good and patriotic cause,' Arthur explained.

'Let me guess, our people were also in attendance?' Jane asked.

Arthur's smile faded slightly, and his brow creased. 'I can't say for all of them because it depends on the report. Certainly, your mother sang at several of them and Frances accompanied a few people. Jenny's name and Ernie and Reggie's names crop up too.'

'I see. Well, well done. It does seem that our theory on how the information is gathered has some merit.' Jane could see how the puzzle was beginning to fit together.

Arthur gathered his notebooks into a pile. 'Now we need to discover who is typing those changes to the scripts that Vince Vaughn and the other announcers are reading out on air.'

Jane drummed her fingertips on the arm of the sofa as she thought. 'It's also how they are being attached to the scripts and announcements. It's more than simply the typing, it's how they get hold of the scripts to make the changes. The whole thing is quite fluid.'

'You mean that the scripts are often only in the building the day of transmission?' he asked.

Jane nodded. 'Sometimes even only a very short time before. The additions or late scripts get couriered over by motorcycle from Whitehall or as Vince said from the Cabinet Office. Or a message could have come through to Tabitha to type it out and add it in I suppose. If she hadn't made changes herself to the older scripts or taken a message, then she would have wondered about the alterations she found after the broadcast. That could have been what initially tipped her off to something being very wrong.'

'The enemy changes I picked up were mainly to news or broadcast items and would have either been couriered as a big, breaking news story or as you say sent via telephone to Tabitha to type and change,' Arthur said.

'Except Tabitha noticed that the changes hadn't been made by her and were on the couriered scripts?' Jane asked.

'She may not have realised until she perhaps caught sight of some of the doctored scripts and knew she hadn't made the changes. Someone else had made them and they were always on the scripts going to the commentary booths. Either news pieces and rarely on story pieces.' The creases on Arthur's brow deepened. 'What happens to the couriered documents when they are delivered? What's the process?'

Jane tried to recall what she had observed. 'I've only seen it once or twice as I'm usually with Mother in the rehearsal rooms or the studio. The motorcycle courier comes in and the receptionist receives the envelope with the scripts. She opens them. I think to check how urgent they are. I believe sometimes things may be for immediate broadcast. You know, the ones where Vince would say "we interrupt your scheduled programme", that kind of thing. Those would go right upstairs, and she would take them—'

'Does the receptionist always take them?' Arthur interrupted.

Jane glared at him. 'No, I think if someone else is in the lobby, Frances for instance, or Leo or Ernie, they might offer to run them up if reception was busy. If they weren't urgent she might leave them in the wire tray on the desk and someone would take them up for her if they were passing. She is supposed to stay on the desk I think.'

Arthur pulled his notebooks closer, his eyes gleaming through the lenses of his spectacles. 'I take it the courier just drops the packages and leaves? The envelopes are sealed?'

'Yes, at least the times I've been there that's what happens. They hand them across and go. I saw one being opened so I take it they would always be sealed on arrival.' Jane could see her companion's mind was busy working something out.

'Different couriers each time?' Arthur asked.

'Yes,' Jane confirmed.

'That means the scripts were definitely doctored once they were in the building,' he said.

'Well yes. I thought we already had established that. We

even know which typewriter they like to use. We need to know who is doing it since they are probably, if not definitely, the same person who killed Tabitha and Jenny.' Jane couldn't help a note of exasperation creeping into her tone. Honestly, Arthur could be very irritating at times.

'There wouldn't be much time to make the adjustments between the scripts coming in and them reaching the booth. If we assume that the slips weren't added in the booth.' Arthur appeared to ignore her frustration at his slowness at getting to the point.

'No, I presume the enemy as we know monitors all our broadcasts as we monitor theirs. If they are looking for specific messages in code then it would help them enormously if they knew the messages were likely to be sent during particular kinds of broadcasts. Whoever is typing these things is acting very quickly. The top floor typewriter is usually quiet with no one around. It wouldn't take long to make the alterations,' Jane said.

'Interesting.' Arthur leaned back again in his chair.

Jane was tempted to shake him.

CHAPTER TWENTY-ONE

'I am assuming then that you believe Vince is unlikely to be our man? He would have no need to alter the scripts in that way. He could just make his own notes in the booth on a notepad and then no one, unless they listened back to the transcripts and compared them to the actual scripts, would have any idea of what had happened,' Jane said.

'I agree. Tabitha must have found the altered scripts after the broadcast and realised she hadn't made the changes. However, we don't know if he noticed these alterations and didn't question them or if he is party to it all in some way. What happens to the old scripts? Tabitha must have had sight of them. Obviously some were sent to me so they must have been collected from a central source?' Arthur asked.

Jane frowned as she tried to think if she had seen or noticed what happened. 'I think they are all bundled up for the paper collection much like the newspapers in this building. Didn't Benson say that as janitor he collected the wastepaper baskets? He would know where they were taken.'

Arthur removed his spectacles. 'I think Tabitha must have caught sight of a change and could have gone to look at some of the other scripts to confirm her suspicions that something odd was happening. In the ones I received to examine there was a gap of about a week date wise.'

'Perhaps those were ones she was bringing to show the brigadier or Colonel Hardacre?' Jane said.

'The murderer may have seen her with them and realised the game was about to be uncovered.' Arthur rubbed his eyes.

'That all fits. What about Jenny? Why was she killed? Did she catch someone typing something odd? Or did she hint to the wrong person that she knew something about Tabitha's death?' Jane shifted uncomfortably on her chair.

'We know Jenny had no money. She was losing work. I think she may have tried a spot of blackmail, either for cash or for more work,' Arthur said.

'Or both. That would imply that the killer is someone who has money or the power to ensure she continued to receive contracts.'

Arthur beamed at her. 'Exactly.'

'I need coffee. I'll put the kettle on.' Jane jumped up from her seat and headed for the kitchen. Everything they had been discussing made perfect sense. She wasn't certain that it narrowed the field of suspects much, apart from possibly eliminating Vince as a suspect.

She glanced out of the kitchen window as she filled the kettle. Her gaze automatically going to the spot where both Leo and the other agents had been watching the building. To her relief there was no one in sight by the plane tree for once. It seemed the message had got through to the Admiralty that the operatives could be called off.

She set up a tray and made the coffee in a pot before carrying everything back through to the sitting room. Arthur had cleared a space on the table, and she set it down in front of him before resuming her seat.

'I rather think that although Vince may not be the one

typing and pasting the alterations on the scripts, there is still the possibility he could be working with the killer,' Arthur said as Jane poured them both a cup of coffee from the chrome pot.

'What makes you think that?' She looked at him curiously before adding milk to his cup.

'While I was observing the room last night, after Vince finished talking to Ernie, he went to meet someone. A younger man.' Arthur gave her a meaningful look.

Jane stirred her coffee, baffled for a few seconds by the loaded meaning in his words. 'Oh, you think that Vince may be fond of the company of men?'

She would not be unduly shocked if he were. Many of her mother's admirers were homosexual, although since it was illegal and would cause all kinds of problems their proclivities were kept secret.

'Knowledge of that could be used to blackmail him. It might be why he has never drawn anyone's attention to the changes to the scripts.' Arthur eyed her over the brim of his coffee cup.

'Or he could have mentioned it to Tabitha and that may be what tipped her off to look for more examples. Her bag was missing when they found her. I definitely think she had some of those scripts with her when she was killed,' Jane said.

'Her murder could have scared Vince into staying silent. I think we need to talk to him,' Arthur said.

Jane nodded her head in agreement. 'Yes, you're right.'

'Are you due at the studios today?' Arthur asked.

'No, believe it or not, I actually have a day off. I'm due there again early tomorrow morning though. Rehearsals of a new piece and then a recording session.'

'Is Vince in today?' Arthur asked.

Jane took a sip of her coffee. 'Yes, our best chance to talk to him would be at around two. There are pre-recorded plays on at that point. He often goes to the café nearby for lunch. Most of the staff there use it. We could go and loiter, see if he comes in,' she suggested.

'I think we should try it. It may be safer than if you try to speak to him alone inside Bush House.'

'What else?' Jane asked. She wondered if he had any other ideas that might help them catch whoever was behind the murders and the script changes.

'Benson is doing what he can today to observe the type-writer. He may have more news when he returns tonight. He'll try to telephone too, I suppose, if he gets a breakthrough,' Arthur said.

'He'll look at today's scripts too and if there are changes then that should tell us if our ideas are correct. We know the enemy monitors our airwaves constantly, as we do theirs. That must be how they get the messages.' Jane felt better for her coffee.

'I assume too that they choose to alter the couriered scripts because the playwrights, etc. would notice changes to their words. These last-minute scripts and changes are rather differ-ent.' Arthur looked thoughtful. 'No one would pick up an oddly worded phrase or addition.'

A shiver ran along Jane's spine. Everything seemed to be coming together quickly and she knew things were about to become dangerous.

* * *

Arthur arranged for Jane to call in for him when she was ready to head across the city to the café. They had decided to go early and take lunch together there while they waited for Vince to appear. Jane had gone back to her flat to attend to her domestic duties and he had taken the opportunity to go through his notes once more in case he had missed anything.

She knocked on his door punctually at twelve and they set

off to catch the bus. Arthur would really have preferred a taxi, but they were hard to get and Jane had given him one of her looks when he had suggested it.

For once though the bus was not too busy and he was able to sit beside Jane as it clattered its way through the city streets. He stared out through the grimy window at the people scurrying in and out of the shops. There was precious little sign of any Christmas gaiety yet even though the festive season was fast approaching.

He had read in the newspaper only yesterday that there was likely to be a shortage of Christmas trees and people were encouraged to make their own or have an alternative. The war seemed to be dragging on with no end yet in sight. The early optimism of a few years ago that it would all be done in a couple of months seemed aeons ago.

Jane nudged him with her arm. 'This is our stop.'

They disembarked from the bus and Jane set off at her usual brisk pace forcing him to speed up if he wanted to walk with her. They passed the entrance to the radio studios and continued along the street until they reached a narrow side road.

'It's just down here,' she informed him.

He nodded and continued to try to keep up. The café was a small, nondescript working-men's affair with a large plate-glass window steamed up with condensation. A board stood outside on the pavement announcing the day's special as potato soup.

A bell on a spring above the door jingled their arrival as Jane went in ahead of him. The café was busy with almost all of the tables occupied. Arthur saw there was a mix of workmen obviously on their lunch breaks, housewives with shopping baskets tucked under the tables near their feet. A young boy in uniform with his sweetheart and an old man reading his newspaper.

Jane spotted an empty table right at the back and led the way. Arthur was quite glad to sit down. He knew Jane didn't intend to rush everywhere; she just couldn't help it. All of her actions were swift, decisive and brisk. She tugged off her leather gloves and placed them in her handbag.

'Brr, it's so cold outside. It's quite nice to come into the warm.' She rubbed her hands together.

Her cheeks were pink from the effects of the cold and the swift walk, and it struck him afresh that Jane was actually an attractive woman. It suddenly dawned on him that Stephen's attitude towards him the previous evening might have been because he saw Arthur as some kind of rival. It would account for the frosty and awkward conversation in the brigadier's office.

It also occurred to him that Jane's mother may have been warning him off her daughter. These dual realisations made him pause and he stared sightlessly at the leatherette-backed menu Jane had thrust into his hands.

'I think I'm going to have the day's special if there is any left,' she declared.

'Oh yes, the soup, sounds, um, warming. Yes,' Arthur agreed.

Jane gave him an odd look. 'Shall we order a drink now or wait until after we've eaten?' she asked.

'I think after. In case we have to loiter.' Arthur blinked nervously and pulled himself together.

They gave their order to the café owner. The table they had chosen gave a good view of anyone coming in through the door. Unfortunately, the condensation on the window meant the view of the street was somewhat foggy and out of focus.

'Do you have a plan if he doesn't come in?' Arthur asked as they ate their lunch.

'I suppose I could call in at the studio on some pretext that Mother may have left something behind. It would be entirely

plausible, she is notoriously scatterbrained with her posses-
sions,' Jane said.

The soup was hot and thick and Arthur could detect the
addition of parsnip to add extra flavour. It was deliciously
warming on such a chilly day and the bread roll accompanying
it was fresh and light.

'Hmm.' Arthur hoped Vince would keep to his routine. He
would prefer that Jane didn't talk to a potential murderer or
murderer's accomplice alone. He also wasn't certain he could
pull off the pretence of being a technician in order to accompany her.

They finished the soup and ordered a pot of tea for two and
apple crumble with custard for dessert. The time was ticking
closer now to two o'clock and the lunchtime rush had thinned,
leaving more of the tables empty.

Jane glanced at her watch. 'He's a little late.'

She had hardly finished speaking when the bell over the top
of the café door jangled and a rush of cold air preceded Vince's
arrival. Jane waved enthusiastically at him and 'cooeed', so he
could hardly refuse to come and join them without appearing
rude.

'Miss Treen and Mr, er...'

'Cilento,' Arthur supplied helpfully seeing that Vince had
clearly forgotten his name.

'Ah yes, of course, do forgive me.' Vince took a seat on one
of the empty chairs at Jane's bright-eyed insistence. 'I do hope
I'm not intruding on your lunch.' Vince looked at their empty
pudding dishes.

'Not at all, we were just having a cup of tea before setting
off home. It's so frightfully cold out today,' Jane said as she
passed him the menu. 'By the way, the soup is quite good, even
though I rather suspect that by the end of the war I may
resemble a potato I seem to have eaten so many.'

Vince smiled at her. 'I know the feeling. The shortages and rationing are rather trying.' He gave his order for soup to the café owner.

Arthur focused on pouring his and Jane's tea until Vince had been served with his lunch.

'What brings you out this way today, Miss Treen? I thought Elsa had said she had a day off,' Vince asked.

'Oh, you know what she is like at misplacing things. I made the mistake of saying that Arthur and I were planning some pre-Christmas shopping and of course she gave me an errand to run,' Jane explained airily. 'I'm relieved though at not being in today. It's a nice break, especially after what happened to Jenny.'

'Yes, a day off is a rare treat these days,' Vince agreed.

'It must be hard in your job when the courier brings in last-minute announcements. So little time to prepare,' Jane continued in a conversational tone.

Arthur saw a wary look flit across the handsome announcer's face.

'Especially when even those scripts seem to have had last-minute adjustments made to them. Why, I expect the glue has barely dried on some of them.' Jane's tone hardened slightly.

'Miss Treen, I'm not quite sure what you're insinuating.' Vince dropped his soup spoon into his almost empty bowl and snatched up his napkin from his lap.

'I rather think you know exactly what Jane means, Mr Vaughn. You must have noticed that some of the scripts you have been given have been doctored with added items for you to read. I think you knew this was unusual,' Arthur said in a calm, level voice.

Colour came and went in the announcer's face as he looked first at Jane and then at Arthur. 'Who are you? What do you want?'

'Two women are dead, and we know those alterations were coded messages to the enemy.' Jane's eyes were flinty.

'I don't know anything about that. The contents of the scripts are nothing to do with me. I noticed the changes and I mentioned them to Tabitha. She seemed surprised and asked me to show her, so I kept back a couple of scripts and gave them to her. A week later she was dead. That's all I know. You have to believe me.'

'You didn't think to mention this to Inspector Winters?' Jane asked.

Vince slumped forward and placed his head in his hands. 'I received some threatening notes warning me to stay quiet. I was frightened.'

'Of being killed yourself? Or of your own secret being revealed to the police and to the public? That would finish your career, wouldn't it?' Jane said.

Vince looked trapped. 'Please, you have to understand. How could I tell the police without revealing the truth? I got the note just after Tabitha was killed.'

'I don't suppose you kept it? Was it handwritten or type-written?' Arthur thought it would probably be too much to hope for that Vince might have retained the message.

'I burnt it. I didn't want it to fall into the wrong hands. It was typewritten though,' Vince replied miserably.

'And then Jenny was murdered.' Jane looked sternly at Vince's unhappy figure.

'I didn't know what to think. Frances was poking around asking questions. Ernie and Reggie seemed to be hinting. I keep looking around all the time, jumping at every shadow. I had no idea who I could trust. Perhaps I'll be next,' Vince said.

His whole demeanour seemed to indicate he was telling the truth.

'Do you have any idea at all who might be behind this?

Anyone who consistently seems to bring the scripts to either the booth or to the technicians?' Arthur asked.

Vince shook his head. 'No, and believe me it's on my mind every time one of those wretched alterations appears.'

He sounded sincere and Arthur could see that Jane believed him. Arthur was not so certain.

CHAPTER TWENTY-TWO

Jane waited until Vince had paid for his lunch and left to return to the studio before turning to Arthur for his opinion.

'Did you believe him?' she asked.

She had felt there was sincerity in what he had told them. Clearly he was a man both in fear of his life and of his proclivities being revealed. After Tabitha's death he had obviously decided that discretion was the better part of valour.

Arthur nodded slowly. 'Yes, I think he was probably telling the truth. Although we can't be entirely certain that he has told us all he knows. We had him cornered so he had little choice when he knew that we had worked out what was going on with the scripts. It's whether he has suspicions about who is responsible.'

'How does this all bring us any closer to catching our killer?' Jane took out her purse to pay for their lunch.

'I'm not certain. I think perhaps we need to talk to Benson when he returns this evening and go from there,' Arthur said.

Jane paid the café owner for their meal and pulled on her gloves ready to brace the cold outside the café. It was already starting to grow darker as the days were so short at this time of year. Arthur, as usual, swaddled himself in layers of wool and they walked back down the street to the bus stop.

The bus was much busier on the return journey back to the flats. Arthur gallantly stood, holding on to one of the leather straps to keep his balance having given his seat to a pregnant lady. The journey took longer too, with more people getting off and on at the stops. By the time they reached their destination sleet was falling from the sky and the pavements were wet and slippery.

Arthur offered Jane his arm when they stepped down onto the pavement. She was relieved they only had a short distance to walk as the icy pellets stung her cheeks. Her shoes slithered on the pavement, and she was glad of Arthur's support.

'I must go and see to Marmaduke.' She wiped her feet on the coconut matting inside the lobby entrance.

'I'll come up with you. After yesterday I think it may be wise just to ensure nothing else has occurred,' Arthur offered.

'Thank you.' She appreciated the offer. It was useless to deny that finding Mr Finch searching her flat the previous day had given her a nasty scare.

She had always regarded her home as a safe space. The only perceived threat before had been the risk of a bomb. Now that sense of security had been shattered and even though she prided herself on being quite tough, it had unnerved her.

Marmaduke, as usual, appeared in the tiny hallway at the sound of her key in the lock. Jane liked to believe it was in happy anticipation at seeing her return. However, she suspected it might also be due to anticipation at receiving sardines.

He twined around her legs leaving the usual stray ginger hairs and Arthur promptly sneezed. Jane took off her outdoor things while Arthur quickly checked out the other rooms to ensure no one had gained entry in her absence.

'All clear,' he confirmed as he returned to the hallway where she was cradling her pet.

He eyed the cat with some disfavour, while Marmaduke stared at him unblinkingly through his one good eye.

'It'll be at least another hour or so before Benson returns. Do go into the sitting room and put the fire on. I'll make us a pot of tea,' Jane instructed as she quickly tidied her hair in the hall mirror.

Arthur, somewhat reluctantly, took off his outdoor things while Jane went to the kitchen to feed her cat and put the kettle on. By the time she returned bearing the tea tray the fire was warming the room up nicely and Arthur was installed in one of the armchairs leafing through the novel she had been reading.

Marmaduke had trotted in behind her and stretched himself out luxuriously on the hearthrug. She placed the draught excluder along the bottom of the door while Arthur continued to watch the cat warily as he stirred his tea. Jane lit a cigarette and leaned back in her seat taking care to keep the smoke away from her companion.

'I was giving the case some thought on the bus.' Arthur sipped his tea. 'Depending on what Benson has discovered today, I believe we need to try and lay a trap for our killer.'

Jane flicked ash from the tip of her cigarette into a small glass ashtray. 'Go on.'

'We need to update Inspector Winters as I think assistance from the police is necessary at this stage. Although, we can be circumspect about Vince Vaughn's involvement. We have no evidence at this stage that he has been anything other than an unwilling tool.' Arthur looked at her.

'I agree. Vince is very popular and well known. He also did go to Tabitha with his suspicions if he has told us the truth. I think it would be a grave blow to public morale if his reputation were to be damaged. I'm certain the brigadier would agree.' Jane stubbed her cigarette out.

She could see the sense in Arthur's suggestion.

'We have to somehow come up with something that will force our murderer to show their hand.' Arthur frowned at his teacup as if it should provide him with a solution to the problem.

'Perhaps we need to arrange a courier delivery of something tempting? We know our traitor has probably gleaned information from The Ritz that would be useful to the enemy,' Jane suggested. 'I mean, I know it depends if Benson has seen anyone trying to use the typewriter today, but a planned courier delivery of some fake news might lure our killer out. Other than the unexpected deliveries, a dispatch rider usually comes at eleven each morning.'

Arthur nodded his head slowly as he considered her suggestion. 'Then we can see who offers to take the parcel up to the booth?'

'There are only certain circumstances when they get the chance to add their cryptic messages. Once they pick up the scripts they then have to get to the top floor, type up a coded alteration, paste it in and deliver it to the booth. They always have them in a format that can be slipped into the official government announcement. Something that's easy to do as the bulletins have set formats,' Jane said.

'Yes, that's true. We would need to work out how to get the courier to deliver at the right moment so that we can track the journey of the parcel without attracting attention.' Arthur scratched his chin thoughtfully.

'We can liaise with the inspector and with the brigadier or Colonel Hardacre to set everything up. The brigadier can arrange a courier bulletin.' Jane was warming to the plan.

'Do you know if everyone we suspect will be there tomorrow?' Arthur asked.

'Leo should be in as he is there most days. Frances and Ernie are rehearsing with Mother, and I believe Reggie is due to record a session too. Vince will be in the booth.' Jane frowned as she tried to recall what Elsa had told her about the work schedule.

The room had grown darker while they had been talking and only the orange glow from the bars on the electric fire illuminated the room. A sudden squall threw sleet against the windowpane and Jane shivered at the unexpected sound.

'We had better put the blackout up and turn on the lamps. Benson should be back anytime now.' Jane moved to switch on the lamp and to tug the stiff, thick black curtain material into place across her window.

'I should go downstairs and do ours. Benson will be cold when he gets in with this sleet. I'll put the fire on. Come down when you're ready, Jane, and we'll see what he has to say. We can work out a plan together then and contact the inspector.' Arthur placed the cups and saucers on the tea tray and rose from his seat.

Marmaduke eyed him suspiciously as Arthur kept his distance to edge out of the room into the hall.

'I'll be down in a few minutes.' Jane followed him carrying the tray as Arthur put on his hat, coat and scarves.

Once he had let himself out of the flat, Jane washed up the tea things and drew the blackout in her kitchen and her bedroom before turning the fire down. She was about to let herself out to go down to Arthur's flat when the telephone rang in the hall.

She picked up the receiver and gave the number in her usual precise manner. At first she thought there was no one there as no one spoke and all she could hear were faint scuffling sounds.

'Hello, is someone there?' She wondered if the exchange might have made a mistake and dropped the call or put the caller through to a wrong number.

She was about to place the receiver back on the stand when

a muffled, sinister voice hissed into her ear, 'Nosy parkers end up dead. Stop poking around in other people's business.' There was a sharp click, and the line went dead before she could respond.

'Well really! How rude!' Jane remarked to Marmaduke who was washing his front paw in the kitchen doorway. 'I suppose that must mean we are quite close to catching whoever is responsible for this.'

*　*　*

Arthur opened the front door to Jane's impatient knock.

'I've just had the most extraordinary telephone call,' she said as she entered the hall.

Arthur could see by the flush on her cheeks and the spark in her eyes that something had riled her up.

'What do you mean? Who called you?' He half expected her to say it was her mother.

'It was an anonymous call. I didn't recognise the voice as it was quite muffled. He warned me to stop poking around in someone else's business or suffer the consequences,' Jane explained, following him into the sitting room.

'Definitely a man, but you don't know who?' Arthur clarified as he moved his newspaper from his seat and sat down.

'It was definitely a man, but the voice was disguised. I'm sure of it.' Jane flung herself down on the end of the sofa.

'Hmm, I wonder if this is a result of the probing you did at the gala or if someone saw us with Vince today,' Arthur was concerned.

'I hope we have not put Vince in harm's way.' Jane sounded concerned.

He knew Jane hated the thought that the announcer might be hurt if someone had chanced to see him talking to her and

Arthur. That she had just received a death threat herself seemed not to be troubling her at present.

There was a sound at the front door and a second later Benson peered into the sitting room. His lean face looked weary and the lines around his eyes more pronounced.

'Good afternoon, Miss Jane, sir.' He took off his cap which appeared quite drenched.

'Oh, Benson, you are soaked. Take off your coat and I shall make you some tea.' Jane bounced up again and disappeared to the kitchen.

For once Arthur's manservant made no objection to her offer. He came in to join Arthur beside the fire once he had removed his wet outdoor things.

'The sleet is getting worse, and the buses were so full I had to let two go past before I could get on.' Benson stretched his hands out towards the bars on the electric fire.

'It was just starting when Jane and I returned.' Arthur quickly told his manservant of their interview with Vince Vaughn and about Jane's telephone call. He had just finished when Jane came in bearing a large mug of tea and a plate with a couple of home-made biscuits which she set before Benson.

'Thank you, Miss Jane. This is most kind of you.' Benson accepted the drink gratefully and sat somewhat primly on the opposite end of the sofa to Jane.

Benson looked tired and Arthur could see that the early starts and strenuous work were taking a toll. He hoped this idea of Jane's would bring the case to a speedy end and they would all be able to resume their normal duties at least for a while. He would be glad to get out of London and back to their quiet life at Pennycombe.

'I assume that Arthur has brought you up to the mark with everything we've learned today?' Jane asked once Benson had drunk some of his tea and looked warmer.

'Indeed, Miss Jane. The telephone call is a most troubling

development, especially after what Mr Vaughn told you about the note he received,' Benson said.

'And how have you fared today, Benson?' Arthur asked. 'Did you learn anything new that might help us?'

'I kept an unobtrusive watch on the typewriter but obviously I couldn't work solely on that floor without attracting attention. I observed Frances Fellowes appeared to be actively seeking people out to speak to them. They, equally, appeared to be attempting to avoid her. She and Mr Leo Cavendish seemed to be quarrelling in the corridor at one point. I heard Mr Cavendish say, "Frances, I don't have time for this," and he stormed off into his office.'

Benson set down his mug of tea and nibbled at one of the biscuits Jane had provided. 'By stormed, I mean he appeared angry and slammed the door in Miss Fellowes's face,' he clarified after swallowing his biscuit.

'I see.' Arthur wondered what Frances had hoped to accomplish. It seemed that she was on some kind of fishing expedition. But was she seeking information for herself or for someone else?

'It seems to me that we have to act quickly now. The situation is growing ever riskier. The telephone call I received, Vince Vaughn, and now these ill-advised actions of Frances could all lead to another murder. I, for one, have no intention of becoming the next victim.' Jane fixed both Arthur and Benson with a firm stare.

'Perhaps we should discuss the plan I suggested with the brigadier. We will need his assistance with the courier,' Arthur suggested. 'If he is amenable to the proposal we can then speak to Inspector Winters about his being at hand to arrest the traitor.'

Jane nodded. 'Yes, you're right. I'll telephone him now.' She went out to the hall, closing the sitting room door behind her. A moment later they heard the muffled bellow of the brigadier's voice emanating from the hall.

'Are you all right, Benson?' Arthur asked as the manservant finished the last of his tea. He was concerned for his manservant's welfare.

'Oh yes, sir. I must confess I am a little tired this evening, but I do find this kind of work most stimulating. One likes to feel as if one is still useful in serving one's country.' Benson smiled gently at him as he set his empty mug down on the table.

Jane re-entered the room a moment later. 'The brigadier is going to liaise with Colonel Hardacre and with Inspector Winters. We are to expect the police to contact us so we can work out the logistics of the trap.' Jane sat down on the sofa and smoothed her tweed skirt neatly into place.

Arthur watched in silent dismay as three ginger cat hairs detached themselves from her person and floated down onto the rug.

'If you will excuse me for a moment, Miss Jane, I shall go and change. Will you be joining us for supper this evening?' Benson asked as he picked his mug up once more and prepared to leave the room.

'Only if you will allow me to assist you. You've been working hard all day,' Jane said.

'Very good, Miss Jane.' He left the room.

'You do know that meant no, don't you?' Arthur said in a low voice when Benson had gone.

Jane sighed. 'I had a feeling it probably did.'

* * *

Supper was a simple affair. It seemed that Benson had acquired a recipe using powdered eggs which he used to create quite a tasty flan-type dish with vegetables. Apparently, he had been experimenting with the government-issued recipes. Jane, as Arthur had warned, found she was relegated to setting the table and washing up.

They had cleared away and were enjoying a post-dinner cup of coffee when there was a knock at the door. Benson went to see who was there and returned accompanied by Inspector Winters.

The inspector looked tired, and Jane noticed the bottoms of his dark-grey trousers were damp. She guessed the sleet must have continued and the pavements were probably quite wet. It might even be snowing. She didn't want to risk peeking out through a window however in case any light showed.

'Good evening, Inspector. I presume Brigadier Remmington-Blythe has contacted you?' Jane said as Benson went to fetch an extra cup and saucer to offer the policeman a drink.

'Indeed, Miss Treen. Perhaps you could enlighten me about the progress you've made in your investigations,' the inspector remarked drily as he took out his notebook.

'Very well.' Jane glanced at Arthur and then began a succinct report of what they had discovered, skirting over Vince Vaughn's secret.

The inspector's demeanour as she spoke was inscrutable and Jane hoped he was not going to be put out by their findings.

'I see. So, what is this plan that you wish me to assist you with?' Inspector Winters asked as Benson returned.

CHAPTER TWENTY-THREE

Arthur accompanied Jane the next morning. They travelled on the bus to the studios. The sleet from the previous night had left the pavements wet and shining in the weak wintry light. Benson had left before them as usual. He already had his instructions and hopefully was in position.

Inspector Winters was due to bring a police car to park unobtrusively near the building. A courier, arranged by the brigadier, would arrive shortly afterwards. Arthur was to wait nearby ready to take action should he be needed. Jane was to observe inside the studios. The stage was set ready, and the trap was about to be sprung.

Jane's heart thumped as she got off the crowded bus and made her way towards the building. Arthur got off at the same stop but headed to the place he had been given to wait. Jane was somewhat taken aback as she entered the lobby to see Frances Fellowes sobbing hysterically on one of the lobby chairs. Her dark-green felt hat was askew, and her coat was dirty. A small crowd surrounded her with everyone talking at once.

Elsa was foremost amongst them, easily visible in her mink-trimmed coat and hat.

'Janey pie, Frances has been attacked just outside the build-ing.' Elsa pounced on her as soon as she approached the group. 'Someone grabbed her and tried to strangle her. Why pick on Frances heaven only knows.'

Jane could see a livid red line around Frances's scrawny neck, as the receptionist tried to press a glass of water on her.

'The police are on their way. Are you certain you don't wish me to call an ambulance or a doctor, Frances?' Leo Cavendish emerged, flustered and slightly dishevelled from his office.

'No, no, I just want to go home,' Frances croaked.

'What happened exactly?' Jane turned to her mother.

Elsa shrugged. 'When my driver dropped me off and I came in, Frances was already in here making an exhibition of herself. She claims that as she was walking along the street she was grabbed from behind and bundled into that little service alley. Whoever grabbed her tried to strangle her.'

'Did she see who it was?' Jane's mind raced. It seemed the murderer must not have liked Frances poking around asking questions and had decided to strike. Did that mean that their carefully laid trap would now fail?

'I don't think so. She said she only got away because the street was so busy and she managed to make a racket clanging on the metal dustbins in the alley, so the attacker fled.' Elsa looked at Frances. 'You can see the state she's in. Her skirt is ruined.'

Leo and the new security guard were busy dispersing the onlookers. He offered his arm to escort Frances into his office to await the police. His gaze locked with Jane's and he made a slight movement with his head indicating she should follow them.

Before she could move, Inspector Winters swept in through the front door. He immediately went to where Leo and Frances were heading through the door to the office. Almost everyone else except Elsa and the receptionist had dispersed and gone about their business.

'Go on up to the rehearsal room, Mother, I'll be there in a minute.' Jane ignored Elsa's huff of annoyance and hurried after the inspector.

Leo seated Frances on one of the chairs in his office and offered Jane the other one. Inspector Winters took Leo's chair behind the desk while Leo himself leaned against the wall, his hands in his trouser pockets.

Frances had thankfully stopped sobbing now and was rubbing at the injury on her neck. She glanced across at Jane as if confused about why she had accompanied them.

'Miss Fellowes, my constable has gone to search the area where you told Mr Cavendish you were attacked. Could you manage to tell me in your own words what happened to you this morning?' Inspector Winters had taken out his notebook.

'I got off the bus at my usual stop. I had arrived early, as I always do.' Frances paused to clear her throat and take a sip of water. 'No one else got off the bus with me. I walked along towards the studios. Then, when I got to the service alley something was thrown about my throat, and I was dragged off my feet backwards into the alley by the dustbins.' Tears leaked down Frances's face once more and she wiped her cheeks with her handkerchief.

'Did you see your assailant's face at all? Or did he or she speak to you? Say anything?' the inspector asked as he scribbled busily in his notebook.

'No, he didn't speak, and I couldn't see anything of them at all. I was fighting for my life. I kicked at the metal dustbins, and I think that was what saved me. There was a terrific noise when they toppled over, and the lids clanged. I think I blacked out then. The next thing I knew I was lying on the floor amongst the garbage. I managed to get myself up and ran here as fast as I could.' Frances blew her nose, clearly distressed at the recollec-tion of what had happened.

'You said he. Are you certain it was a man?' the inspector asked as he reviewed what he had written.

'I can't be certain but they were taller than me and very strong so I suppose I assumed it must have been a man,' Frances said.

'They didn't take your handbag? Or try to rob you?' Inspector Winters asked.

'No, at least I don't think so.' Frances looked down to where her handbag, an old black leather affair was at her feet. She picked it up and checked the contents. 'No, nothing is missing.'

'Very well, I think you should go home, Miss Fellowes, and rest after your ordeal. You are certain you don't wish to see a doctor? I understand Mr Cavendish offered to send you to the hospital,' Inspector Winters said.

'No, I'll be all right in my own house. My neighbour, Mrs Pegg, she's ever so good. I know she'll look in on me,' Frances said.

Leo peeled himself away from the wall. 'I'll call a taxi then. Would you like Miss Treen or someone else to accompany you?'

Frances blinked and looked at Jane. 'No, no. I just want to go home.'

Leo picked up the telephone receiver and contacted a taxi company to dispatch a car. Jane rose from her chair, her gas mask bumping against her hip in its box.

'Thank you, Miss Treen, for accompanying us during the interview. It's always good to have another woman present when interviewing a lady,' Inspector Winters said.

Jane knew this was for Frances's benefit to explain why she had been present in the office.

'Not at all, Inspector. I'm happy to be of assistance. Shall I go, if you are certain I can't help any further? Only Miss Macin-tyre will be waiting for me.'

'Yes, thank you,' the inspector said.

'I do hope you feel better soon, Frances,' Jane said as she left the room.

She glanced at her watch when she reached the lobby. The courier was due in an hour, and they really needed the inspector to be gone and everything to be back to normal by then. She hoped that Arthur was aware of what had happened and wouldn't think the plan had been aborted.

'Is Miss Fellowes all right, Miss Treen?' Louisa at the reception desk asked.

'She's dreadfully shaken as you might expect. Mr Cavendish has sent for a car to take her home.' Jane used the opportunity to sign in and check that all the suspects had also arrived. She saw that Vince, Ernie and Reggie were all accounted for, having arrived after Elsa. From the times given she guessed they had arrived while she had been in the office with Leo, Frances and the inspector.

Depending on their mode of transport they could all have been in the vicinity when Frances was attacked. As indeed could Leo Cavendish himself. She scurried up the stairs to the rehearsal room.

Her mother was already standing beside the piano sorting music with Reggie. Ernie was pacing about, a script in his hand, muttering to himself. Jane guessed that Vince had already gone to the studio to take over from the other announcer.

'About time, Janey. Where have you been?' her mother demanded as Jane scurried to remove her outdoor things to hang them on the coat hooks.

'Sorry. The inspector wanted me to stay with Frances while he interviewed her. He thought having another woman with her might help her,' Jane explained as she straightened her grey tweed skirt and came over to the piano.

'Is Frances all right? Elsa told us what happened. It seems Ernie and I arrived after the event,' Reggie asked.

'She's frightfully shocked. I think she's gone home. She wouldn't see a doctor,' Jane said.

'I'm not surprised. She was dashed lucky from what Elsa told us to have escaped with her life.' Ernie looked up from his script.

'It would seem so, although heaven knows why anyone would attack Frances,' Elsa said. 'It makes a gal feel most unsafe. I think we should suggest that we switch to the Maida Vale studios until this lunatic is caught. It's clearly someone with a vendetta against this place, don't you think?' She turned to Reggie.

'It certainly seems rather strange. I think you and Miss Treen would be advised to be careful. Whoever is doing this seems to be only attacking the ladies,' Ernie said.

'I'm afraid I agree. Better safe than sorry, Elsa, my dear,' Reggie agreed.

'You and Ernie must have passed by just after it all happened. Did you arrive at the same time?' Jane seated herself at the piano stool and flexed her fingers ready to commence playing.

'What? No, I came in with Vince, he caught me up as we walked by that alleyway. We saw the constable in there poking about near the dustbins and wondered what he was doing,' Ernie said.

'I came in just before you then. I don't recall seeing him there when I got here.' Reggie gave a careless lift of his shoulders.

'Ugh, I swear Frances made the whole place stink of garbage downstairs.' Elsa wrinkled her nose and shuddered. 'Anyway, we haven't much time. Here, Janey, honey, let's start with this one and run through.' She handed her a pile of music and Jane set it up on the piano, glancing through to see how many of the pieces she was familiar with.

Reggie and Ernie took themselves over to a far corner of the studio. It appeared that Reggie was standing in for Frances to feed Ernie his lines as he ran through his script. Jane had to force herself to concentrate on her music while the clock ticked on towards when the courier would be due.

They stopped the rehearsal just before eleven as the woman with the tea trolley clattered her way into the room. Jane watched as both Ernie and Reggie slipped out after they had been served a cup of tea.

'Honestly, Janey, I don't know what you were thinking but you made so many mistakes this morning. You'll have to do better than that when we go in to record,' her mother reprimanded her as she peered in distaste at the insipid-looking fluid in her cup.

'Sorry, Mother. I think I was distracted by what happened to Frances this morning.' Jane could see it was eleven now and wondered if the dispatch rider had arrived.

Elsa rolled her eyes and took her cigarettes from her bag to offer one to Jane. Normally she would have accepted with alacrity but now she wanted to find out what was happening.

'Maybe in a moment. I think I need to just pop to the ladies.' Jane made good her escape and slipped out into the corridor. The rehearsal room they had been allocated was on the floor above the lobby.

There was no one in sight as she crept quietly towards the staircase, listening out for whatever might be going on downstairs. She could hear a male voice and a feminine voice floating up from the reception desk.

Benson was stationed near the room where the typewriters were kept in case the killer had not yet prepared his adaptations in advance. The studio where Vince was situated in his announcer's booth was on the floor between.

Jane knew that the inspector had a man concealed on that floor ready to pounce at a signal to capture whoever might be delivering the adapted scripts. Her pulse pounded in her ears, and she hoped their killer would take the bait. The brigadier had promised a script marked as urgent to be broadcast immediately on receipt. Just the kind the traitor liked so there was no opportunity for scrutiny or questions over the content before it was read out live on air.

She glanced at her watch, ten past eleven. They had another ten minutes before they were all due to regroup and go to the recording studio. At the sound of footsteps coming up the stairs she darted quickly into the ladies' lavatory not wishing to be seen loitering on the landing.

A door creaked just along the corridor, and she risked a quick peep to see where whoever had come up the stairs had gone. She was certain whoever it might have been hadn't gone into the rehearsal room since that door hadn't creaked when she had entered or exited from it.

The other doors along the corridor led into another rehearsal space, the gentleman's lavatories and a store cupboard. There were more doors further down, but she was unlikely to have heard the noise of the door from any of those as they were too far away.

It was entirely possible that some perfectly innocent gentleman was in the lavatories answering a call of nature. However, Jane was not so sure. If the killer had taken the bait, they would require a few moments of privacy to examine the contents of the dispatch. Then they would head for the typewriter to make and attach their own amendments to it before continuing to where Vince was busy linking the currently playing light music programme.

To her alarm she saw the door of the rehearsal room start to open so she darted quickly back inside the ladies and placed herself in front of the mirror by the sink to tidy her hair.

'Janey pie, are you all right, honey? You've been gone for

ages. Your tea is getting cold.' Elsa put her head around the door.

'Just coming now.' Jane fixed a smile on her face and followed her mother back across the corridor wondering how she could give her mother the slip to try and discover who had come up from the lobby and where they might have gone.

'You really are behaving very oddly, Janey. Are you sure you're all right?' her mother asked, peering at her as Jane swallowed her cold cup of tea. 'You maybe should try and get some vitamins. You do seem quite pasty today.' Her mother reached out to try to pinch some colour into her cheeks.

'Mother!' Jane sidestepped her attempts.

There was the faint sound of a whistle outside the door. Jane abandoned her tea and hurried over to look out into the corridor.

'Mother, stay here. Don't move!' Jane warned as she took off down the stairs to the lobby, her pulse racing as she ran.

'Janey!'

She ignored her mother and rushed down to the reception area. Arthur ran in through the front doors.

'I heard the police whistle. Have they got him?' he asked.

'I don't know. I heard the whistle too.' The reception desk was empty with no sign of Louisa.

'What's happening? I heard a whistle?' the security guard asked.

'You don't think she took the package up?' Jane ignored the guard who headed for Leo's office, presumably to alert him.

Arthur shook his head. 'No, the police had arranged for someone to keep her busy at the desk so she would let someone else volunteer to take it. She's missing now though.'

'Then what's happening?' Jane looked around but Leo Cavendish's office door was closed and no one else appeared. The guard, having got no answer, rushed off up the stairs.

The police whistles sounded again closer this time and there was the muffled sound of shouting.

'It's coming from upstairs!' Jane went to the bottom of the stairs to see what was happening just as a man came hurtling down them.

'Jane, take cover. He's got a gun!' Arthur shouted a warning.

CHAPTER TWENTY-FOUR

Jane had no time to react to Arthur's shout as Reggie caught hold of her arm and started to drag her towards the door.

'Stand back or I will use this.' Reggie raised the gun and pointed it towards Arthur who had moved to try to block their exit.

Arthur raised his hands and was forced to move slowly out of the way.

Jane wriggled furiously in Reggie's grasp. 'Let me go!' She tried to stamp back onto his foot, but he dodged the move.

'I don't think so, you're my ticket out of here.' He pushed her towards the door.

Behind her she heard more footsteps on the stairs.

'Bosun, stop!' Inspector Winters's voice rang out around the lobby as Reggie struggled with her towards the exit.

Jane fought him every step of the way, wriggling furiously in his grasp. Her efforts slowed him down and he pressed the barrel of the gun against her side. 'Keep walking or I'll kill you right now.'

The cold, hard end of the gun was jammed against her ribs,

and she had little choice but to comply. Arthur watched help-lessly as she was forced out of the door.

'My car is just along the street. Walk normally and don't draw attention to yourself unless you want to end up like Tabitha and Jenny.' Reggie's breath was warm against her ear as he forced her to walk beside him.

'Why are you doing this? You know you'll hang.' Jane glared at him as she tried to walk as slowly as she dared under the circumstances.

'I don't think so. I have a place where I can lie low until I can get across the Channel.' He met her gaze, and she recog-nised the gleam of fanaticism in his eyes. A chill ran down her spine and she knew it was only a matter of time before he killed her.

She spotted the police car parked on the opposite side of the street and wondered if it was manned. Reggie's car was in sight, parked in a bay at the kerb. She recognised it from when he had been ferrying her mother around town. Now, she suspected he had been the one trying to scare them off the night they had been at The Ritz.

'Bosun!' a shout rang out. The call was swiftly followed by the crack of a gun being fired.

Jane automatically flinched and attempted to drop down to the pavement. Her unexpected action seemed to throw her captor temporarily off balance. She made the most of it by twisting in his grasp at the side of his car.

For a split second she was free and ready to run to safety. Then the next thing she knew was a sharp pain at the back of her head and everything went black.

* * *

Arthur was joined in the lobby by the security guard, the

inspector and by Benson, all of whom had charged down the stairs.

'He's taken Jane.' Arthur rushed to the door to peer down the street to see where they were headed.

'What do you mean, he's taken Jane? Who's taken her? And where?' Elsa appeared and before they could prevent her she had darted through the door.

'Miss Elsa, come back. He has a gun.' Benson went after her with the inspector and the guard hard on his heels.

Arthur followed, but instead of remaining with the group he plunged across the road, narrowly missing the front of a passing bus. As he ran he heard the sound of a gunshot and hoped whoever was firing hadn't aimed at Jane. He dared not stop to find out what was happening.

His chest was sore and his breathing ragged and uneven as he ran. He was relying on his somewhat rusty knowledge of the London streets and alleyways to bring him around to where Jane and Reggie were headed. His intention was to somehow cut off Reggie's escape route.

The man always had his car so he guessed that would be where he would go, using Jane as a shield to prevent the police or anyone else from stopping him. His breathing was laboured and whistling now and he was forced to slow his pace as he rounded the last corner and emerged once more onto the main street. He was now looking back down the road towards the entrance to Bush House. The pavement was mercifully devoid of pedestrians between Reggie and the group outside Bush House. In the distance Arthur could see Benson apparently tussling with Elsa.

Reggie was at the side of a sleek, expensive motor car not far away from him as Arthur weaved across the road once more. His heart was in his throat when he saw Jane's crumpled form lying on the pavement at Reggie's feet. The gun was still in the bandleader's hand as he used his free hand to fumble in his trouser pocket, presumably for the car key.

His attention was on the group down the street and his back was to Arthur, apparently oblivious to what or who might be behind him. For once, Arthur wished he had brought his own gun. They had discussed it while making their plan but the risk to civilians had been thought to be too great. Now, seeing Jane lying injured or dead, he thought the decision was a mistake.

There was no time to lose. Once Reggie found his key and was in his car he would be gone. Their chance of catching him and bringing him to justice greatly diminished. Arthur swiftly calculated the risks as he drew closer to his target then launched himself on Reggie.

The weight of his body carried his unsuspecting opponent to the ground next to Jane and he grappled with the bandleader to try to force the gun from his hand. His chest felt as if it were on fire, and he gulped in air as he struggled to overcome the other man.

He grabbed Reggie's wrist and banged it down hard on the kerb in a bid to make him drop the gun. There was a clang of metal on metal and the gun disappeared from the bandleader's hand, slithering between the metal grating of a drain to disappear from sight.

Reggie let out a roar of fury and threw Arthur off before scrambling to his feet and running away through a small knot of pedestrians who had just disembarked from the bus. Arthur lay gasping for breath on the pavement beside Jane as Inspector Winters, Benson and Elsa raced to join them.

'Janey pie.' Elsa's face was ashen beneath her make-up as she bent over her stricken daughter.

Inspector Winters and a uniformed constable took off in pursuit of Reggie, while Benson joined Elsa to check on Jane.

'What happened? Did he shoot her? Is she alive?' Arthur sat on the pavement, his gaze fixed on Jane's still form. He was too shaken and breathless to stand just yet. At least he saw no signs of blood.

'I believe Miss Jane is unconscious. There is no sign of a bullet wound.' Benson's gaze skittered towards Elsa who was stroking Jane's hair back from her face.

'An ambulance is coming. I got the guard to telephone.' Leo Cavendish accompanied by Ernie Simons came to join them, forming a semi-protective circle around Jane. Benson removed his jacket, folded it and slid it carefully beneath Jane's head.

She moaned at the movement and Arthur's spirits lifted at this sign of life. The distant sound of a bell grew closer and louder as Benson assisted Arthur to his feet. The ambulance halted and Jane was swiftly and efficiently bundled onto a stretcher. Elsa accompanied her daughter into the ambulance.

'Do you also require medical attention, sir?' Benson murmured in Arthur's ear.

'No, I think if I go home and take my usual medication all will be well,' Arthur said. His hands trembled and he shoved them inside his jacket pockets before anyone could notice. To his surprise he encountered something hard, metallic and gun-shaped in the pocket closest to his manservant.

He looked questioningly at Benson who remained as inscrutable as ever. 'Perhaps if we return to the studios, we can obtain a taxi,' the manservant suggested quietly.

The small crowd that had gathered at the sight of an ambulance and two people on the pavement dispersed once the ambulance had driven away.

'What on earth was all that about? Did Reggie just attack Miss Treen?' Ernie looked at Leo and then at Arthur, a bewildered expression on his face.

'I'm not certain exactly what has happened.' Leo also glanced at Arthur and Benson, before offering his hand for Arthur to shake. 'I must say, I was impressed with how swiftly you managed to get around him.'

Arthur shook Leo's hand but refrained from speaking. He knew he really needed to get home and sit quietly inhaling his medication. Benson spotted a taxi and raised his hand to call it to a halt.

'Mr Cilento studied the knowledge in his youth,' Benson explained. 'I shall accompany Mr Cilento home, sir. I am familiar with his address.' He opened the taxi door and assisted Arthur inside before climbing in beside him.

Leo nodded in acknowledgement. 'Very good. If I hear from Inspector Winters, I'll inform him of where you've gone. Hopefully, they'll soon have Reggie under lock and key.'

Benson gave their address to the cabbie, and they set off. Arthur closed his eyes and focused on his breathing. There would be time enough to examine the mystery gun in his pocket and ask questions once they were back.

He was grateful once more for his trusty manservant's assistance from the cab and up the flight of stairs into the flat. Arthur sank down in his chair.

'Take a little brandy with water, sir, while I set up the tubing.' Benson pressed a crystal tumbler into his hand before moving around the room with a calm economy of motion.

A few minutes later, his mask was in place, and he was inhaling the mixture of medications his consultant had prescribed for him. Benson tutted over the state of his trousers where he had fought with Reggie Bosun and ministered to the soiled patches with a damp sponge.

He wondered if Inspector Winters had captured Bosun. There were still so many unanswered questions Arthur would have liked to ask. He knew too that Colonel Hardacre would also have a great many questions for the bandleader. His contacts in Germany, who had recruited him, and any sources of information here in England.

He closed his eyes and focused once more on trying to keep his breathing even and unhurried, resisting the urge to gulp in the mixture. The heavy feeling finally started to recede from his chest, and he opened his eyes once more.

The telephone rang in the hall and Benson went to answer it. Arthur strained his ears to try and catch who might be calling. His curiosity was satisfied when he heard the familiar rumbling roar of the brigadier talking to his manservant.

His medication was finished by the time Benson returned to the sitting room.

'That was the brigadier, sir. He had received information that a gun had been fired in a public place and Miss Jane had been taken to hospital.' Benson switched off the machinery and started to dismantle the tubing.

'I presume the gun that was fired wasn't Reggie's gun? It was this one?' Arthur dug down into his jacket pocket and extracted the mystery weapon, placing it on the table.

'That is correct, sir, yes,' Benson agreed.

Arthur examined the gun. It was American and he could see it must be quite a rare model since he didn't immediately recognise it. It was .22 calibre and small enough to be easily concealed in a pocket or a lady's handbag.

'The gun belongs to Miss Elsa. She attempted to shoot Mr Bosun when she realised he had Miss Jane,' Benson explained.

'Elsa had a gun?' Arthur blinked at his servant. It certainly explained why it was of American manufacture.

Benson coughed apologetically. 'She produced it and fired before I could prevent her. She called it her popgun and claims she is an expert shot. Apparently, she thought she should have it with her in the light of Jenny Jackson's murder. She thought she might be attacked herself.'

'That was what you took off her just before I tried to stop Reggie from escaping?' Arthur asked, placing the gun back down carefully on the table.

'I was concerned she might attempt another shot. The first one seemed very close and then Miss Jane was on the floor. I wasn't certain at first if Miss Elsa's aim was as good as she claimed,' Benson explained.

'No, quite.' Arthur took some more of his brandy. 'I hope Jane will be all right. I presume Reggie must have hit her fairly hard. She was out cold for a few minutes.'

Benson carried some of the equipment away to clean it ready for the next time it was required. Arthur was impatient now to discover if Bosun had been captured. He would have thought that either the brigadier or Winters would telephone once the bandleader had been apprehended.

It also struck Arthur that if Jane were to be detained by the hospital, something that was very likely, that left an orange feline problem in her flat. Someone would have to brave the wrath of Marmaduke and go in to feed the beast. He winced at the thought and glanced at the back of his hand. He still bore the mark from the last time he had been in there to care for Jane's precious pet.

The telephone rang once more and he sprang to his feet, keen to answer it himself this time.

'Is that Mr Arthur Cilento?' He immediately recognised Elsa's American accent.

'Speaking, Miss Macintyre, how is Jane?' He could hear the hustle and bustle of hospital noise behind her.

'She's come around but is bothered over that cat of hers. Say, you couldn't make sure it's all right? She said you knew where everything was. There's a spare key with your lovely Mr Benson.'

'Certainly, tell her not to worry. Is she being kept in?' Arthur asked.

'Overnight, but she's complaining already. Say, does Mr Benson have my popgun?' Elsa asked. 'Only, he said he'd keep it safe. I want it back, you know.'

'He has it safe.' Arthur glanced through the open doorway

into the sitting room to where the tiny gun lay on the coffee table.

'Right, thanks. Darn it, the pips are going and I've no more change, I...' Whatever Elsa might have been about to say was cut off as her money ran out in the booth.

Arthur replaced the receiver and went to tell Benson what Elsa had said.

'I'm glad Miss Jane is recovering. I can attend to Marmaduke later, sir, if you prefer,' Benson suggested.

'Thank you.' At least he wouldn't have to risk life and limb with Jane's cat. He would rather risk running across Reggie Bosun again than feed Marmaduke.

The afternoon wore on with no word from the inspector or from the brigadier. Arthur was pretty certain that this was not a good sign. If Reggie had been successful in giving the police the slip he could be anywhere by now.

Benson prepared supper and went and fed Marmaduke, returning miraculously unscathed. The blackout was in place and there was still no word from anyone on Reggie Bosun's whereabouts.

CHAPTER TWENTY-FIVE

Jane's head ached as she stared up at the ceiling from her hospital bed. Her mother had thankfully been banished by the ward sister earlier in the afternoon and it was now night-time. The unfamiliar noises of the other occupants of the Nightingale ward were keeping her awake. Women snoring, moaning, rustling, asking for bedpans.

She had no idea what had happened after Reggie had hit her and knocked her out. She remembered a gunshot, but Elsa had avoided all her questions about that. She didn't even know what had happened to Reggie. Had he been captured? Where was Arthur and why had no one come to tell her anything? It was incredibly frustrating.

She had asked her mother to call Arthur and Benson so they could look in on Marmaduke. It was not a task she could have entrusted to Elsa. Luckily, Benson had her spare key so at least that was one less worry. She tried to move her head on the rock-solid pillows to make herself more comfortable. The effort made her wince with pain, and she was forced to stay still.

The odour of disinfectant was heavy in the air, mingling with the perfume from the vases of flowers on the centre table in the middle of the ward. First thing in the morning she intended on getting out of there, no matter what.

* * *

Arthur telephoned the brigadier early the next morning.

'Arthur, dear boy, I've no news for you, I'm afraid. Inspector Winters has men combing London for Reggie Bosun. They've been at the stations and spread the word amongst the cab drivers. Colonel Hardacre also has agents seeking him. He'll be captured very soon, I have no doubt,' the brigadier boomed in his ear.

'Any news on Jane, sir?' Arthur wasn't even sure which hospital she had been taken to. He also knew better than to try and telephone Elsa at this time of the morning to ask.

'She was reported to have had a good night.' The brigadier didn't sound as certain about this.

'Thank you, sir. You will keep us informed I hope, if we can be of any assistance,' Arthur said.

'Certainly, certainly. I understand you did your utmost to try to prevent Bosun from escaping. Most commendable.' The brigadier's tone was approving, and he passed a few more pleasantries before ending the call.

The knock at the front door came as he was finishing his toast and marmalade. Benson went to answer it and returned with a pale but determined-looking Jane. She had changed her clothes from yesterday and her hair was brushed and her lipstick freshly applied.

'Jane, how are you? Do sit down, have some coffee, there is some in the pot. I wasn't expecting to see you until later today at the earliest.' Arthur rose to pull out a chair for her.

'I discharged myself. I couldn't stand it in there any longer. Thank you for looking after Marmaduke, by the way. I'm most grateful. Now, is Bosun in custody? Tell me everything. I haven't a clue what happened after that gunshot and he knocked me out,' she said as Benson went to fetch another cup and saucer.

'Ah, I'm afraid he isn't. At least not quite yet.' Arthur told her what had happened while she had been unconscious and hospitalised.

'So, he's still on the loose?' Jane exclaimed as Benson placed a cup of coffee in front of her. She rummaged in her handbag for her cigarettes and lit up. 'That's better. I couldn't smoke on the ward, something about the woman next to me being on oxygen.'

Her gaze fell on her mother's gun still lying on the coffee table. 'That's Mother's popgun. She's had that thing for ages. It was a gift from one of her admirers back in the States.' She stared at it in bewilderment. 'What is it doing here?'

'Um, the gunshot you mentioned. That was Elsa.' Arthur looked at Benson for support.

'Miss Elsa was aiming for Mr Bosun, I believe,' Benson confirmed.

'Good heavens. She is a very good shot but honestly, she could have killed me. Did she hit him, do we know?' Jane asked.

'I don't think so. There was no blood at the scene,' Arthur said.

Jane rolled her eyes. 'Then, what's happening now? Are they out looking for him?'

Arthur told her what the brigadier had said during his call.

'We have to do something to try and find him. We can't just sit back now and do nothing.' Jane stubbed out her cigarette in a small ashtray that Benson had produced.

'What do you suggest we do?' Arthur asked.

Jane frowned and rubbed her head. Arthur saw her wince as she did so, and he wondered if she was recovered from her injury. He suspected that she should really be resting, not sitting at his breakfast table trying to work out where Reggie Bosun might be hiding.

'He said something to me about having a place to hide. Mother spent quite a lot of time with him. He used to ferry her around in his car. If we return her popgun we might get something helpful that could tell us where to look,' Jane suggested.

Arthur supposed it might be worth a shot.

Benson ordered a taxi and Arthur wrapped up warmly ready to venture back out with Jane to Stephen's mother's apartment. Benson agreed to let Inspector Winters know where they were going.

'Mother's roof is almost repaired, so she'll be able to go back to her own house soon,' Jane informed him as they drove through the city.

'I expect she'll be pleased to go home. It's been a few weeks now since her flat was damaged.' Arthur could see that some of the shops now were trying their best to look festive despite the shortages. 'She'll be home for Christmas at least.'

It was a crisp, dry morning with no fog or smoke for once. The streets were busy with people and Arthur wondered how they could possibly find Reggie amongst the crowded streets. That was if he was still even in the capital.

Stephen's mother's apartment block was much more impressive than the one where Jane lived, and he and Benson were temporarily residing. It seemed too that they had managed to call on a day when Elsa was the only person at home. Stephen's mother was at the hairdresser's and the maid had gone shopping.

'Janey, you should be in bed, at the hospital. What are you doing here?' Elsa exclaimed on opening the door to discover her daughter on the step.

'I'm perfectly fine, Mother. They let me go,' Jane fibbed as they followed Elsa into the luxuriously appointed flat.

Elsa raised her carefully pencilled eyebrows at this. 'What

brings you both here? Did you bring my little popgun back? I've been having kittens in case that inspector tried to confiscate it.'

Jane produced the small gun from her bag and passed it over to her mother. 'Do you even have a licence for this?'

Elsa pounced on her gun and stroked the handle lovingly. 'Honey, I'm a US citizen remember.'

'I suggest you keep it somewhere safe and refrain in future from firing it on a public street,' Arthur said.

'You could have killed me,' Jane added.

'Oh pish, Janey, I'm an excellent shot. You know that.' Elsa tucked the gun inside her cream leather handbag and snapped the clasps shut.

'We wanted to talk to you about Reggie.' Jane took a seat on the end of the sofa, tucking her skirt neatly about her legs. Arthur remained standing near the door, his hat in his hands.

'I still can't quite believe what happened yesterday. Has he been caught?' Elsa asked as she too sat down.

'No, not yet. The police are out looking for him. We wondered, since you knew him quite well and spent time with him when he was giving you lifts, if you knew where he might be?' Jane said.

A faint frown puckered Elsa's brow. 'You mean like a hiding place, a bolthole?'

'He told me he had a place he could go until he got across the Channel,' Jane said.

'The police seem to believe he is still in London, so we think it may not be too far away,' Arthur added.

'I don't know. I mean, I can't believe the police haven't caught him. Obviously, he won't have gone to his home or his clubs,' Elsa said.

'Is there anywhere else at all that he mentioned or a particular friend who may be sheltering him not knowing what he's done?' Jane asked.

'His friends are all artistes and musicians, and word has

probably gone around that he's in a mighty big pickle.' Elsa looked at Jane. 'You know how that goes, honey. I'm trying to think if there is anything he said.'

Jane waited patiently for her mother to try to recollect something that might be of interest. Arthur noticed only the fidgeting of her fingers betrayed her concealed impatience.

'There is one thing. He mentioned it in passing once. There's a small weekend cottage he has, a bungalow. He inherited it from an uncle. He goes there sometimes to paint he told me. It's kinda a hobby of his. It's near the Thames in a little village close to the railway just outside London.' Elsa looked at Jane. 'You can tell the police. Blissett-on-Thames, that's the village. The cottage is just outside it. It had a quaint kinda name... The Birdhouse, that was it.' Elsa snapped her fingers.

'That's perfect. Thank you, Mother.' Jane leapt up and kissed her mother on the cheek. 'Come on, Arthur.'

Arthur barely had time to bid Elsa farewell before Jane had swept them out of the flat and was flagging down a passing taxi outside the apartment block.

'Blissett-on-Thames,' Jane directed the driver as she slid onto the back seat of the taxi.

'That'll be quite a fare, gel,' the driver warned. 'I used to 'ave an aunt lived out that way.'

'That's quite all right. This is something of an emergency,' Jane assured him.

'Jane, don't you think we should have let Inspector Winters know about this?' Arthur asked as the car set off.

'It may be a wild goose chase and there isn't much time. If he has gone there then we need to know. There will be time enough to alert the police once we've found him,' Jane said.

Arthur looked at the determined set of her mouth and tilted up chin and wished they had kept hold of Elsa's popgun in case Reggie was in residence at The Birdhouse.

* * *

Jane settled back in the seat of the taxi and prayed the incipient headache she had would disperse by the time they reached their destination. She could only hope they were doing the right thing by going to Blissett-on-Thames. Time was of the essence, however, and if Reggie was there then they needed to catch him. Any information he could provide might lead to other traitors in their midst. This was about more than just the murder of two innocent women.

'This is the village 'ere now, miss,' the driver said as they sighted the first of a couple of cottages.

'The house is called The Birdhouse, it's a bungalow. Can you drive slowly so we can look for it?' Jane asked.

The driver, clearly thinking them to be eccentric but rich to have undertaken such a journey by car, obligingly slowed down.

'There, Jane.' Arthur pointed to a hand-painted sign almost buried in an overgrown privet bush.

The driver halted. 'Do you need me to wait for yer?' he asked.

'Yes, please.' Jane pulled a white five-pound note from her purse and pressed it into the cabbie's hand before she and Arthur stepped out of the car.

The hedge around the perimeter of the tiny front garden was overgrown and untidy. A wooden gate stood partly open. The taxi driver produced a newspaper and settled down to read.

'I'll go first, he's less familiar with me,' Arthur suggested.

Jane nodded her agreement. Her heart was racing at the thought of having to potentially confront her assailant once more.

She loitered near the gate while Arthur made his way to the house. From her vantage point peering through the branches, Jane could see it was a small, single-storey building. It was made of or faced with wood, black now with age. Dead plants stood in dilapidated wooden tubs on either side of the front door. Reggie obviously didn't visit often.

The house appeared deserted with no signs of life. Arthur went to the front window and placed his hand above his eyes to peer through the glass trying to see inside. He apparently had no luck as he straightened up and signalled that he was going to try the rear of the house.

Jane crept down the drive to the corner of the building while Arthur made his way along a narrow, overgrown path at the side which she assumed must lead to the back garden. Her heart thumped as he carefully and quietly walked down until he rounded the corner out of sight.

Without warning, a flock of magpies flew up, squawking noisily from a large tree at the rear of the bungalow. There was the bang of what sounded like a door, and she hurried down the path after Arthur.

'Jane, quickly, he's getting away!' Arthur's shout sent more birds flying up from the hedges surrounding the back garden.

As she reached the corner she found Arthur wincing and nursing his arm. The rear door of the house was swinging open. Reggie was fleeing through the long grass of what must once have been the back lawn down to a wooden gate at the bottom of the garden.

'Stop!' Jane set off in pursuit with Arthur following more slowly behind her.

The pale half-dead meadow grass swished painfully about her legs and the hidden brambles almost sent her flying as she ran after Reggie. She was aware of Arthur following her but had no time to look back if she was to catch her quarry.

Reggie reached the gate and opened it, and Jane realised they were right alongside the railway line. Only a wire fence prevented them from going onto the track. He sprinted up the side of the rails heading towards a white painted set of steps that led to a narrow metal footbridge that crossed over the track.

He started to climb the steps and Jane followed after him. Arthur reached the bottom of the steps as Jane got to the top. Reggie was on the bridge, and she wondered why he hadn't descended on the other side.

'Stay back!' Reggie whirled around to face her and something metal glinted in his hand.

'Give yourself up! There's no way out!' Jane continued to block his exit.

She realised now that he had no way down the other side since an ancient iron gate barred the way which was secured with a chain and padlock.

'Never!'

Arthur panted his way up the steps to join her on the bridge.

'Why did you do it? Why kill Tabitha and Jenny?' Arthur asked. 'Did Tabitha work out that you were the one sending coded messages to the enemy? Is that why she had to die?'

'What enemy? You two are fools if you think you can win this war. She started asking questions and I knew she had some of the scripts.' Reggie spat the words out, his handsome features contorted with rage.

'You followed her that night and realised she intended going to Whitehall?' Jane guessed.

'I knew she had come from the typing pool there. She was bound to take her suspicions to someone in homeland security,' Reggie said. 'My role was too valuable to allow that to happen.'

'I presume Jenny tried to blackmail you and then Frances was asking questions wasn't she?' Arthur had his gaze fixed on the knife in Reggie's hand. A serrated long-bladed kitchen knife that gleamed in the sunlight.

'That pathetic drunken has-been. I couldn't take the chance that she might betray me. Then Frances and you, Miss Treen, asking questions, spying on everyone. I knew you were up to something. When I learned from Leo that Elsa was your mother I tried to get information from her.' Reggie glared at Jane.

'Good luck with that. My mother has no idea what I do,' Jane said.

Reggie scoffed. 'Yes, she was a waste of time but still useful for keeping tabs on your whereabouts.'

'What about the fires at the studios? I presume that was you, too?' Arthur asked.

'Sabotage, delays and interruptions to broadcasts designed to demoralise and destabilise. I was proud to do it.' Jane saw the gleam of fanaticism once more in Reggie's eyes.

'Who were you working with? Who are your contacts?' Arthur made an attempt to try to get more information.

'Do you really think I would betray my fellow patriots?' Reggie sneered.

In the distance Jane heard the familiar sound of an approaching steam engine.

'Arthur go down the steps, a train is coming,' she urged her companion to move so he would not be enveloped in the smoke from the engine as it passed under the footbridge. 'Give yourself up, Reggie. There is no way out of this. Even if you harm me and Arthur you will still be caught and punished for your crimes.'

The train was drawing closer, she could smell the smoke as the clanking of the metal wheels on the track grew louder.

Reggie's expression changed to a smirk.

'I would rather die a hero.' He clambered up onto the wooden guard rail of the bridge, balancing on the edge as the train approached at speed. Jane was powerless to prevent him.

'*Heil* Hitler!' He saluted.

Jane coughed and turned her head away as choking grey smoke enveloped her and the train passed under the bridge. Its whistle screaming as it went by. When she opened her eyes and looked back the train was receding, and the footbridge was empty.

She rushed forwards to the centre of the bridge where Reggie had been standing, Arthur following her. Coughing and with eyes streaming they looked down to see what remained of the bandleader on the track. Jane turned away quickly as Arthur gathered her in his arms to shield her from the terrible sight.

CHAPTER TWENTY-SIX

Jane, Arthur and Benson were in the brigadier's office a few days later. Colonel Hardacre had joined them for a full debrief on everything they had learned about Reggie Bosun's operation.

The daily newspaper was open on the desk where they had seen the official government spin on Reggie Bosun's death.

Suicide of Popular Bandleader

Star of radio and dance halls, Reginald Bosun, died after throwing himself in the path of the 12.20 train to Euston the day before yesterday. A popular figure, Mr Bosun was noted for his musical skills and his hard work raising funds for the war effort. His most recent event being a gala at The Ritz hotel which was attended by HRH the Princess Elizabeth in aid of the Red Cross. It is thought that the pressures of work and the recent loss of a close friend led to this tragic event. He will be much missed by members of the artistic community.

Jane knew that Stephen had been tasked with working with the press to conceal the true reasons behind Reggie's death. He had been popular with the general public, and it was vital that morale be maintained. Not that she personally liked or approved of this whitewashing of Reggie's true nature or his beliefs.

'I wish to extend my thanks to all three of you on behalf of the department,' Colonel Hardacre said. 'This was a dangerous and tricky mission. I saw from the report that each of you placed yourselves at great personal risk.'

'Thank you, sir, but we were only doing our duty,' Arthur spoke on their behalf.

'I know that Mr Cavendish has also expressed his own personal gratitude when we informed him privately that the investigation into his fiancée's death had been concluded.' The brigadier gazed at them all, his eyes shrewd and assessing.

'I shall be in touch, Mr Cilento, with you and Mr Benson about a role after Christmas which I believe you would be most suited for.' Colonel Hardacre looked at Arthur.

'I think, Jane, that you have already discovered your work has accumulated in your absence from your desk.' The brigadier smiled at her.

'Yes, sir.' She had already started to tackle the mountain of files and messages in her office.

'By the way, it concerned me that Mr Cavendish managed to acquire your address quite early in this case. It seems a friend of Tabitha Moore gave him the information. The young lady in question works in the typing pool. She has been severely reprimanded,' the brigadier said.

'Thank you, sir.' Jane was relieved to finally have the answer to that particular conundrum. She had been concerned that she might even have to try to move if her home address was known outside the department.

Now, it seemed the brigadier had taken steps personally to ensure her privacy and safety. She had no wish to discover any more Albert Finches in her flat.

Once they had been dismissed, Benson went downstairs to find a car to take himself and Arthur to the station. Their luggage had been left in the lobby and they were to return to Pennycombe.

'I shall quite miss having you as a neighbour,' Jane remarked as she accompanied Arthur down to the lobby. 'I shall especially miss Benson's cooking.'

He gave a wry smile as they reached the foot of the stairs. 'I daresay it won't be too long before we are working together again.'

'Have a lovely Christmas.' She could see Benson had managed to get a car and was taking their luggage out of the building.

'You too.' Arthur smiled at her once more and as if on impulse he quickly kissed her cheek before joining Benson at the taxi. He raised his hand in farewell and got into the car.

Jane stood still on the pavement as the taxi pulled out into the traffic before touching her cheek lightly with her hand and hurrying back inside to her desk.

A LETTER FROM HELENA DIXON

Dear reader,

I want to say a huge thank you for choosing to read *Murder Most British*. If you did enjoy it, and want to keep up to date with all my latest releases, just sign up at the following link. Your email address will never be shared and you can unsubscribe at any time. You will also a receive a free short story featuring Alice, from the Miss Underhay series.

www.bookouture.com/helena-dixon

I hope you loved *Murder Most British* and if you did I would be very grateful if you could write a review. I'd love to hear what you think, and it makes such a difference helping new readers to discover one of my books for the first time.

Keeping up morale during the war was a challenging task. The entertainment of the nation and the fighting forces was invaluable. It was also highly controlled so that people were shielded from the worst of losses and victories were celebrated. Radio broadcasts were used to spread propaganda from all sides and coded messages sent and received hidden in the most innocent of programmes.

The locations of many studios, rehearsal rooms and stations were subject to attack and even the government was not entirely certain where the BBC was basing its operations from. Although many could make a best guess.

Therefore, I wrote this story based on probabilities mixed with hard facts with the help of some excellent advice from experts in this field. I hope I succeeded in creating a realistic fictional world for Jane and Arthur.

I love hearing from my readers – and you can get in touch through social media or my website.

Thanks,

Helena Dixon

www.nelldixon.com

 facebook.com/nelldixonauthor
x.com/NellDixon

ACKNOWLEDGEMENTS

With many thanks to Sophia Pritchard for her endless hours of research and advice. Also to my lovely local history society friends and colleagues for answering numerous questions. The staff at the Imperial War Museums for their generous assistance. Thanks also go to my agent, Kate Nash for her unfailing support and faith in my ability to write these books. My hardworking editor Cerys and everyone at Bookouture who work so hard to make these books succeed. Thank you.

PUBLISHING TEAM

Turning a manuscript into a book requires the efforts of many people. The publishing team at Bookouture would like to acknowledge everyone who contributed to this publication.

Audio
Alba Proko
Sinead O'Connor
Melissa Tran

Commercial
Lauren Morrissette
Hannah Richmond
Imogen Allport

Cover design
Debbie Clement

Data and analysis
Mark Alder
Mohamed Bussuri

Editorial
Cerys Hadwin-Owen
Charlotte Hegley

RAISING READERS
Books Build Bright Futures

Dear Reader,

We'd love your attention for one more page to tell you about the crisis in children's reading, and what we can all do.

Studies have shown that reading for fun is the **single biggest predictor of a child's future life chances** – more than family circumstance, parents' educational background or income. It improves academic results, mental health, wealth, communication skills, ambition and happiness.

The number of children reading for fun is in rapid decline. Young people have a lot of competition for their time, and a worryingly high number do not have a single book at home.

Hachette works extensively with schools, libraries and literacy charities, but here are some ways we can all raise more readers:

- Reading to children for just 10 minutes a day makes a difference
- Don't give up if children aren't regular readers – there will be books for them!

- Visit bookshops and libraries to get recommendations
- Encourage them to listen to audiobooks
- Support school libraries
- Give books as gifts

There's a lot more information about how to encourage children to read on our websites: **www.RaisingReaders.co.uk** and **www.JoinRaisingReaders.com**.

Thank you for reading.